"I think we'd better stop,"

Lila said breathlessly.

"Why?" Jeff's eyes were glazed with passion. "I could go on kissing you all day. Do you have any idea how soft your lips are?" he added whimsically.

"Things are moving too fast," she murmured unsteadily. With a firm motion, she extricated herself from his arms. "Last night . . . and earlier this afternoon . . . maybe it was excusable. We were both elated, on an emotional high, thrown off balance because of circumstances. But now . . ." Her voice trailed off.

"Now the kisses are all the sweeter because it's just for you and me and not due to any outside influence."

"We barely know each other, Jeffrey."

"How well do we have to know one another after the night and day we've been through? How long do we have to be acquainted before we demonstrate the undeniable truth that we're attracted to each other?"

Dear Reader,

Sophisticated but sensitive, savvy yet unabashedly sentimental—that's today's woman, today's romance reader—you! And Silhouette Special Editions are written expressly to reward your quest for substantial, emotionally involving love stories.

So take a leisurely stroll under the cover's lavender arch into a garden of romantic delights. Pick and choose among titles if you must—we hope you'll soon equate all six Special Editions each month with consistently gratifying romantic reading.

Watch for sparkling new stories from your Silhouette favorites—Nora Roberts, Tracy Sinclair, Ginna Gray, Lindsay McKenna, Curtiss Ann Matlock, among others—along with some exciting newcomers to Silhouette, such as Karen Keast and Patricia Coughlin. Be on the lookout, too, for the new Silhouette Classics, a distinctive collection of bestselling Special Editions and Silhouette Intimate Moments now brought back to the stands—two each month—by popular demand.

On behalf of all the authors and editors of Special Editions,
Warmest wishes,

Leslie Kazanjian
Senior Editor

SONDRA STANFORD
Through All Eternity

Silhouette Special Edition
Published by Silhouette Books New York
America's Publisher of Contemporary Romance

For Denise and Javier
May your love be unshakable
Through All Eternity.

SILHOUETTE BOOKS
300 East 42nd St., New York, N.Y. 10017

Copyright © 1988 by Sondra Stanford

ISBN: 0-373-09445-0

First Silhouette Books printing April 1988

America's Publisher of Contemporary Romance

Printed in the U.S.A.

SONDRA STANFORD

wrote advertising copy before trying her hand at romance fiction. Also an artist, she enjoys attending arts and crafts shows and browsing at flea markets. Sondra and her husband live happily with their two children in Corpus Christi, Texas.

Chapter One

Even with all the financial problems she had, and they were many, Lila Addison felt strangely free, oddly happy. The difference between her former life in New York City and her existence now was drastic. She'd made a clean break.

Except whenever she thought of Nick and what he had done. Then her anger caused raw, open wounds to fester.

But this was a beautiful spring afternoon and as she drove the five miles from the farmhouse into town, Lila refused to dwell on either the unalterable past or the uncertain future. Today the world was awash in golden sunlight. Mimosa trees were blooming profusely with pink and purple blossoms; the fresh scent of pine sharpened the air. Here and there, vegetable gardens thrived in glorious shades of green beneath the life-giving sun.

Lila's artistic soul responded to nature's beauty as though it were expanding to include the universe itself. She inhaled deeply and thought that in this vicinity alone there was enough scenery to provide subjects for her paintings for ten lifetimes. Her fingers itched to grab a paintbrush and go to work.

Tomorrow, she assured herself. She'd begin tomorrow. In the meantime she'd promised Amy Mathis that she would give this talk to the girls in Amy's high school gym class.

Only two weeks ago Lila had settled into her grandmother's house and already she felt at home. Her own possessions seemed to mingle happily with her grandmother's. She was glad that last year, after her grandmother's death, she had stored her grandmother's furniture and knickknacks, while she rented out the house. Now the renters were gone, Lila was in residence, her grandmother's things were back in place beside her own and Lila had a real sense of belonging, of firmly putting down roots. She was convinced that despite all advice to the contrary, this major change in her life was for the best.

Cattail, Texas was a small community of fewer than two thousand citizens. East Texas was pine country and lumbering was big in the area. For the rest, there were a number of farms sprinkled about the hilly, red-dirt countryside. It was in no way an overwhelmingly prosperous community, but then it wasn't poverty stricken either. The residents were, for the most part, solidly middle-class with firm values of God, country, family and a deeply held reverence for the land.

Lila had always enjoyed coming here for summer visits. Her father had died when she was only four and her northern-bred mother had taken Lila back to New York to live, but Lila's mother had been conscientious about allowing her daughter to spend ample time with her late husband's widowed mother.

Lila's childhood memories of visits to Texas were sweet. The slower pace of life enchanted her. There'd been time to make homemade ice cream and to learn to swim in Cattail Lake along with Amy and the other children she had met; time, too, for gathering food from the garden and sitting on the front porch in the evenings listening to the crickets and frogs or dashing about catching fireflies in a fruit jar. Recently, when she'd felt a desperate need to escape the multiple pressures of a fast-paced life in the city, the firmly entrenched memories of her youthful stays in Cattail drew her back. She had the honed instinct of a homing pigeon. Here she could lick her wounds, rejuvenate in peace and quiet and perhaps find the real Lila Addison beneath the thick layers of acquired sophistication.

She drove through the outskirts of town and slowed her speed. Only two more blocks and she would reach her turn.

But she only made it one block further.

As she drew into the center of the next intersection, another car came hurling out of the cross street. From the corner of her eye, Lila saw a flash of blue, but too late. There was nothing she could do to save herself.

The sound of crunching metal was sickening. The violent jolt when the two cars collided sent shock waves vibrating through Lila. Terror thudded in her heart, paralyzing her, and she gasped as her Volkswagen spun dizzily like an old-fashioned toy top.

After an endless moment the car lurched to a halt at a crazy angle, half on the pavement, half off. It had narrowly missed smashing into a nearby electrical pole.

Silence and stillness came swiftly in amazing contrast to the noise of a moment ago. Lila drew in a ragged breath, amazed to find herself still alive and seemingly uninjured. Then she remembered the other car and her gaze went swiftly to the rearview mirror to see what had become of the vehicle.

A late model blue Porsche with a damaged fender and splintered headlight rested a few yards behind her. Lila saw a man leap out of it and begin running toward her car.

Still slightly dazed, Lila didn't attempt to move. She continued to watch the man through the mirror as he narrowed the distance between them. He was tall and dark headed and had long lanky legs. He was dressed neatly in khaki-colored slacks and a matching casual jacket over a dark brown shirt that covered massive shoulders. He looked incredibly large and strong and had an athletic build and stride, but it was the expression on his face rather than his size that arrested her attention. He was consumed by some tortured emotion that was frightening to observe. Somehow Lila sensed that whatever it was, it went far beyond concern for her safety or worry over the damage to both automobiles.

The man reached her opened car window and bent over to peer inside the car. "Are you hurt?" he asked gruffly.

Lila looked up into deep brown eyes that held a strange and compelling intensity. His face, which she was certain normally had a healthy complexion, was extraordinarily pale and there were deep, dark shadows under his eyes. He was either very ill or very tired, but Lila couldn't decide which. However, his jaw was firm, as though he was used to being in command, and his lips were hard and grim, stark slashes across his teeth.

"I don't think so," she answered uncertainly. She averted her eyes from his oddly disturbing gaze.

The man pulled open the car door. "Can you stand?"

"Yes, of course I can." Lila tried to concentrate on her body. Every muscle was still tense from the fear and adrenaline that had raced through her, but she wasn't conscious of any real pain, only of being sore and bruised. She twisted on the seat, extending one leg, planting her foot on the ground.

The man offered his hand to help her. Lila placed hers within it. Her hand was immediately swallowed up by a large, warm palm and strong, firm fingers as he steadied her while she stepped out of the car.

"Now how do you feel?" he asked anxiously as she stood before him. His hand released hers and Lila felt a sense of relief. For some reason, this large man was a bit overwhelming. Instinctively, she took one step back, enlarging the small space between them.

"Fine. I'm really okay," Lila responded. Belatedly, she thought to ask, "How about you? Were you injured?"

"I'm all right," the man answered shortly. "Sorry I hit you. I was in a hurry and I wasn't paying enough attention to traffic."

"Obviously," Lila said dryly. She glanced around at the empty road. No other vehicles had come along. There had been no witnesses to the mishap. "I suppose we'd better call the police," she added. "Maybe someone in that house across the road will call them for us."

"I don't have time for that," the man told her. He reached inside his jacket and pulled something out of his shirt pocket. It was a business card and he thrust it into her hand. "Here, that's my name and office phone number. Get in touch with me and I'll pay for the damages to your car."

Without another word or glance, he turned abruptly and began to lope off. His behavior was so unexpected that it took Lila's breath away. Incredulously, she watched him go but a sudden, spirited anger revived her from her state of shock. She chased after him.

"Hey!" she yelled as they both neared his car. "Hey, mister, you can't just drive away like this! We have to call the police and wait for them!"

The man jerked his car door open. He half-turned and shouted back at her, "I have to be someplace and I'm already late. I've got to go!"

"It's against the law to leave the scene of an accident like this," Lila sputtered furiously. But her protests fell on deaf ears. It was as though the man had completely forgotten her.

He got into the car and switched on the ignition.

Lila put her hands firmly on the window frame of the car door, determined to stop him.

But before she could even catch her breath, much less speak, he growled ferociously. "I don't have time for this, lady! Now get out of my way!"

Something in his eyes told her he was ready to commit murder if she didn't comply. Shaken and suddenly fearful of him, Lila hastily withdrew her hands from the car window and backed away.

The Porsche tore off down the road, tires squealing, and quickly vanished from sight as Lila gazed after it, helpless, impotent, and furious.

Finally, she crossed the road and knocked on the door of the only house in the vicinity. Fortunately the owner was at home, though she hadn't seen or heard the accident, and she telephoned the police while Lila went back to her car to wait.

While she was waiting, she glanced at the card the man had shoved at her. *Jeffrey Chappel, Chappel Lumber Company,* it read in bold, masculine print. A Tenth Street address and telephone number were listed in the lower corners.

Lila's indignation increased. *Chappel.* Naturally, she'd heard the name before. Her grandmother had once said the Chappels were the wealthiest family in town. They owned a timber mill and lumber company and a lot of real estate in addition to farming and ranching interests. If she remembered right, there was oil money behind them, too. With a powerful background like that, no wonder Jeffrey Chappel felt he could run roughshod over her! Just like Nick. People like that thought they were above the law. Well, so far she hadn't been able to touch Nick, but this man was in for an unpleasant surprise. She intended to see that justice was done.

Fifteen minutes later two patrolmen arrived. They took her statement, carefully examined the skid marks on the pavement, and looked at the dented passenger side of her car.

Lila showed them Jeffrey Chappel's card. "He was driving a blue Porsche and he wouldn't wait for you to be called," she told them indignantly. "As soon as he saw I was all right, he sped away like a crazy man! I certainly expect you to track him down and give him a ticket. The way he drives, the man ought to have his license taken away from him!"

The two men exchanged knowing glances before one of the officers said in a tone that obviously meant to cool her down, "You really don't need to worry, ma'am. He gave you his card, and Mr. Chappel will pay for the damages to your car like he said he would."

"How do you know that?" Lila demanded in exasperation. She wasn't about to be placated so easily. "He was in the wrong and he refused to wait around for you as he should have because he probably didn't want this accident put on his insurance record. How do I know he'll pay for anything unless you ticket him?"

"We'll talk to him, ma'am," the other officer assured her. "Now let's see if your car is still drivable."

Lila wasn't at all satisfied with the officer's lackluster enthusiasm for chasing down Jeffrey Chappel, but there was little she could do about it. However if, in the next few days, she hadn't been notified that they had ticketed this Jeffrey Chappel as he deserved, she intended to contact the police chief himself. She'd had quite enough of men taking advantage of her lately, and she was determined Chappel wasn't going to get away with it.

By the time she was able to drive away, Lila was thoroughly disgruntled. She was still unnerved by the accident, angry with Jeffrey Chappel and his callous disregard for proper procedure, vastly irritated with the patrolmen who were obviously indifferent to what the villain had done, and last but not least, upset because it was now too late to keep her commitment to speak to Amy's class. Amy and the girls must think she was awful for reneging on her promise to them.

Lila sighed heavily, trying to calm her temper and frayed nerves as she carefully turned her car around and headed toward home. She only hoped and prayed the Volks would make the trip.

When Jeffrey Chappel sped away from the scene of the accident he only hoped and prayed he'd be on time, that the unexpected delay wouldn't throw a clinker into things. He was frantic to reach his destination and his foot pressed hard on the accelerator as he kept one eye on the dashboard clock.

The accident had been more bad luck. Since his mind was elsewhere, not to mention that he was exhausted from lack of sleep, he simply hadn't come to a complete stop at the intersection. It had been his own foolish fault, pure and simple.

Thank God the woman in the other car was not hurt! Jeff didn't need an injured victim on his conscience, especially while he had this other worry consuming all his attention.

He hadn't had the time to ask the woman her name or address and, as he sped through the town's only red light at Main Street, he was mildly curious about her. He knew practically everyone in Cattail, but he'd never seen her before. He would certainly remember her if he had.

She'd been stunningly beautiful. Even as distracted as he was, Jeff's mind had filed away that fact. But then, what man wouldn't notice a flawless, classically oval-shaped face framed by spectacular red-gold hair? Her eyes had been an unusually dark shade of green and when she'd stepped out of the car, he'd seen that she had a body that was as beautiful as her face. She'd been tall, coming up to his chin, which had surprised him since not many women he knew ever reached beyond his shoulders. Her slender, well-shaped figure had been attractively adorned by a deceptively simple suit of slacks and jacket, but Jeff had recognized that the eggshell-colored fabric was nubby silk, that the copper-toned blouse was expensive, that her high-heeled shoes had probably been Italian leather. She did not dress at all like most of the locals he knew. More than likely, she was only in town visiting someone, he concluded.

Jeff dismissed her from his thoughts in the next instant. He reached the opposite end of town and he slowed the car just a fraction because he would soon be making a turn off the highway. He couldn't afford to overshoot the dirt road he was to take. Again he prayed silently that he wasn't too late. If he was...

But that possibility didn't bear thinking about. If he did think about it, he would go completely mad.

At four o'clock the next afternoon, Jeff sat in his office, elbows propped on the desk, his face buried in his hands. He'd never been so disconsolate in all his thirty-two years. He was exhausted, both mentally and physically, and emotionally he was torn into bits and pieces.

Yesterday he had missed his appointment by ten minutes. Ten vital all-important minutes. It had been just enough time, apparently, to mean the difference between success and failure. And as the hours crept by, with the telephone remaining ominously silent, it was increasingly evident that he had failed.

The intercom buzzer rang, jolting him out of his exhausted stupor. Electrified, he sat up abruptly and with trembling fingers he pressed the intercom button. "Yes?" His voice was garbled and thick with both anguished fear and rising hope.

"George Duncan here to see you, Mr. Chappel," said Mary, his secretary.

Jeff's shoulders slumped. It was not the message he'd wanted. "Show him in," he said dully. His tone had become lifeless and flat.

A moment later a man in a patrolman's uniform stepped into Jeffrey Chappel's pine-walled office. Jeff rose wearily from behind his desk. Nodding, he said, "Good to see you, Pokey. How are you?"

"I'm fine." George Duncan, better known as Pokey since the third grade when Jeff himself had coined the nickname, slightly tilted his head and, unsmiling, asked, "A better question is, how are you holding up?"

"You know?" Jeff asked cryptically as he sank heavily into his leather chair.

George nodded and took a chair on the other side of the desk. "The chief told Tom and me, but that's all. He knows what good friends the three of us are. He swore us to secrecy, so I haven't even told Esther," he added, referring to his wife. "I hope you don't mind our knowing."

"No." Jeff waved his hand dismissively. "I would've told you myself, only I haven't had a minute to breathe, much less to talk to anybody except for the people involved in this nightmare. The main thing is trying to keep the media from getting wind of it and maybe botching things up for good."

"I'm damned sorry, Jeff," George said somberly. There was genuine concern in his gray eyes. "Any word at all today?"

"Not so much as a whisper." Jeff got out of his chair and walked to a window. Gazing out, he ran his hand agitatedly across his forehead. "I'm going crazy, Pokey," he said, his voice cracking. "I can't eat; I can't sleep; I sure as hell can't concentrate on business. I only came to the office today to get away from that tomb of a house. Today's the fourth day and I don't know how much more I can take."

George rose and went to stand beside his old friend. "Don't lose the faith, pal," he said softly. He clasped his hand on Jeff's shoulder in a gesture of sympathy. "Something's bound to break soon."

"Yes, but it might be too late! Maybe it's already too late."

"Don't talk like that!" George spoke sharply. "Don't even think it!"

Jeff managed a wan smile as he turned toward George. "You're right," he said at last. "I just have to hang on to hope a little longer, that's all."

"Atta boy!" George said with gruff heartiness. He paused a moment, then said, "I hate to bother you with anything else at a time like this, Jeff, but actually I'm here on business."

"Business?" Jeff looked confused. "About the case?" he asked anxiously. "Do you know something I don't?"

George shook his head quickly. "Of course not. Patrolmen don't usually get involved in things like that, though Tom and I are keeping our eyes peeled for strangers or anything unusual when we're out on our beat. No, this is about your accident yesterday afternoon."

"Oh," Jeff said in a flat voice. "That."

"Yes," George replied. "That. I saw the Porsche outside. Looks like you bashed it up pretty good."

Jeff shrugged. "It's repairable."

George nodded. "Sure. So is the other car. But the woman you hit is furious about the way you took off." When Jeff opened his mouth to speak, George held up a hand to stave him off. "Oh, Tom and I both knew why you had done it. The chief told us about your appointment. Of course we couldn't tell her why you'd left so fast, so we weren't able to do much to smooth her ruffled feathers. She's out for blood and determined that we throw you in the jail house or hang you from the handiest tree."

"So give me the ticket already," Jeff said indifferently. "I can't be bothered with such things right now."

"I'm not going to give you a ticket," George said, "and I know you feel like you can't be bothered with her, but I think you ought to try." He pulled out a scrap of paper and handed it to Jeff. "There's her name and phone number. At least pick up the phone and call her. Reassure her you'll pay for the damages to her car. That ought to calm her down.''

Jeff looked at the paper, then back at George quizzically. ''This is a local number,'' he said. ''Is she visiting relatives or something? She's not from around here, that's for sure.''

''She is now,'' George replied. ''You remember Mrs. Addison who died last year? She lived on a small farm a couple of miles this side of your place.

Jeff nodded. ''Sure. She used to sew costumes for us kids for the Pine Festival Parade every year. Nice lady.''

''That's her,'' George answered. ''Well, this Lila Addison is her granddaughter and from what I hear in town, she's come to live on the old place.''

Jeff shook his head. ''Can't be true,'' he protested. ''A looker like her? She'd be a fish out of water. She's the city type for sure.''

''Maybe so,'' agreed George. ''But that's what Mrs. Cheetham at the post office told me and you'd think she'd be likely to know.''

''Hmmm. She looked vaguely familiar to me, but I'd swear I never saw her before in my life until yesterday.''

George shrugged and glanced at his watch. ''I gotta get going, Jeff. Call her, will you? Get her off both our backs?''

''Okay,'' Jeff agreed without showing much enthusiasm. ''I suppose I can do that.''

''Good. It'll save our hides for not sticking you with a fine. Meantime,'' George turned back as he neared the door, ''if there's anything Esther or I can do for you...'' He trailed off lamely, his face a portrait of shared pain and grief.

''I'll let you know, Pokey,'' Jeff said in a choked voice. ''Thanks.''

As soon as George left, Jeff sat down behind his desk and punched the intercom. ''Any other calls, Mary?''

''No sir,'' she answered regretfully. ''I'm sorry. You know I would have put it through at once if they'd called.''

Jeff sighed. "I know," he said softly. He punched the button again, disconnecting Mary and himself and swiveled his chair toward the sunlight flowing through the window.

A beautiful day, he thought. A day in which to appreciate being alive.

A day when his sorrow knew no bounds.

Chapter Two

Lila put down her brush and stretched. She was really tired and stiff, but she was satisfied with her beginning. Already the new painting was taking form.

This morning she had driven out to Cattail Lake and made sketches and notations about light and color. During the afternoon at home, she had outlined the shapes of trees and lake on the canvas and made a small start at actually painting. She decided that if tomorrow was another nice sunny day she would take her easel and canvas to the lake and work there.

Unless, of course, she mentally amended, a miraculous job offer should materialize first.

Lila left the sun porch, which she had converted into her studio, and went into the kitchen to pour herself a glass of orange juice. Then she carried the glass into the living room where she sat down in her grandmother's rocking chair.

She had earned a good rest and, yet again amending her plans for tomorrow, she thought she might just take the day off completely and do nothing except indulge herself. She could sleep late, for one thing, then begin reading a novel she hadn't had time for, then have a late breakfast. After that . . . well, she'd think of something.

The telephone rang, interrupting her pleasant reverie. Groaning, Lila got out of the rocking chair to cross the room to the sofa, next to which was the telephone.

"Hi. How're things down in Hicksville, U.S.A.?" asked a familiar voice.

Lila chuckled. "Rowdy. I've been going to wild parties every night."

"Sure. The excitement puts New York to *shame*, huh?" asked Clotilde Gold.

"Yep. I'm exhausted by the social whirl."

"Actually, you do sound a little tired," Clotilde scolded. "Aren't you getting enough sleep or are the crickets keeping you awake at night?"

To Clotilde Gold, owner of Gold Modeling Agency, one of the most prestigious in the business, there was no sin greater than one of "her" girls neglecting to get adequate rest. She always knew when they didn't. It showed beneath the glaring lights and through the merciless eye of the camera lens.

"I'm sleeping like a baby," Lila answered. "It's the daytime that's wearing me out. Only yesterday I finally finished unpacking and getting settled into the house. I've been job hunting as well and today I began my first painting."

"Hmmph. If you think I'm going to congratulate you on *that*, you're horribly mistaken."

Lila laughed softly. "Okay, okay, I already know you disapprove. You don't need to remind me."

"Painting for a *hobby* is all very well, my dear, but to make a *living* at it? Artists have been starving for *centuries* and I'm sure they'll continue to do so, whereas models, highly *successful* models, can afford to eat in the *best* restaurants." Clotilde had a way of talking with great stress on certain words, as though she was punctuating all her sentences with exclamation points in the middle of them.

"Yes, and order salads when they do," Lila retorted. "I'm eating very well, Clo. As a matter of fact, I've already gained two pounds since I've been here."

"Ugh! You make me *shudder*, Lila, you really do! I've called you with an offer for a *marvelous* assignment, but if you're becoming grossly overweight, I'll have to give it to someone else."

"You'll have to do that anyway, Clo. I thought I made it clear to you that I've retired from the business."

"Retirement sounds so *old*, and you're only twenty-six—still in your prime. This insanity of yours has gone on *quite* long enough, Lila. I want you to take this assignment. It's a fashion spread and the setting is Greece. Surely you can't turn *that* down?"

"Yes, I can. I'm here now, Clo, and I intend to stay put. At least long enough to put myself to the test and find out if I can make it."

"And by then you might find out you're no longer salable as a model. Be *sensible*, Lila. You and I both know you could use the money."

Lila sighed. Could she ever! Doing the assignment could make the difference between losing the condo or hanging on to it long enough to find a qualified buyer. But she had sworn to herself when she left New York that come what may, she was never going back to her old life.

"I'm sorry, Clo. I love you dearly as a friend, but our business relationship is over. I like going without makeup and wearing jeans and eating an ice-cream cone if I feel like it."

"What're you trying to do, give me a *heart* attack?" Clotilde wailed. "Please, spare me the *grisly* details of your chosen life-style. But just tell me this, have you met any *men* in that godforsaken hole?"

"You know that's the last thing I'm interested in right now, but as a matter of fact," Lila teased, "I have. Yesterday I met the richest man in the county."

"*Did* you? Well, that's more like it. Now tell me he's good-looking and single and I might forgive you for moving there."

"He's good-looking," Lila said, remembering every detail about him, including that anguished expression on his face, "but as to his marital status, I don't know. Nor do I care. We met when he rammed his car into mine."

"*My dear!* Were you hurt?"

"No. Just furious. The maniac took off before we could even call the police!"

"That *is* an exciting place. I thought things like that only happened in New York!"

"Obviously he thinks he's such a big shot that he doesn't have to follow the rules like the rest of us."

"Sounds like Small Town, Texas has a Nick, of sorts, all its own."

"Isn't that the truth? Why do men think they can get away with anything they like?" Lila asked in despair.

"I hope you don't expect an answer in twenty-five words or less," Clotilde said. "Listen, I'm going to hang up now, my dear. Frances is waving her hand at me. My latest client must be here and I have to see her."

"Sure. Thanks for calling, Clo. And for the offer of the assignment."

"Won't you reconsider?"

"Afraid not. But I'll call you soon."

After the phone call, Lila remained seated on the sofa for a long time. Forgotten was her drink and she was unaware of the evening shadows beginning to fall. She was thinking of Nick, and what a fool she had been.

When she had met him two years ago, Nick Barrow was the owner of a successful investment firm. She'd gone to him to make some investments and in turn he'd invited her to dinner.

Later they had become engaged, but they never got around to setting a wedding date because both of them were engrossed in their careers. Lila was one of the most acclaimed models in New York, gracing numerous magazine covers, selling many different products in advertisements and television commercials. Nick made frequent trips to the Bahamas and Switzerland for business and Lila hadn't given any thought to the legality or illegality of what he was doing. Certainly she hadn't realized he was a thief. Only recently had she learned that—at the same time that she had discovered that most of her own money had vanished without a trace.

Nick's parents were now dead. They had been highly respected. His father had been a Wall Street stockbroker, his mother an acclaimed hostess. They'd owned a lovely country home in Connecticut, where they had often entertained. Nick grew up with the best—servants, private schools, summer vacations at Martha's Vineyard or in Europe.

He'd had everything going for him—his family background, the family estate he'd inherited, a successful business and the respect of the business community, charisma, and youthful good looks somewhat similar to those of John Kennedy—the sort that inspired trust and admiration. Only in Nick's case, the impression had been deceptive.

Lila's sole comfort, if comfort it could be called, was that she hadn't been the only one duped by Nick's charms. There'd been at least a dozen other investors who had also been swindled by him. But what singled her out from the others, much to her chagrin, was that she had planned to marry the man.

Six months ago Nick's scheme had unraveled. Someone had wanted to withdraw his investments, only to find that his money had somehow evaporated. Investigations were to begin, but before anything meaningful was done, Nick had vanished. Since then, there'd been reports that he was living somewhere in the Caribbean where the long arm of the U.S. law couldn't touch him.

Lila's life had abruptly turned topsy-turvy. There were meetings and depositions at the D.A.'s office, consultations with attorneys and as if that weren't enough, there'd been the circus atmosphere created by the media. Because Nick had been from a well-known family and because Lila, with her own "celebrity" status as a top model, had been his fiancée, reporters dogged her footsteps relentlessly. Outrageous misrepresentations of facts were headlined on the front pages of newspapers, tabloids and in TV reports.

Sickened and disgusted by it all, completely disillusioned by men, love and her own increasingly unfulfilling career, Lila had decided it was time to make a complete change in her life. She was at the top of the modeling profession and made a substantial amount of money at it, but the truth was, she was burned out. She'd been modeling since she was seventeen years old. It seemed she'd spent a lifetime placing too much emphasis on glitz, glamour, intense competition and the shallowness of fame. Very few people in the business could be considered true friends. Far too many were two-faced, ready to stomp on others if it furthered their own way to the top. Lila was tired of it all and Nick's betrayal was the catalyst that prompted her to make the change. She'd felt that if she didn't get back to the true, basic values of life now, she'd be lost forever.

For the past couple of years she'd been painting as a hobby, as a way of unwinding and relaxing from the demands of her work. A handful of paintings had been good enough for a New York gallery owner to' sell. Now she hoped to develop her talent and turn her hobby into a career. But until she was established, she would need to subsidize herself with a job. A job she hadn't yet found.

Money was her big bugaboo right now. Fortunately she'd had a savings account that hadn't been entrusted to Nick.

The money from that account was all that was keeping her going. When she'd decided to make this drastic change in her life, she'd been lucky enough to unload her Mercedes and replace it with a modest Volkswagen. The problem was her Park Avenue condo. So far she hadn't been able to sell it and the mortgage was quickly gobbling up her reserve funds. In a few short months she was going to lose her investment in it if the condo hadn't sold by them. She hated the thought of losing that money, too, and now she wondered if she shouldn't reconsider Clo's offer. The money from the new assignment would stave off the wolf for a few more months.

But Lila knew if she went back, she'd be caught up in the old web again once and for all. It had taken a lot of courage for her to make this break and she wasn't sure she could do it a second time.

The telephone was still silent. The office line was also connected to his house phone, so Jeff knew no call had gone there either. His bleary eyes were stinging as he glanced at his watch. After six. Another day almost gone and still no word.

He might as well go home, he decided. There was nothing to keep him occupied at the office. But home felt so empty, even with all the hubbub going on there.

Jeff walked out of his private office into the reception room. Mary had long since left for the day and the room was as silent and oppressive as his own office had been.

As he started to pass Mary's desk, his eye was caught by a magazine she had left there. The face on the cover attracted his attention and he paused to look at it more closely. The young woman's smiling face was oval, her eyes a deep green, her hair a halo of gold highlighted with fire-red.

It was the woman he'd collided with yesterday—the one Pokey had asked him to telephone. Preoccupied as he was,

Jeff had forgotten his promise the minute his friend had left the office.

Now he understood why she had seemed familiar to him. Lila Addison was a model. He'd seen her photograph before somewhere, probably gracing another magazine cover or perhaps featured in a television commercial. Now his curiosity was mildly piqued once more. What in the world was a woman like that doing in a small, unpretentious community like Cattail?

Since he hadn't gotten around to calling her, Jeff abruptly decided to stop by her place on his way home. After all, it wasn't out of his way. He could write out a check for the damages to her car and hand it to her in person. Also, it would give him an excuse to delay going home, even if only for a few short minutes. If the call came during the interim, which his heavy heart told him wasn't going to happen after this much time had passed, Bud Himes would take it as he had done once before.

The Addison farm house looked the same to Jeff as it had the last time he'd been there, which had been at least six or seven years ago. His mother had been alive then and sent him there with some homemade sausage and jams to give to Mrs. Addison. Country people were like that, always giving each other small gifts out of their own bounty.

The house was a simple white, frame building with green shutters on the windows. A huge pecan tree graced the front lawn and behind the house was a cluster of pines. Mrs. Addison's beloved rose bushes were grouped next to the house, though none were blooming.

Two rocking chairs were on the wide front porch. Jeff climbed the steps and knocked at the door. A moment later it opened and Lila Addison stood facing him.

"Good evening," he said politely. "I'm Jeff Chappel, the man who ran into you yesterday."

"I remember," she said coldly. "The man who was in too much of a hurry to wait for the police."

It wasn't a good beginning. Jeff could tell she was still outraged and in no mood to be forgiving. Still, he had to try to make amends.

"May I come in?" he asked quietly. "I'd like to settle up with you for the damages to your car."

At first Jeff thought she was going to refuse. Her green eyes were narrowed as she glared at him with obvious dislike. She hesitated for a long moment, then finally pushed open the screen door, allowing him to enter.

The living room was different than he remembered. An elegant blue silk-covered sofa was placed against one long wall. Adjacent to it was an old rocking chair Jeff recognized as having belonged to Mrs. Addison. A small table that was also hers stood beneath a window with an expensive crystal lamp on it. The room had a cozy look to it, even with its eclectic furnishings. Somehow everything blended together into a harmonious whole.

Jeff gave Lila Addison a small smile. It had been so long since he had last parted his lips in that pleasant manner that the smile felt strange and unfamiliar on his face. "Very nice," he told her. "Your things go well with your grandmother's."

She looked surprised. "You know who I am?"

Jeff nodded. "You're a model from New York, and you're Mrs. Addison's granddaughter. George Duncan, the patrolman, told me your relationship to her. I'm sorry about her death. I always liked her."

"Thanks." Lila Addison's voice had suddenly turned husky. She fell silent for a brief instant, then said firmly, "Shall we get on with our business?"

Jeff studied her before replying. She wore faded jeans that hugged her slender hips and long legs and a loose-fitting, paint streaked T-shirt. Her hair was caught at the nape of her neck by a blue band. Instead of exuding the expensive French perfume that one might reasonably expect a beautiful model to wear, Lila smelled of turpentine and linseed oil.

"Certainly," he said at last, answering her question. "I came to write you a check to cover the damages to your car."

"Of course," she replied sarcastically. "A check solves everything, doesn't it?"

It was Jeff's turn to be surprised. "What else am I supposed to do?"

She shrugged one delicate shoulder. "Oh, nothing at all. This is exactly what I'd expect from a man like you."

Jeff's eyes narrowed. "Just what is that supposed to mean?"

"That you're a rich, spoiled person who thinks he's above the law! Why didn't you wait for the police yesterday as you were supposed to do? Too many accidents on your insurance record already? People like you disgust me! You're careless, carefree and you run roughshod over everyone else! I'll bet that officer was too intimidated by your power and your money to even give you a ticket, wasn't he? It must be nice to have everything going your own way, to be able to settle every problem with money!"

"Everything my own...my own way? My God, but that's f-funny!"

Jeff turned blindly in the direction of the door. A second later a strange lightheadedness overtook him and he slumped against the door frame, trembling as though he had a chill.

Something was terribly wrong here!

Lila stared in shocked dismay as the man staggered toward the door and then collapsed against the frame. Instead of the satisfaction of seeing how her words had riled him, and perhaps shamed him, as she'd intended, his strangely pale face had gone even whiter as he had stammered those few inexplicable words.

She rushed to his side and clasped his arm, afraid he was about to fall to the floor. This man was either very, very ill or he was under a tremendous amount of stress.

"Please," she said gently, "let me help you. Lean on me and try to reach the sofa."

Weak as he felt, Jeff's mind somehow recorded the fact that what she was suggesting was absurd. Lean on her? Why, he could make two of her. She wasn't strong enough to carry his weight.

All the same, he recognized her suggestion as a good one. This weird weakness had him shaken and he didn't think his legs were going to carry him outside to the car.

"I'll make it by myself," he said gruffly. He withdrew his arm from her clasp and lurched toward the sofa where he sat down with the abruptness of a person who had reached the end of his stamina.

"What is it?" Lila asked anxiously. She had followed him closely and now she bent over to touch his forehead. "Are you ill? Should I call the doctor?"

Jeff was already feeling somewhat recovered now that he was sitting and he shook his head. "No. I'm not sick. There's no point in calling anyone."

"Then what can I do for you?"

"May I have a glass of water?" Jeff asked quietly. He was ashamed of his unaccountable weakness in front of this woman.

"Certainly." Lila straightened and hurried to the kitchen.

A moment later, she came back and gave the glass to him. "I beg your pardon," she told him. "I was an idiot to pitch into you like that! I knew something was wrong, you looked so pale. I should have had more sense, better manners, but I let my temper get the best of me. Please forgive me."

Jeff finished the glass of water and leaned his head against the cushions and closed his eyes. "It's forgotten," he said in a weary tone. "Do you mind if I just sit here and rest a few minutes before I go? I don't think I'd better attempt to drive just yet."

"Of course not! But isn't there anything else I can do for you?"

"Nothing, thanks."

"If you're not ill, what made you have such a strange spell?" she wondered aloud.

Jeff struggled to open his eyes. "I can't imagine," he said. "It's never happened to me before. I apologize for alarming you like this."

Lila eyed him anxiously. He really did look dreadful. His eyes were red, bloodshot; there were still those dark smudges beneath them that she'd noticed yesterday, and his skin had the ghostly pallor of death.

Sudden instinct struck her and she asked, "When was your last meal, Mr. Chappel?"

"Jeff," he said softly. He squinted at her as though in thought and finally he replied, "Yesterday at breakfast, I think."

"No wonder you're practically fainting! I'll get you something to eat." She turned toward the kitchen door.

"Please, don't bother. I'm better already and I'll be able to go home in another minute?"

"Driving yourself?" Lila asked scornfully as she swung back toward him. She shook an admonishing finger at him and added sternly, "You'll sit right there while I get you some food. Otherwise you'd probably get yourself mixed up in yet another accident and I don't want that on my conscience."

"All right." Jeff gave in. The truth was he still felt too weak to argue. As she started to walk away he noticed the telephone on the table beside the sofa and asked, "Do you mind if I use your phone?"

"Help yourself," Lila said over her shoulder.

In the kitchen Lila opened a can of beef and vegetable soup and poured it into a saucepan. While the soup was warming on the stove, she made a couple of sandwiches from the chicken salad she had left from lunch and poured a glass of milk. Then she put on a pot of coffee. As she busied herself, she could hear the low murmur of Jeff's voice in the background as he spoke on the phone. She hoped he was calling someone to come and drive him home. She wasn't sure she trusted him to drive, even after he had eaten. The man looked exhausted as well as ill and Lila was still mentally kicking herself for the things she'd said to him.

When the soup was ready, she put everything on a tray and carried it into the living room.

"Thanks," Jeff said quietly as he took the tray from her. "This is very kind of you, considering the way I left you in the lurch yesterday."

"I'm tough, but I'm always kind to dumb animals and men who practically faint at my door." The words were needle sharp, but Jeff looked up just in time to see Lila Addison's smile. It was breathtaking and for a moment he forgot his food, until she reminded him.

"Eat," she ordered firmly. "Meanwhile, I'll have a cup of coffee while I keep you company."

She went into the kitchen and, grateful for the food that was now stirring an appetite he hadn't known he had, Jeff began to eat.

When she returned, Lila sat down in the rocking chair and silently sipped her coffee while she watched him eat. When he had finally polished off the last crumb, he said, "Thanks again, Miss Addison. I feel much better now."

Lila nodded in satisfaction. "Your color is better, too. But call me Lila. Two people who crashed into each other shouldn't be so formal."

"Agreed." Jeff placed the tray on the table in front of the sofa and asked, "Could I stretch your hospitality a little further, Lila? I'd love a cup of coffee. It smells delicious."

"Sure." Lila picked up his tray and carried it away. When she returned, she had a plate of cookies and a mug of coffee. "The cookies are only store-bought, but they're not too bad," she told him.

Jeff looked at her as she sat down in her chair again and he said softly, "You know, you're as kind as your grandmother was, Lila Addison."

Her eyes shimmered as they widened and suddenly she favored him with another knockout smile. It lit up her entire face. "That's about the nicest thing anyone could ever say to me, even if it's not really true." Lila shook her head. "I'd like to think I measured up to my grandmother, but I'm not sure I'll ever manage. She was one in a million."

"Yes," Jeff agreed. "She was. There's no end to the good things she did for the people in this community."

"Or for me," Lila said softly. "Except for my mother, I loved her better than anyone in the whole world." She paused and looked thoughtfully at Jeff. Then, changing the subject, she said, "You say you aren't ill, but something is really wrong in your life or you wouldn't look as though you haven't slept in a month or forget to eat for almost two days. I have a feeling that whatever it is was also connected to your leaving the scene of the accident so fast yesterday, wasn't it?"

Jeff set his coffee on the lamp table beside him. "You're a very perceptive person," he said slowly. "As a matter of fact, I haven't had more than three hours of sleep in four days and you're right about yesterday, too."

"Is there anything I can..." Lila hesitated. "Look, I don't want to be pushy or seem idly curious, but would you like to talk about it?"

Jeff's expression was one of such unadulterated anguish that Lila almost cried out. Brokenly, he said, "It's my sister. My...baby sister. She's been kidnapped."

Chapter Three

Lila's grandmother's living room appeared the same as it had only moments before...comfortable, cheerful; a snug, safe, secure harbor from the rest of the world. From outside the open windows came the sound of frogs croaking, reinforcing the sense of country solitude and insulation from the vicissitudes and dangers of what is termed civilization. Everything seemed so dear and familiar, yet in but an instant nothing any longer seemed safe and comforting. An element of horror had been injected into the mood, dispelling the mythic atmosphere of serenity and peace.

Jeffrey Chappel's words were so shocking, so far outside the range of ordinary, normal experience that at first the true meaning of them passed over Lila. She stared at him blankly, unable to assimilate the hideous significance of what he had just said. For a timeless moment she simply stared at him in uncomprehending silence.

But then the impact of the simple, devastating statement was absorbed and she gasped and cried out protestingly. "My God, no!"

Lila felt the color drain from her own cheeks, matching Jeff's. There was no doubting the veracity of what he told her. That Jeff was suffering the tortures of the damned was abundantly evident in his grief-haunted eyes, the haggard, parchment white of his face, the hopeless manner in which his shoulders slumped, the unsteadiness of his hands.

Without conscious awareness of her actions, knowing only that she had to comfort this large, heartbroken man somehow, Lila left her chair and went to sit next to him on the sofa. She reached out and with the simple caring of one human being for another who happens to be in trouble, she did the only thing she knew to do. She took his hand into her lap, clasping it tightly with one hand and covering it with the other. His fingers were icy, cold as death.

"How terrible!" she whispered as she looked up into his ashen face. "Jeff, I'm so dreadfully, dreadfully sorry! You must be out of your mind with worry."

He nodded mutely and his cold fingers wrapped themselves around hers as though he needed to cling to something, or someone, for support. Finally he said in a thick, emotion-riddled voice, "It's a nightmare that has to be endured to be believed. I never thought a person could live through this much pain." His voice broke and he drew in a long, ragged breath.

"What... how?" Lila murmured softly. "When did it happen?"

"Four days ago," Jeff answered in despair.

"Four?" A chill rippled through Lila. It sounded like forever. "Has there been no word at all?"

Jeff's lips formed a grim line. "Oh, yes. They called. They wanted money. A lot of money, and in a hurry. I had a hell of a time coming up with enough cash in the short period of time they gave me. And then..." His voice cracked and he fell silent.

"And then," Lila said, picking up the story with an odd, but unshakable instinct, "you had the accident with me on the way to give it to them. The accident delayed you."

Jeff looked at her in surprise. "How did you know?"

She shrugged. "Easy. It explains perfectly why you rushed off the way you did."

"Yes." Jeff's voice was scarcely above a whisper. "I was ten minutes late. Ten lousy minutes. I dropped the money where I was told to, but they never picked it up. The place has been under surveillance ever since. Either the kidnappers suspect the spot is being watched or they got scared off when I didn't show up exactly on time. Whatever the reason, there hasn't been a word from them since." He paused and rubbed his forehead. "I just telephoned my house to check and they still haven't called again. I hope you don't mind... I left your number in case they need to reach me while I'm here."

"Of course I don't mind. Jeff, I'm so terribly sorry. Sorry, too, for being so hateful to you. If I'd had any idea..."

Jeff didn't actually smile, but his expression became softer as his eyes met hers. "How could you have known? Under the circumstances, you had every right to be angry with me, but I just couldn't spare the time to explain yesterday."

"Certainly not! Oh, if only we hadn't had that accident!" Even though it had been Jeff who had run his car into hers and not the other way around, she felt a heavy responsibility for having been involved, for having delayed him for those few vital minutes. If the accident hadn't happened, his sister might very well be home right now, safe and sound. It was a dreadful burden to carry, and if she were feeling so badly about it, she could only imagine the guilt

Jeff felt. "The authorities . . ." she asked helplessly. "Can't they do anything?"

"They're doing everything they can." Jeff shrugged wearily. "The FBI and local law enforcement agencies in several counties are beating the bushes, but they don't have any solid leads. Two agents are camped in my house, monitoring the telephone, but the kidnappers have never stayed on the line long enough for the agents to trace where the calls are coming from. The first night the kidnappers put Janey on the phone herself, just to prove that they had her." He shuddered. "She sounded so frightened and there's not one damned thing I can do about it! And after this long, I'm not even sure she's still alive." His voice broke again, and he looked away from Lila briefly as he struggled to keep control.

"She has to be all right!" Lila exclaimed fervently. Sudden, unexpected tears had welled in her eyes and throat while she listened to his story. Her voice was raspy and harsh over a suppressed sob, but her tone and manner were as staunch and firm as a military commander giving orders to his troops. "Don't you dare give up hope, Jeffrey Chappel! Your sister needs that from you! Don't you dare stop believing, even for one little instant, that she'll come back!" Unconsciously, she squeezed his hand tighter and felt a responding pressure from his fingers.

"Thanks," he said huskily. "I guess I needed to be reminded."

There was an odd expression in his eyes as he looked at her and her heart skipped a beat. She saw gratitude there, but also something more, a warmth, an awareness of her as a person, as a woman and suddenly she felt herself being drawn to him in a way that went beyond simple compassion. It disoriented and confused her. Masking her feelings, she said sharply, "Well, don't you forget it again!"

Jeff was somewhat amazed at the whole situation. In spite of his grief and anxiety, he felt a magnetic pull toward Lila.

They were complete strangers, and yet he felt a closeness to her that defied comprehension. He was aware of her appealing beauty, yet he found himself responding more to her inner beauty than to her physical charms. He hadn't realized how desperately he had needed kindness and compassion until she had freely given them to him. Even more amazingly, there were tears of genuine concern shimmering in the depths of her lovely green eyes, and yet she was barely acquainted with him and she didn't know Janey at all.

He voiced a little of what he was thinking. "I don't know why I've been telling you this. We've been very careful to keep the situation hushed. Most of my closest friends don't even know. But somehow...you're very easy to talk to. And you really care." Involuntarily, he raised his free hand and gently wiped a tear away from her cheek. "You're crying."

"No I'm not!" Lila denied hastily. She gave him a wobbly smile, then amended, "Well, maybe a little. Anyway," she went on softly, "who wouldn't care?" Suspecting he needed to talk still more, and slightly unnerved by the warm flood of sensations she'd felt when his large hand had tenderly brushed across her face, she demanded, "Now, tell me about her. What does she look like? How old is she? What are the things she likes? All I know about her so far is that her name is Janey."

Jeff sighed. "She's fifteen. Our parents are both dead and we only have each other. I've been responsible for raising her for the past five years."

"Hmmm. I'll bet *that* job keeps you on your toes."

She got a smile out of him for her efforts and it heartened her.

"That's a fact." Jeff paused and gazed off into space for a moment. "She's beautiful," he said softly. "As beautiful as you are," he went on as he glanced at Lila again. "But in a different way. She has long dark hair and teasing brown eyes. She's a sophomore in high school and a cheerleader. She loves clothes." He chuckled at the thought. "Teenage girls are something else! They need a new outfit for every-thing. She badgers me constantly for more money for clothes. Sometimes I think that's all I work for, to feed her closet.''

"And you spoil her shamelessly and give in to her."

Jeff's smile widened. "Sure, I do. What else am I going to spend my money on? *I* certainly don't need that many clothes.''

"What else does she like besides clothes? Does she have a lot of friends?''

He nodded. "Janey's always the life of the party and the telephone never stops ringing." He frowned abruptly. "The past few days I've been telling all her friends she's sick and can't talk on the phone. I don't know how long I'll be able to keep up that story.''

"What about school? Does she enjoy it?"'

Jeff grimaced. "Oh, she loves the social aspect of it, being with all her friends. But as a student, she's just average. She's smart, and she could do a lot better if she only tried harder, but she's content to get by with passing grades. As a matter of fact, she wants to be a model just like you when she gets out of school. She would love meeting you.''

"She will," Lila stated with absolute conviction. "And soon.''

"I wish I could feel as certain as you do."

Lila didn't feel certain at all. She only knew she had to maintain a positive attitude for Jeff's sake. She couldn't let down for an instant because he was close to the breaking point after so many days of constant alarm and he needed whatever moral support she could offer him. She couldn't do much else for him, but she knew somehow that it was important to be as emphatically optimistic as she could. Her cheerfulness would help him keep from letting down and letting go, because once hope was gone... well, she just couldn't let him give up. Not yet.

"Tell me more about her. Does she like sports or have any hobbies? At least she's interested enough in her schoolwork to keep passing grades. So many kids don't these days."

Jeff suddenly grinned again and Lila liked the way his brown eyes lit up as he talked about his sister. "That's because I have one powerful weapon to use as a bribe. She enjoys sports all right, but the one thing she loves most in all the world is her horse, Toby. If she doesn't keep up her grades to a respectable level, I've threatened not to allow her to ride him and that's incentive enough. Sometimes, I think she loves that horse more than she does me."

They both laughed and Lila was about to ask about boyfriends when a shadow crossed Jeff's face once more. "She was riding Toby along the roadside on her way to a friend's house the afternoon she was kidnapped. When the horse came home alone, it was the first indication that something was wrong. I went out looking for her, thinking that Toby had thrown her and she was lying injured somewhere. Bad as that would have been, the reality is so much worse!"

Withdrawing his hand from hers, he covered his face with both his hands and hunched forward, elbows on knees, a portrait of desolation, of a man who by slow degrees, was dying inside.

Lila had never before felt such deep, cutting pain over another person's problems. Her heart ached for Jeff and she battled her own rising tears as she wrapped both her arms around his broad shoulders. For long minutes, they remained that way as she held him in silent sympathy.

Finally, he lifted his head. His eyes were red, but he was better. "Sorry," he murmured gruffly.

Lila released him immediately and clasped her hands in her lap. "Nonsense. There's nothing to be sorry about. You're under a tremendous strain."

Jeff looked away from her, and she sensed that he was embarrassed. "I could use another cup of coffee if you don't mind," he said at last.

"Sure." Lila stood up at once and carried their cups to the kitchen. The mundane request broke the intense tension for both of them and she was relieved to have something to do. She would take her time, giving them both an opportunity to get their emotions under control. She knew she needed to do that, and certainly Jeff did. She suspected that ordinarily he was a man with supreme control over his feelings and she had sensed his acute humiliation over her having witnessed his vulnerability.

Jeff was glad when Lila left the room. He needed a few moments to get a grip on himself. He could hardly believe how he had spilled out his most inner feelings to this woman, and it made him feel peculiarly uneasy, as though he'd lost all control. Yet she didn't seem to judge him or think him less of a man for it, and he appreciated that. He appreciated, too, her readiness to leave him alone for a little while. It was strange, but somehow she seemed to understand exactly what he needed.

Exhausted, he leaned his head back against the sofa cushion and closed his eyes. They were gritty from lack of sleep and they pricked like sharp, stabbing needles. He would rest them until Lila returned. As soon as he drank the coffee he'd asked for but didn't really want, he would get up and go home. Not that there was anything to go home for, but it was time. He certainly hadn't meant to stay this long and surely by now Lila must be wishing he'd leave and take his problems elsewhere.

Still, she sure had been nice to him, after her initial coldness. Who would have thought a woman who'd posed for magazine covers and appeared in television commercials would have come to live in a small country town like Cattail? It didn't make sense. Jeff yawned and decided he would ask her when she came back. It was better if they got completely away from the subject of Janey so that he wouldn't break down again, and asking about Lila's life seemed a logical way to do it.

But the question floated away as sleep overtook him.

Lila was returning with the coffee, but she paused in the doorway when she saw that Jeff was asleep. His head was tilted to one side, nestled against the mound of pillows at the corner of the sofa, his eyes were closed and his breathing was soft and regular. His long legs were stretched out before him and one arm was flung out across the sofa in a pose that reminded Lila of a completely relaxed, unconscious child. Her heart melted and, smiling to herself, she turned and tiptoed back into the kitchen.

She sat at the kitchen table and sipped her own coffee while Jeff's went cold. She didn't know whether to wake him up and send him home, or allow him to sleep a while. In the end, she decided it was better to leave him alone and allow him to get what rest he could. The man was plainly exhausted in every way, physically, mentally and emotionally and she just didn't have the heart to disturb him yet.

When her coffee was gone, she went back to check on him and Jeff was still soundly asleep. This time she approached him and bending down, she gently removed his shoes. He never stirred.

Lila chanced lifting one long leg at a time and stretching them out on the sofa. He would be so much more comfortable that way. Now that full darkness had fallen, the evening had grown cooler and she went to shut the windows and then cover him with a blanket. Deciding it best to leave the lamp on in case he woke up and became disoriented, she turned off the overhead light. Satisfied at last that she'd done all she could for him, she crept silently away.

While Jeff slept, Lila prepared and ate her own supper, but she found she had little appetite for it. She was too disturbed about the girl, Janey.

Four days! In such circumstances, it seemed like a life-time! Now that she was alone with her own thoughts and having no need to maintain an encouraging demeanor for Jeff's sake, she privately entertained the same doubts he had expressed. After this much time had passed, was it possible that the girl was still alive?

And if she was, what was she going through? The hideous possibilities didn't bear thinking about. Dwelling on them could make a person insane.

Since she couldn't eat, Lila got up from the table and washed the few dishes. When she was done, she finally returned to the living room.

Jeff had turned over onto his side, but he was still sleeping deeply. Lila watched him for a moment in consternation, still wondering what she should do about him. She'd never had a strange man fall asleep in her home before. It didn't seem right to let him remain all night, if indeed he slept that long; on the other hand, these were unusual circumstances, to say the least, and she hated to disturb him. If she woke him, he'd just have to endure his agony of mind again; asleep, he could have a brief respite from it.

But what about the agents in his house? Surely they would be expecting him back soon and glancing at the clock, Lila saw that it was already nearly ten o'clock. She nibbled at her lower lip indecisively, then abruptly reached a decision.

She found her purse and fished out the business card Jeff had thrust at her at the time of their accident. Under the business phone number, his home telephone number was also listed.

The only telephone in the house was next to the sofa. It was where her grandmother had left it and Lila hadn't yet gotten around to having another phone installed in the bedroom. She went to it and dialed. She would just have to chance waking Jeff by talking, but she had a suspicion that he was under so deeply that he would never hear a word.

"Chappel residence," said a voice at the other end of the line after the first ring.

"My name is Lila Addison," she said softly. "Mr. Chappel called you earlier to say he was at my house."

"Yes? What's wrong?" The other voice became sharp, anxious, and somehow Lila had the impression that whomever she was speaking to was no FBI agent. He sounded too personally concerned.

"Nothing," she answered hastily. "I'm sorry to have alarmed you. It's only that he's fallen asleep on my sofa and I hate to wake him up."

"I . . . see."

"Do you think I should?" Lila asked now. "He seemed so exhausted, I thought it best to let him get what rest he could, but I'll wake him and send him home if you say so."

"No. No. Let him sleep," the man said. But then an odd note crept into his voice, cautious, yet curious. "You know what's going on?"

"Yes. He told me," Lila admitted. "You still have my number? You'll call at once if there's news?"

"Sure. Thanks for calling, Miss Addison."

Lila cradled the receiver and glanced at Jeff. He hadn't roused at all during her brief conversation. She stood for a moment, watching him. One hand was now tucked beneath his face and his brown hair was tousled. His face looked young and untroubled in sleep, and it made her glad, since his conscious world was so grim.

In the shortest span of time possible, she had come to feel a strong attraction to this man. Part of it was compassion, certainly, but that wasn't it entirely, and she knew it. She found she liked Jeff Chappel a lot . . . maybe too much, and it vaguely disturbed her. Only a short while ago, she had believed herself in love with Nick, and then had come his treachery and her disillusionment. So now, what was this response to Jeff? Was she so fickle that she could become interested in another man so soon?

Lila didn't want to feel anything for any man again, at least not yet. She needed to get her own new life squared away, and anyway, hadn't Nick taught her anything? Hadn't she learned a bitter lesson, that trusting a man, any man, was a dangerous thing?

Setting her mind against the involuntary emotions this large man somehow aroused in her, Lila left the room and went to take a shower.

As she stripped off her clothes in the bathroom and stepped into the water, she suddenly realized that back in New York, under no circumstances would she have dared to undress and take a bath while a strange man slept in her apartment, yet tonight she had no fear. There was something about Jeff Chappel that she instinctively trusted. Somehow she simply knew that even if he woke up, he would make no attempt to harm her. She felt perfectly safe with him in her house.

By a quarter of eleven, Lila was tired and ready for bed. The emotion-packed evening she'd spent with Jeff, coupled with her own anxiety about his sister, made her feel as though she'd been put through a wringer herself. She went back to check on Jeff one last time and he was still dead to the world. She locked up and went into the bedroom and closed the door.

When the telephone rang, Jeff was dreaming about Janey, and it was a pleasant dream. She wore her cheerleader outfit—tights, a short white skirt and a blue and white sweater with a large C emblazoned on the front. She was feeding sugar cubes to Toby and telling Jeff that she wanted to invite fashion models to her birthday party. Then someone else entered the dream—a beautiful woman with long red hair. She clasped hands with Janey and told Jeff that Janey must have a new dress.

Jeff opened his eyes and for a split second, gazed about in confusion not knowing where he was. But in the next instant he was fully alert. He was on the sofa in Lila Addison's living room and the telephone next to it was ringing.

Without even thinking about the fact that this wasn't his home, he sat up abruptly, fully alert, and reached for the phone.

"Yes?" he barked, his voice gruff with alarm.

"Mr. Chappel?"

"Yes." Jeff sat up straighter and a chill of tension raced through him. Something had happened or the FBI agent, whose voice he recognized as belonging to one of the men stationed at his house, wouldn't be calling here.

Exultation rang in the other man's voice. "We've got her, Mr. Chappel! Your sister is safe!"

Lila had also been awakened by the telephone, even through the closed bedroom door. When she flipped on her bedside lamp, she saw that it was after two in the morning.

Still half-asleep, she forgot that a man was in her house. She stumbled toward the door in her red nightshirt, not bothering to put on a robe. She got to the living room just in time to see Jeff grab the phone.

Remembering why he was here, remembering that his sister had been kidnapped, Lila was suddenly wide awake. Tensely, she listened to Jeff as he spoke.

All at once a wide grin broke over his face and a wild excitement stampeded through Lila's veins. She went swiftly to stand next to Jeff, eager to hear what was obviously good news. He glanced up at her while he continued to carry on his conversation and when he winked at her, it confirmed all she really needed to know.

His conversation was mercifully brief. The instant he hung up, Lila demanded, "Tell me! Tell me!"

With a lightness that was unusual for so large a man, Jeff swung to his feet. His gaze encompassed her...slender arms and legs visible above and below the shapeless nightshirt that concealed everything else, the mussed cloud of red-gold hair, a delighted, expectant smile curving her lips, the sparkle of joy that glittered in her eyes.

Exuberantly, Jeff did what came naturally. He wrapped his arms around Lila's waist, lifted her from the floor and swung her around and around. "She's all right!" he exclaimed in a deep, vibrant voice. "They found her! She's safe! Janey's alive and safe!"

"Thank God!" Lila gasped breathlessly somewhere in the vicinity of his left ear.

"Thank God is right!" Jeff slowly lowered Lila to her feet, but he did not release her. He looked deeply into her eyes and what she saw in his expression made her tremble. Then he drew her closer until her body was pressed tightly to his and she could feel the rapid thudding of his heart against her breast.

Jeff saw his own joy mirrored in Lila's eyes and he thought, this woman is incredible. Beautiful and wonderful and incredible. Earlier, she had really cared about him in his ordeal; now she was genuinely thrilled that Janey was all right. Somehow the details seemed perfectly right, like puzzle pieces fitting together—her caring, his being here to share with her the thrilling news when it finally came. What seemed incredible was the fact that they had known each other but for scarcely a single evening.

It also seemed natural and right when he bent his head at last and kissed her. He couldn't have stopped himself had he wished. He was too ecstatic, her smile too lovely, her rosy lips too near.

She didn't try to stop him, but responded willingly, as though she, too, felt that it was the only possible conclusion they could reach.

When they drew apart a few moments later, they were both breathless as they gazed at one another in wonder.

Chapter Four

The heater inside the Porsche blew warm air on its occupants, overriding the chill of the predawn darkness. The highway wound its way through stretches of woods that cast ghostly dark shadows over the pavement. Then the road abruptly emerged into deep gray open spaces, fields and meadows. A waning moon clung to the black, starless sky, affording little light. The bright beams of the car's headlights picked out a curve in the road, an occasional farmhouse on a hilltop, a road sign, a startled jackrabbit—and the luminous red taillights and the flashing light atop the roof of the escort car ahead of them. Except for the short convoy, there was no other traffic on the road at this hour.

Despite the two cars that accompanied them, one ahead, one behind, isolated as they were inside Jeff's car and by the slumbering countryside, it seemed to Lila almost as though she and Jeff were the only two people in the world. It was a strange, and yet somehow, a snug, comfortable feeling—as though they belonged together like this.

Lila dismissed the foolish thought and rubbed her hands against her arms. She turned her head to gaze out the window at the swiftly passing blur of indistinct shapes and reminded herself that they were together this way only because Jeff had felt it might be a good thing, for his sister's sake, if a woman came along. There was nothing more to it than that she might be useful.

"Cold?" Jeff enquired. From the corner of his eye, he had noticed Lila rubbing her arms.

"No. I'm fine, thanks."

He tossed a quick glance in her direction. "I really appreciate your coming with me," he said. "After all, none of this trouble belongs on your shoulders."

"Don't be silly!" Lila responded spiritedly. "You'd have had a hard time leaving me behind. I'm so excited I can hardly sit still. I feel like I want to get out and give the car a push."

Through the darkness, Jeff couldn't actually see her smile, but he could hear it in her lilting voice. She really was elated that Janey had been rescued, even though she'd never met his sister, never ever heard of her before tonight. On the face of it, it seemed absurd and illogical that Lila should care so much, that in a few short hours she had seemed to become a vital part of his life. Yet it was true and Jeff was very, very glad they had met, that she was sitting beside him now, sharing his eager impatience to reach Janey.

Impulsively, he took one hand from the steering wheel and reached out to touch hers. "My sentiments, exactly. Where've you been all my life?" he asked huskily. "We've only just met, yet I feel closer to you than I've felt to anyone in a long, long time."

Something caught in Lila's throat. Things were moving entirely too fast! She had barely met this man, yet already she'd told him off, then fed him, allowed him to sleep in her house and even let him kiss her!

And what a kiss it had been! Sure, they'd both been jubilant, caught up in the joy of the moment, and anybody might be excused for getting a little carried away at a time like that. But somehow she couldn't quite rationalize away all of the extraordinary feelings that had engulfed her during that kiss. His lips had moved warmly upon hers and the touch of them had seemed to pull up something from the very depths of her soul. She had suddenly gone weak-kneed and all tingly inside. Her heart had begun to race and her blood had flowed hot. In all the time she'd been with Nick, she'd never once felt like that! It was a revelation.

It was also alarming.

Now she became aware of the gentle pressure of Jeff's hand on hers. She felt an almost overwhelming desire to turn her hand palm up and lace her fingers with his.

But she resisted the urge and sternly reminded herself once more that things were going too fast. After Nick, the last thing she needed was to get involved with another man right now—any man.

Besides, everything was out of sync. She and Jeff both were off-balance from the emotionally charged evening and then from the exhilaration of learning his sister was alive and well and free. Probably under ordinary circumstances they wouldn't have even given each other the time of day.

"It's just the excitement of everything," she said prosaically. She forced a laugh. "I think you'd probably have felt this way toward anyone who happened to be with you when that phone call came."

Jeff withdrew his hand at once and Lila's felt suddenly chilled. She wondered if she detected a note of hurt in his voice as he responded, "I suppose you're right."

As soon as they had drawn apart from the impulsively shared kiss, Jeff had asked Lila if she would accompany him to the Tyler police station where Janey had been taken. His tortured, "She might need a woman's comfort right now, and Martha, my housekeeper is away," had been all he'd needed to say. Lila had understood that he was afraid his young sister had been molested. Even if she hadn't wanted to go along, she would have been unable to turn down his anxious request, more for the girl's sake than for his.

After that, there hadn't been time to talk. Lila had rushed back to her bedroom to throw on slacks and a lightweight sweater. Then she had hastily gathered a jacket, blanket and pillow to carry along in case Janey needed them.

They had gone first to Jeff's residence. The FBI agents stationed there met them at the gate in their car; two local policemen were also present in a patrol car. Without wasting a moment, all three cars sped away, the patrol car ahead with its warning flashing light, then the Porsche and finally, the unmarked FBI men's car.

Now, to ease the suddenly strained tension between them, and also because she wanted to know all the details she hadn't taken time to question him about before, Lila asked, "How and where did they find her?"

"The kidnappers finally showed up to collect the money," Jeff explained. "Around midnight. Thank goodness the FBI still had men watching the area. They trapped them and then one of the kidnappers talked. They'd been keeping her in an old farmhouse a few miles north of Tyler. I just hope they didn't . . ." He broke off, unable to say the terrible words.

"Take it easy," Lila said soothingly. Forgetting she'd been worried about things going too fast, she reached over to cover his hand on the steering wheel with hers. "She's alive," she reminded him. "And she's safe. That's what's most important."

Jeff did what she hadn't had the courage to do. He turned over his hand and clasped hers tightly. "Thanks," he said thickly.

"For what?"

"For helping me keep my head screwed on." After a moment, he released her hand, but by this time the comfortable, close feeling had returned between them.

It was three-thirty in the morning when the little caravan arrived at the Tyler police station. Its passengers were escorted down a hall and into a private office.

Lila's immediate impression was of a large crowd. There were three men, one a police officer, the other two, she later learned, were the FBI agents who had rescued Janey, and a police matron who sat in a chair next to a young, frightened-looking girl who could only be Janey. Then there were Jeff and herself, along with the four men who had escorted them here.

When they entered the room, the girl looked up and as soon as she saw Jeff, she burst into tears. During the time it took for him to swiftly cross the room, she threw off the blanket that had been wrapped around her slim shoulders and stumbled to her feet, arms outstretched.

Jeff caught her in his arms.

It was a long, emotionally charged moment. Brother and sister clung to one another as though they would never let go. Janey sobbed into Jeff's jacket lapel while his trembling hands stroked her head and shoulders.

Lila's eyes misted over and she had to brush the tears away and take a deep breath so she would not make a fool of herself.

Finally she had control of her emotions and she glanced toward the others in the room. They looked touched as well, and some of the men's eyes were suspiciously moist. Then, one of the men jerked his thumb in the direction of the door and they all quietly trooped out into the hallway, leaving brother and sister alone together.

The men began to drift down the hall, but the policewoman remained with Lila. Her smile was friendly. "This is one of the rare rewards of my job."

"I can well imagine," Lila answered, smiling back. Abruptly she became serious and asked in a low voice, "How is she, really?"

"Okay as far as we can tell. A bit bruised on her arms and legs, but essentially she's fine. Pretty shaken up, though, which is understandable."

Lila nodded. "Do you know whether she was assaulted? Her brother's been worrying about that a lot."

"She says she wasn't, although she hasn't had a physical examination to determine it. I believe she's telling the truth. She's upset and scared, but she doesn't act like a victim of a sex crime."

Lila sighed with deep relief. "Thank God! She's so young and she's been through enough without that!"

"I'll say," the policewoman replied. "They had her tied up inside a dark closet. She said they only let her out to take her to the bathroom and then they blindfolded her. She even had to eat in that closet. She had no idea where she was."

"Poor kid," Lila murmured to herself.

They stood in the hallway a few more minutes talking softly and then the policewoman offered Lila coffee. She was just about to follow the woman down the hall when the door of the office swung open.

Jeff stood there. His eyes were moist as rain, but his smile was dazzling, like the sun, and his voice was steady and under control. "Lila, would you come in, please? I'd appreciate it if you'd stay in here with Janey while I have a talk with the agents who rescued her."

"Nothing I'd like better," Lila responded heartily. She nodded pleasantly at the policewoman and stepped inside the room.

Jeff's hand pressed the back of Lila's waist as he escorted her across the room. His touch was warm, even through the wool sweater she wore, and it sent a pleasant sensation through Lila. It felt as though his hand belonged there and always had. It was a silly notion, of course, but somehow Lila found she liked the fantasy. Tomorrow, when this extraordinary night was over, there would be time enough to bring herself back to stark reality.

His sister had resumed her seat in the chair next to the wall. Her shoulders were hunched, her eyes dark with unmistakable fatigue. She showed no expression at all while Jeff made the introductions.

"Janey, this is Lila Addison, the lady I told you about. She's going to stay with you while I talk with the men outside." His smile was soft as he gazed at his sister and added, "Lila's as good a listener as she is beautiful. I brought her along because I thought you might like to have a woman to talk to."

"Or not to talk to, if that's how you feel." Lila smiled and said gently, "Hello, Janey. I can't tell you how delighted I am to be able to make your acquaintance and how thrilled I am that you're all right."

"Hi." Janey didn't smile back. She shivered and looked up at Jeff. "You won't be gone long, will you?" she asked pitifully. Her face was troubled and her voice trembled.

"Not a second longer than necessary," Jeff assured her. He tossed a concerned glance at Lila as if to ask silently "Are you sure you can handle this?"

Lila nodded at him, then sat down in the chair beside Janey. "While you're gone, Janey can fill me in on all your faults. I doubt she'll be finished by the time you get back."

Jeff grinned, relieved at Lila's light tone. "That ought to keep you busy, all right," he agreed. He bent and kissed Janey's cheek and then turned and quietly left the room.

After they were alone, Janey Chappel and Lila studied each other frankly. The girl wore dingy jeans and a dirty, yellow T-shirt. She had long dark hair that right now was in a frightful mess. It obviously hadn't been brushed in days. Her face was streaked with tears and altogether she looked as though she could use a hot bath. All that notwithstanding, Lila saw that Janey was uncommonly lovely. Her face was squarish, but with high, prominent cheekbones. Her dark brown eyes were wide spaced and fringed with beautifully thick black lashes, although at the moment there was deep pain evident in those eyes, pain that no fifteen-year-old girl should know. Her mouth was well shaped and in spite of her need for a bath, her skin had a flawless, youthful glow. There was an innocent beauty about her and the artist in Lila told her that, properly groomed, Janey would make a marvelous subject for a portrait.

Janey looked her over just as curiously. Finally, she blurted, "Are you Jeff's girlfriend?" There was a tinge of resentment in the question but Lila instinctively knew the reason for it. The girl had been through a terrible ordeal and it must cut her to the quick to think her brother had been concentrating on romance while she'd been missing.

Lila determined to nip that idea in the bud at once. She managed a small laugh, partly to relieve the girl's anxiety and partly out of genuine amusement. "Nothing could be further from the truth. We only met day before yesterday and my main ambition at the time was to see him tossed into jail."

She was rewarded by an expression of real interest. "Honest?" Janey gasped. "What did he do?"

Lila chuckled again, leaned back in her chair and picked up Janey's hand. It was icy and to warm it, she covered it with both of hers, rubbing her fingers back and forth. "Have I got a story to tell you," she said.

She made an amusing tale out of the car accident, how outraged she'd been when Jeff had sped away and how she'd wanted the police to apprehend him. Then she described his visit to her home last night, the way she'd angrily jumped all over him, then had to nurse him back to a state of health with food and a bed on the sofa.

She had Janey laughing by the time she finished. "Poor Jeff," she finally murmured. "That accident sure was rotten timing."

"The absolute worst," Lila agreed. "But how was I to know? I just thought he was a first-rate creep trying to flaunt the law." Turning serious, she added, "But after he nearly collapsed at my house, I knew something was terribly wrong. When he finally explained what was going on, I felt horribly ashamed of myself for having been so rude to him.'' She patted the younger girl's hand and suddenly smiled. ''You should have seen his face when they called to say you'd been rescued, Janey. It's obvious you're the light of his life.''

Janey's lips quivered and fresh tears sprang to her eyes. Lila didn't pause to think. She simply did what came naturally. She gathered the girl into her arms and pressed the dark head against her own shoulder. ''Cry all you want, honey,'' she said softly. ''You've been through a lot and you need to get it out.''

Janey began to sob and Lila just sat quietly, holding her and stroking her hair from time to time. She was no psychology student, but she was certain that the girl would feel a great sense of relief once she'd cried it all out of her system.

They remained that way for some time. Lila waited patiently for the storm to subside, while her heart went out to Janey. The poor child had been through only God knew what, an experience so hideous, so terrifying that most people couldn't even begin to imagine it. There was no telling how long it was going to take for her to recover from the ordeal, to be able to put it out of her mind, if she ever could.

Or Jeff. He had been terrified for his sister's life. It wasn't going to be an easy thing for him to get over, either. Lila was just glad that she could be supportive of them both, even if only in the smallest way. Somehow it didn't seem at all strange that she should suddenly be so intimately involved with this family. It only felt right.

Finally the sobs ended. Janey sniffled and Lila dug in her purse for some tissues. Janey lifted her head, mopped at her eyes and blew her nose. ''I'm s-sorry,'' she stammered.

''Don't be silly,'' Lila said matter-of-factly. ''It's the best thing you could have done.'' She fished inside her purse again and pulled out a brush. "Why don't you let me brush your hair," she suggested. "It'll make you feel better."

Obligingly, Janey turned her back and Lila, working as gently as she could, began to run the bristles through the mass of matted tangles. "Do you feel like talking about it now?" she asked quietly.

A tremor ran through the girl and she was silent for a long moment. At last she said, "I was so—so scared. They kept me in a dark closet. The told me...they said if I tried to get away, they would find me and k-kill me and Jeff, too."

Lila paused from her task of brushing and wrapped her arms around Janey once more. "Go on," she urged softly.

"There's not much to tell," Janey said. "They didn't talk to me at all, except to make threats."

"Did they..." Lila paused, trying to think of a way to delicately ask the question that had been paramount in Jeff's mind, once he knew she'd been found. The police-woman had said Janey told her she wasn't molested, but Lila knew, for Jeff's sake, she had to ask it, too. "Did they hurt you, Janey? Did they touch you...intimately...or force themselves on you in any way?"

"No," Janey replied gruffly. "One of them would have, but the other man stopped him. He said getting the money and getting away was all they had time to be concerned with."

"Thank heaven for that!" Lila exclaimed. "But I notice you have some bruises."

"Most of them are from when they first grabbed me and threw me into the trunk of their car. Some of them are from when they'd take me out of the closet to go to the bath-room. I was blindfolded and they'd grab my arms pretty roughly and shove me."

Lila squeezed Janey's shoulder sympathetically. "Well, you're safe now. Nobody is ever going to hurt you again."

She began brushing Janey's hair once more and had it in some semblance of order when Jeff returned.

He was cheered when he saw what Lila was doing. The very ordinariness of the activity was somehow comforting. It was like a promise of things to come, that life was going to be normal and safe once again.

Lila could have no possible idea of how deeply he appreciated all that she had done. She'd given him a kind, sympathetic ear when he'd badly needed one and now she had done the same for Janey. He could see it on Janey's face. She wasn't as tense and fearful as she'd been when he'd left them alone. It was something he wasn't likely to ever forget or cease to be grateful for. Lila was virtually a stranger to them both, yet she had willingly bolstered them when they had needed someone.

She looked up at him at that moment and smiled. The warmth of it seemed to spread right through him, and for a second he caught his breath. She was beautiful, inside and out. Who would have thought it of an acclaimed model? Jeff had always believed such women were hard to the core, intent only on themselves and their vanity, but Lila wasn't like that. Except for a touch of peach-pink lipstick, she hadn't bothered with makeup when she'd dressed to come with him. Even the clothes she wore were far from glamorous. She was neat and attractive in her beige slacks and aqua sweater, but there was nothing about the outfit that leapt to one's attention like the fantastic clothes models usually displayed in fashion magazines. She was lovely, of course, even without makeup, but otherwise there was nothing about her looks, her clothing or her demeanor that seemed sophisticated or out of the ordinary.

"How would you girls like to go home now?" he asked with a wide grin.

Janey jumped to her feet and ran to hug Jeff around the waist. "I thought you'd never come back and say that. Let's go!"

Jeff gazed at Lila across Janey's head and he mouthed the words, "Everything okay?"

Lila smiled again and raised her hand, forefinger and thumb together in the "OK" sign. His face immediately lit up with relief.

In the hallway, the FBI agents and police officers milled around, waiting to say goodbye. Jeff paused to shake hands with each of them; Janey left the shelter of his arm long enough to briefly embrace the two agents who had actually rescued her.

"Thank you doesn't . . . seem like enough," she said in a choked voice.

"Honey," answered one of the men as he gave her a fatherly pat on the shoulder, "finding you made our day!"

"Our year," corrected his partner with a broad grin. "You take care of yourself."

Janey gave him a smile and then they were ready to leave. The two Cattail policemen who had accompanied them here preceded them toward the door.

As they went, Jeff draped an arm over both Lila's and Janey's shoulders and held them close. Lila was startled and her mouth went dry at his nearness. She was remembering that tender kiss they had exchanged earlier and once more, she pondered the fact that she seemed to be getting involved with this man very fast. But when he looked down at her and smiled, it softened something within her. She wouldn't have drawn away from the warmth of his arm for anything in the world.

Outside, they were startled by the presence of TV cameras. A loud clamor arose immediately as the journalists vied with one another to elicit comments from the participants of the drama that had been carefully concealed for days. Now they were determined to make up for lost time.

"Hey, Janey, how do you feel?"

"What did they do to you?" screeched a woman's voice.

"What thoughts went through your mind while your sister was missing, Mr. Chappel?" An aggressive man shoved a microphone directly into Jeff's face.

A muffled sob came from Janey and she pressed her face against Jeff's sleeve. Lila looked up and saw that Jeff's jaw had turned to stone. "Get that thing out of my face, if you know what's good for you!" he growled with such ferocity that the reporter hastily stepped out of his path. "Damned barracudas!" he muttered beneath his breath. "How'd they find out, anyway?"

"Keep your cool and keep walking," Lila advised in a low undertone. "Just ignore them."

With the two policemen clearing a path for them, they made it at last to the car, while the reporters followed, still shouting questions.

"Give us a break," yelled one man before Lila could close her door. He rushed forward and stooped to peer into the car, getting in the way so she could not shut him out. "Just one quick statement," he insisted.

"Give this girl a break," Lila shot back. "She's exhausted and you ought to be ashamed of yourself for upsetting her like this after all she's already been through." Behind her in the back seat, Janey was sobbing hysterically over all the ruckus.

The reporter had the grace to look chagrined as Lila's gaze held his, and then he fell back so that she could pull the door shut.

"Burn some rubber!" she ordered Jeff in a voice like iron.

Jeff laughed raspily in a far-from-amused voice and did just that. Tires squealed as he followed the lead police car. Lila, meanwhile, occupied herself by turning to comfort Janey.

Little by little, Janey calmed down and the sobs subsided.

"That was a narrow escape," Jeff said at last. "I can't believe those clods have so little respect for people's feelings. Are you okay, honey?" he asked Janey.

"Yes," she answered in a quavering voice. "They just surprised me, and I got scared when they all started coming at us at once." She sighed. "I'm glad we got away from them."

"Me, too," Jeff seconded. "Reporters are the last thing we need right now."

"Oh, they'll be back," Lila predicted with grim certainty. "You haven't heard the last of them yet."

"How do you know?"

Lila's eyebrows lifted. "Are you kidding? With a hot story like this? No way they're going to give up without a fight. Obviously you've never had to deal with the press before."

"Can't say as I have," Jeff replied thoughtfully. "But you sound like you've had plenty of experience with them."

Lila's voice was harsh. "Far too much. Enough to last a lifetime."

After the scandal had broken about Nick, reporters had pursued her relentlessly for weeks. It had been a nasty experience, one she most certainly didn't want Janey to have to endure, but now wasn't the time to go into all the details. The main thing was to calm Janey and make her comfortable.

Dawn broke over the hills as they drove back to Cattail. Janey dozed in the back seat wrapped in the blanket Lila had brought, her dark head nestled against the white pillow. While Jeff drove, Lila turned from time to time to check on Janey, who sometimes cried out or moaned in her sleep.

"Poor baby," she murmured in a soft undertone. "She truly is exhausted." She tilted her head and peered intently at Jeff. "You, however, look a hundred percent better than you did when you showed up at my door last night. I wonder why?" she teased.

Jeff grinned at her. "It's amazing what relief and happiness can do for a man. I feel like I've been reborn."

"I think Janey will feel the same way once she's had a bath and a good, long rest. She's a pretty strong girl, Jeff. I'm amazed at how well she's held up through such an ordeal."

"That's my Janey," Jeff said with pride. "Stubborn, strong spirited and spunky. In this case, I'm glad she's the way she is. She doesn't give up. However, when she wants to do something I don't think she should, we can have some mighty fierce arguments." He shook his head. "Believe me, it's not always easy being the guardian of a teenage girl."

"That's a big, fat fib, Jeff," Janey said, sitting up in the back seat. "You know what a meek, mild, easy-to-get-along-with person I am."

"Sure," Jeff retorted dryly. "As long as you're getting your way."

They all laughed, but then Janey changed the subject and asked earnestly, "Toby? Is he all right?"

"He's fine," Jeff replied. "Came straight home. That's how we first realized you were missing."

"I'm glad he's okay. I've been so worried about him. I was afraid he might get hit by a car or a truck while he was on the loose like that."

Lila turned to stare at Janey in astonishment. "In the predicament *you* were in, you worried about your horse?"

Janey shrugged. "Sure. I love Toby and I don't want anything to happen to him. Anyway, I had to think about something besides myself most of the time or I would have gone crazy. I thought about a lot of things."

"Such as?" Jeff asked quietly.

"You, of course. And about Mom and Dad." Her voice became sad. "I was wishing they were still here."

"So do I, honey," Jeff said softly. "They'd be very proud of you, you know. Just as I am." He paused, then asked, "What else did you think about?"

"School. I missed that algebra test I was so worried about." She sighed. "I guess Mrs. Gunther will make me stay after school and take it."

Jeff chuckled. "Well, we'll worry about that later. Right now we could all use a big breakfast. I'll bet Bud already has it going."

"Ummm. I hope so. When is Martha coming back? I even daydreamed about her fried chicken."

"Next week, I think." Jeff glanced at Lila and said, "Bud and Martha Himes and their son Lionel take care of our place. But their married daughter lives in San Antonio. She had a baby just before Janey was taken and Martha went to be with her. Bud's been holding down the fort while Martha's away, so he's as worn out as the rest of us after this crisis, but knowing him, he won't be able to get any rest until Janey's home safely. He's a pretty fair cook himself. I called him just before we left the police station to let him know we're on our way and he's sure to have breakfast ready. You'll join us, of course," he stated flatly.

"Oh, I don't think so," Lila protested. "You'll want some time alone together now and I'd just be in the way. You'd better take me home."

"I want you to come with us," Janey said unexpectedly. "Please, Lila?"

Jeff grinned. "Maybe you can refuse me," he told her, "but surely you can't turn down Janey."

No, she couldn't. She was a little surprised that either of them still wanted her company once they got home, but strangely enough, it pleased her enormously. Perhaps she'd been more lonely than she thought all by herself out at her grandmother's house.

Surely that was the only reason. It had nothing at all to do with Jeffrey Chappel's warm smile or the memory of his kiss. Of that she was certain.

Almost.

Chapter Five

During the predawn darkness, when they'd stopped outside the gate and met their escort, Lila had not been given the opportunity to visit the Chappel house. Of course she had seen it many times before from the road, but now, as Jeff waved goodbye to the men in the patrol car and drove past the gate, curiosity stirred inside her.

The house was two stories, of white brick, set atop a small rise, so that enticing glimpses of it were visible from the road beyond a thick stand of pines.

The car pulled to a stop in the curving driveway in front of the house. Thick antebellum columns graced the porch. Beyond them, on either side of the massive, carved front door, were large terra cotta pots containing shrubs. Edging the porch were neat flower beds.

The grounds were sweeping and grass luxuriantly carpeted the gentle slopes. At the foot of the rise were pecan and elm trees and beneath one of them was a wooden swing where one could relax in the shade on a hot summer day.

Jeff pressed the car horn to announce their arrival and even before the three of them could mount the steps, the front door swung open.

A man of medium height, with burly shoulders and thinning gray hair came outside to greet them. Janey went straight into his open arms.

"I'm so glad you're home, Sweet Pea," he said gruffly. "How are you feeling?"

"I'm fine," Janey replied as the man drew her inside the house. "It's sure good to see you, Bud."

Jeff grinned at Lila and indicated by a wave of his hand that she should follow the others. Inside the marble-floored entranceway, she heard Janey add, "I'm starving. Do I smell biscuits?"

Bud grinned and nodded. "I just put 'em in the oven. I got busy cooking as soon as Jeff called to say you were on your way. I figured you'd be hungry." His gray eyes studied Janey with keen scrutiny before he asked, "What do you want first, a bath or food?"

"Food," Janey said decisively. "I'm afraid if I take a bath first, I'll fall asleep."

For the first time the man looked beyond Janey and saw Lila standing behind her. Jeff introduced them. "Lila Addison, this is Bud Himes. He and his wife Martha boss us around and keep us in line," he said lightly.

Bud nodded affably. "Somebody has to," he said. He gave Lila a pleasant look without exactly smiling. "Nice to meet you, miss. You're the lady who called last night to tell me Jeff had gone to sleep on your sofa."

Lila smiled. "That's right. It's nice to meet you, too, Bud."

Bud swept an arm out in an inviting manner. "All of you go sit down at the table. I'll pour the coffee while you wait for the biscuits to get done." To Janey, he added, "You look like you could use a little fattening up. You'll drink milk with your breakfast."

"Ugh!" Janey affected a shudder of disgust.

Jeff grinned at Lila. "See what I mean about bossing? Janey hates milk, but if Bud says she's going to drink it, drink it she will."

"Good for Bud," Lila laughed softly. "I'm with him. Besides, it'll help her sleep better later."

Janey and Lila sat down at the small round table in a cozy breakfast room while Jeff excused himself to make a quick phone call to the doctor. Janey protested that she felt fine, but he refused to heed her. He wanted the doctor to check her over.

Janey glanced around the room at the floral blue and white wall paper, the hanging plants at the window, and sighed. "I was afraid I'd never see all this again," she said shakily.

Lila reached across the table and touched her hand. "It's all right now," she reminded huskily. "You're back with the people who love you."

Breakfast was a happy event. Bud brought in a mountain of food—bacon and sausage, fried eggs, hash browns, orange juice and of course, the hot fluffy biscuits. Then he sat down and joined them, something that obviously surprised Jeff and Janey, though they didn't appear to disapprove.

Bud saw the surprise on their faces and said simply, "I just gotta look at Janey for a while. Make sure she's really here and all right."

Jeff nodded. "I know. I feel the same way." His gaze was infinitely tender as it went to his sister.

"She's a sight prettier than those FBI men who've been camping here the past few days," Bud declared as he held the platter of sausage and bacon while Janey helped herself.

"I imagine they think she's prettier than you, too," Jeff teased. "Where's Lionel?"

"He'll be in soon. He's brushing Toby. Wanted to make sure he's shiny and ready for a visit from Janey."

"I want to see Toby as soon as we're through eating."

"Only to say 'hello,'" Jeff said. "Then it's upstairs to bed for you, young lady."

Janey nodded. There were dark circles of fatigue beneath her eyes and despite her claim that she was starving, she ate slowly, as though she was too tired to bother. "If you're expecting a fight about that, you're wrong."

A small silence fell while they ate, but after a little while, Janey broke it. "How's the new grandbaby, Bud? Jeff told me it's a girl."

Bud grinned proudly. "Martha says she's beautiful. They named her Jacqueline Annette. Seems like an awfully big name for a little mite of a thing, but I reckon she'll grow into it."

"When's Martha coming home?"

"Next week. I called her this morning at daylight to tell her you were safe. She was so happy she started bawling like a calf." Bud glanced toward Lila and said, "I'm glad you're here, miss, since Martha ain't. Seems like Janey could use a woman's company right now."

"That's exactly what I thought," Jeff said.

He smiled across the table at Lila and something caught in her throat. It was such a warm, intimate look that it made her feel all shaky. How could she keep responding like that to a man she hardly knew? She disapproved of her weak reaction, but somehow she couldn't summon the discipline to resist. In spite of herself, she found herself smiling back.

"I'm glad to be included as long as Janey needs me."

"Well, I do," Janey said firmly. She flashed a smile in spite of her tiredness. "After I wash my hair, I'll need you to brush the tangles out again."

"Done," Lila answered. She turned to the older man and her eyes twinkled. "You make such terrific biscuits, Bud, I think I've fallen in love with you. Mind if I have another?"

Bud grinned with delight and passed the plate of biscuits. "Martha's nose would be out of joint, for sure, if she heard that. Have some honey on the next one. It really brings out the flavor."

Jeff glanced at Lila when she reached for her third biscuit. "I thought models always starved themselves to stay slender."

Lila laughed. "They do," she said lightly. "That's why I decided I needed a new profession. Eating. It's a lot more satisfying, especially now I've met Bud."

Both men laughed, but Janey looked at Lila in surprise. "Is that true? Are you a model?"

Lila nodded. "I used to be, until I decided to move to Cattail."

"That's what I want to be someday," Janey said. "Will you give me some pointers?"

"I'd be happy to," Lila said mildly. "But not today. You're much too tired to pay attention. Finish your milk," she added, looking at Janey's half-full glass, "and then we'll see about getting you a bath."

Janey wrinkled her nose in distaste. "Do I have to, Jeff?"

Jeff grinned at her. "I guess you do. It's two against one. Bud and Lila seem determined."

Janey grimaced again. "Seems to me there's an awful lot of bossy people around here," she complained. "I'd think you'd all be ready to spoil me."

"We'll spoil you all you want, Sweet Pea," Bud said. "After you drink your milk."

Saucily, Janey stuck her tongue out at him. All the same, she obediently finished her milk.

When the meal was over, they all made a brief trip to the stables where Janey could reassure herself that her horse was indeed unharmed. Lila was introduced to Lionel Himes, a young man about Jeff's age, who was plainly delighted to see Janey.

"Hey, kid," he told her. "Toby and I've sure missed you around here."

Janey draped her arms around the gelding's sleek neck and laid her head against it. "I've missed you, too. I can see you took good care of Toby while I was gone. Thanks, Lion."

Lionel grinned at her. "I'll give you a couple of days to rest up and then the job is all yours again."

Janey looked like a wan little street waif as she leaned against the magnificent animal. Her hair had tangled again and she still wore her dirty jeans and T-shirt. Her face was pale and the dark smudges beneath her eyes were more pronounced than ever. Lila realized Janey was about to fall on her face from fatigue, yet was gamely fighting it. She stepped to the girl's side and said softly, "I think it's time to get you ready for bed."

"Lila's right," Jeff said. "You can visit Toby again tomorrow."

Back in the house once more, Lila followed Janey upstairs to her bedroom. While the girl stripped off her clothes, Lila went into the adjoining bathroom and ran the water, pouring bath oil and bubble bath into it. If anybody ever deserved a luxurious bath, Janey was that person.

While Janey bathed, Lila sat in the bedroom, staying nearby in case she was needed. The room was pleasantly decorated in cheery yellow and white. She sat near a window overlooking the back lawn, and felt herself finally relaxing. She was extremely tired, but for the time being, Janey's needs came first. Lila fought the urge to doze.

After Janey had bathed and dressed in a nightshirt and a robe, the doctor and Jeff arrived.

"Well, Janey, it's good to see you." Dave Mathis came into the room, bearing little resemblance to most physicians, who affect a more formal style. He wore faded denim jeans and a bright yellow western shirt. He looked more ready to rope a steer than to attend a patient.

"Hi, Doc," Janey said easily. All the same, she objected to his presence. "Jeff shouldn't have called you. There's nothing wrong with me."

"Well, since I'm already here, it won't hurt to let me look you over a bit, will it? Just to reassure Jeff."

"I suppose not," Janey sighed.

Dave gave Lila a pleasant nod as he set his medical bag on the floor beside the bed and sat down in the chair next to it while Janey slid into bed. "How're you doing, Lila? I didn't expect to find you here. I didn't even know you were acquainted with Jeff and Janey. How'd you get involved in all this?"

Dave Mathis was married to Lila's good friend, Amy, and there was a comfortable familiarity between them since they'd known each other for years. Now Lila chuckled and shook her head. "It's a long story you'd have a hard time believing anyway, Dave. It's entirely accidental. I'll tell you and Amy all about it sometime over dinner."

Dave didn't push for an explanation. He was more interested in his patient. He glanced back at Jeff and suggested, "Maybe you ought to leave the room while I examine her."

Lila immediately headed toward the door to follow Jeff out of the room. Behind them, Janey suddenly burst into tears.

"What is it?" Jeff asked anxiously, rushing back to his sister's bedside. "Are you in pain, honey?"

Janey shook her head and rasped out over her sobs, "I don't want you to leave."

Jeff and Dave exchanged understanding glances. Dave turned back to Janey and patted her shoulder. "You're not afraid of me, are you, Janey?"

The girl shook her head again. "No. I just don't want Jeff to go away."

"He'll be right outside the door," Dave said in a soothing voice. "Why don't we have Lila stay instead? I was going to ask her to, anyway. Will that do?"

Janey nodded and dashed a hand to her eyes, wiping away her tears. "Lila?" she asked questioningly.

Lila went to the opposite side of the bed and took Janey's hand. "Of course I'll stay with you." Her gaze lifted and she met Jeff's eyes across the room. His gaze expressed unvoiced gratitude.

"I'll be just outside the door, Janey," he said.

Dave kept his examination mercifully brief. Interspersed with penetrating questions about her ordeal, her treatment, the amount of food she'd been given, how much rest she'd had, he cracked silly jokes. Though Janey remained teary eyed and clung to Lila's hand as though to a lifeline, he managed to get her to laugh a little and it made the whole episode easier on everyone.

When Dave called Jeff back inside, he smiled kindly at his patient and said, "Janey's a tough gal, and she's just fine. I'd say not many grown-ups could go through what she has and emerge so strong. The bruises will fade in a few days. She's a little undernourished, but I know Bud will soon take care of that. Meantime, she's just worn out and needs a lot of rest. I've given her an injection to help her sleep, but once she's rested up, she ought to be good as new."

"Thank God!" Jeff exclaimed softly. He expelled a long breath.

"I told you so," Janey said drowsily.

"So you did," Jeff conceded. "But I just wanted to make sure."

"Do you want me to stay with you until you fall asleep," Lila asked, "or do you want us all to clear out now?"

"Stay," Janey said promptly. "You too, Jeff." She flushed with sudden embarrassment. "I know it sounds sissy, but..."

"There's nothing sissy about needing people now and then, Janey," Dave told her. "We all do."

"That's a fact," Jeff said vehemently.

For a brief instant his eyes met Lila's and her blood raced, responding to his warmth. Hastily, she withdrew her gaze and turned her full attention to Janey again as she sat down on the edge of the bed. "We'll stay as long as you want us," she said.

"I'll just see Dave out and then I'll be right back, okay, honey?" Jeff said.

"Okay," Janey answered. Already her eyelids were heavy and she was having a hard time keeping them open.

While Jeff was gone, she suddenly opened her eyes wide and asked, "Will you still be at the house when I wake up?"

"Sure, if that's what you want," Lila answered. "I'll stay as long as you think you need me, Janey."

"Why?" she asked curiously, struggling to hold her eyes open. "Why're you being so nice to me?"

"Because I like you, silly. I thought you were bright enough to figure that out."

Janey grinned, appeared satisfied and mumbled sleepily, "I like you, too. Know what?"

"What?"

"I'm glad you had that wreck with Jeff."

"Glad? Why?"

"You wouldn't be here otherwise."

Lila chuckled softly and smoothed Janey's hair away from her face. "True. I can't say I'm glad we had the accident, but I am glad I got to know you. Now close your eyes and get some sleep or I'm going to become very annoyed with you." Impulsively she leaned over and kissed Janey's forehead. Her original pity and compassion were quickly turning into fondness for this girl.

By the time Jeff came back, Janey was already asleep. He sat down on the opposite edge of the bed and took her other hand in his. "She's really out of it, isn't she?" he whispered.

"Yes," Lila whispered back. "I think we ought to stay a little while longer, though, just to make sure she doesn't wake up and find us gone."

They stayed another fifteen minutes, companionably silent, each of them holding one of the girl's hands. Jeff seemed unable to tear his eyes away from Janey's face. Lila felt emotion swell in her throat. It choked her up to see how much he loved his sister.

Finally, she whispered, "She seems to be sleeping deeply. I think we should go."

They tiptoed out into the hallway and Lila told him, "She asked me to stay, at least until she wakes up. I hope you don't mind."

"Mind?" Jeff said the word as though it were foreign. "Are you kidding? I'm just grateful to you for how much you've done for her. Janey really took to you, and she doesn't take to many strangers."

"I like her a lot, too." Lila yawned abruptly, then apologized.

Jeff smiled at her. "We're both worn out. There's a guest room right next door," he said, pointing to a door. "Go on and get some sleep yourself. I intend to do the same. Bud'll keep an eye on Janey and if she wakes up and wants one of us, he'll rouse us."

"Don't mind if I do," Lila said wearily. She went to the door Jeff had indicated. Then she glanced back at him and grinned. "Doesn't it strike you as a bit strange that we hardly know each other, yet we keep falling asleep in each other's houses?"

Jeff's answering grin was quick. "It is a little odd, now that you point it out. Crises create strange circumstances, I guess, but somehow it doesn't feel so strange, does it?"

"No," Lila admitted, surprised. "It doesn't." She turned the knob and opened the bedroom door. "See you later," she said softly.

* * *

Jeff felt wonderful. A few hours of sleep—not to mention a shower and shave—had revived him.

He supposed Lila was still sleeping because, when he went into the hallway, her door was closed. Jeff went to Janey's door and opened it quietly. She was sleeping peacefully, so he closed it again and went downstairs.

Bud was in the kitchen, sitting at the counter bar, sipping coffee. "I just brewed some fresh," he told Jeff. "Want me to pour you a cup?"

"Don't bother to get up," Jeff said. "I'll get it myself. I think I'll pour a second cup for Lila and take it up to her. I imagine she's awake by now."

"Where does she come into all this?" Bud asked curiously. "I never saw her before."

As Lila had told Dave Mathis, Jeff echoed her words. "It's a long story," he answered as he poured the coffee. "Maybe I'll tell you some other time."

Bud shrugged. "Well, I like her, no matter where you found her."

"You just like her because she loves your biscuits," Jeff teased.

Bud grinned. "It's as good a reason as any. It ain't every day a beautiful woman tells me she's in love with me." He became serious and added, "Mostly, I like her because she's so good to our Janey."

"So do I," Jeff agreed. "Though I was somewhat surprised at how quickly Janey took to her."

"You oughtta think about marrying her," Bud said, half-serious. "She'd fit in here a heap better'n that Dallas woman you brought last year."

Jeff was startled and annoyed. Bud had a way of blurting some of the darndest things, especially when they weren't any of his business in the first place.

"I'm not the marrying sort," he muttered brusquely, putting a stop to that line of talk. He put both cups of coffee on a silver tray, picked it up and left the room before Bud could think up any more outrageous statements.

But as he climbed the stairs, the older man's words rankled. The thought of the Dallas woman, Angela Thompson, still left a bitter taste in his mouth. She had taught him a hard lesson about women. He didn't trust any of them anymore, at least not where marriage was concerned.

It didn't matter that Lila was vastly different from Angela in personality as well as looks. Just because she'd been extraordinarily kind to him and Janey in a difficult situation, it didn't necessarily follow that she was different from other women when it came to serious relationships and the motives behind them. Jeff was gun-shy at the mere idea of marriage and as far as he was concerned, it was a good way to stay. That attitude would save him a lot of heartache and disillusionment.

Besides, the suggestion of marriage between him and Lila was preposterous. How long had they known each other, anyway? Three days, if you counted their first brief encounter at the time of the accident! Bud's suggestion was absurd, and anyway, he'd only been joking. Normally Jeff wouldn't have taken such joshing to heart. Any other time he would've laughed and shrugged it off. It was just that he'd been through so much this past week that he was beyond such teasing. He was still too shaken by what had happened to Janey. His nerves, always rock-steady in the past, were shot.

What he probably needed was a long vacation. He'd never been a man who required such periods of idleness before, and frankly, he'd been a bit scornful of those who did. Work had been his life. Yet now the idea of a trip, a change of scenery, suddenly appealed to him. It might be the best prescription for Janey's recovery, too, if they went away somewhere different and put this nightmare behind them.

When he reached Lila's door, he balanced the tray with one hand and knocked softly with the other. If she was still asleep, he didn't want to disturb her.

But from beyond the door, he heard her voice. "Come in."

Jeff opened the door, took a step inside the room and when he saw her, he was bowled over. Gone in a flash were his cynical thoughts of a minute ago about women in general and Lila in particular. For a moment, he was paralyzed as his eyes drank in every detail about her.

Lila was in bed, half-turned away from him, vigorously plumping the pillows. Then she twisted around and leaned back against them, half-reclining, half-sitting.

Obviously she was wearing only her underwear because Jeff could see dainty white satin straps crossing her exposed shoulders. The bedcovers were tucked securely above her breasts and beneath her arms.

Her hair, caught in a shaft of light from the window, reminded him of the warmth and comfort of flames leaping in a fireplace on a cold winter's evening. Fire red vied with yellow gold, gleaming within the path of dancing sunbeams. The exquisite cloud of hair curled riotously about her head and shoulders in bewitching disorder. Jeff's mouth went dry and he felt a compelling urge to touch Lila's hair, to run his fingers through it.

Unexpected desire scalded his blood, inflaming his flesh. Despite his cynical view of women when it came to serious relationships, Jeff had a healthy appreciation of their charms. He dated frequently, though he had a strict rule of seeing only those who lived elsewhere, women he met on business trips to Houston, Dallas, Austin and of course, Tyler. Some attracted him more than others, but his attraction to Lila was altogether different. He didn't understand why or how; he only acknowledged that it was so. He had felt it last night when Lila had shown such unexpected concern for his and Janey's welfare. Now it flared again, stronger, more powerful, as he looked upon the alluring picture she made.

She gazed at him quizzically before smiling. Her soft pink lips parted, showing a glimpse of startlingly white teeth. Even her eyes were smiling. They glowed with a luminescence that drew him like a magnet.

"If you're bringing me coffee," she said in a warm tone, "I'll be your friend forever and ever."

Jeff felt himself smiling back. His momentary paralysis ended and he crossed the room and set the tray on the bedside table. He handed Lila one cup, then took the other for himself before he sat down on the edge of the bed.

"It doesn't take much, then, to earn your gratitude," he said lightly. "My coffee, Bud's biscuits. I'm beginning to think you're obsessed with your stomach."

Lila chuckled softly, and Jeff found that he adored the sound of it. When she laughed, her eyes glittered like emeralds and then they narrowed, so that they became partially hidden behind a sweeping screen of thick eyelashes. "It's due to having starved myself all those years I was a model. Now I indulge myself and eat whatever I want. I'm likely," she sighed, "to turn into a blimp one of these days."

"I doubt there's much danger of that," Jeff said, scrutinizing her face. "You've got a long way to go before those cheeks fill out." Impulsively, he reached out and trailed a finger along her right cheekbone and down through the hollow valley beneath it.

His touch caused Lila to catch her breath. Her eyes grew wide as she gazed back at him, but she didn't push him away.

"I don't think I've ever known anyone as lovely as you," he said softly. "Even without makeup, as you are now, you're utterly beautiful."

"Jeff..." Lila began uncertainly.

Jeff leaned forward and stole a kiss. It had been an overwhelming desire in him ever since he'd entered the room.

Her mouth was soft and sweet and warm from sleep. The taste of her was sensuously delightful. Jeff sipped at her lips as though he were drinking spring water or some delicious tea sweetened with honey. A melting softness came over him as her mouth quivered and moved against his. He slid his hand up her throat and shoulder, finally embedding his fingers into the tresses that so enticed him.

Jeff was caught up in the magic of her, the flavor of her lips, the silkiness of her skin, the fine luxuriousness of her hair. Her scent was faintly reminiscent of roses. He was completely engrossed in the gentle womanliness of her and he forgot entirely his earlier wariness. In that moment, an intense yearning spread through his body. He wanted her totally and completely.

But after a timeless moment, Lila put her free hand on his chest and pushed him away. She wasn't abrupt or harsh about it, but the pressure of her touch was insistent.

Her face was flushed softly, her lips berry-red from his kisses, her eyes wide and luminous once more. Her loveliness was so devastating that Jeff's heart constricted.

"I think we'd better back off a little," she whispered breathlessly. "This is . . . getting to be a little too intense."

Jeff smiled and decided it was prudent to follow her lead. Enough was enough while he had her in such a compromising position. Beautiful and alluring as she was in bed and much as he might wish he had the right to crawl in with her, he knew he'd gone far enough for one day. If he pushed any further, he was liable to lose whatever ground he'd gained.

He dropped his hands at once, but he couldn't resist teasing her. "Are you sure about that?" he asked. "Personally I thought things were just starting to get good."

Lila responded with a quick twinkle in her eyes and her lips curved into an involuntary smile at the hang-dog expression he assumed, but she didn't rise to the bait. "Out," she ordered imperially. "Out, so I can get dressed."

"I could help," Jeff said hopefully. "I'm real handy with buttons and zippers and such."

Lila's lips twitched. "Thank you very much, but I'm a model, remember? I'm an expert at handling such complicated tasks by myself."

Jeff sighed, but got to his feet. "Well, if you're sure?"

Lila openly laughed at him then. "Quite sure."

Jeff went toward the door and just as he reached it, Lila said, "Jeff?"

He turned to look at her enquiringly.

She smiled at him and her voice was warm. "Thanks for the offer, anyway."

He chuckled and nodded, then let himself out of the room.

Once he was away from her, he paused thoughtfully in the hallway and wondered if he had already gone and done the unthinkable . . . fallen in love.

Chapter Six

When Lila had dressed and gone downstairs, Jeff was nowhere in sight. She stood uncertainly for a moment in the spacious family room, then headed for the kitchen.

There she found Bud, busy already with his dinner preparations. He sat at the kitchen table with a pan of fresh green beans before him.

"Sleep well?" he asked pleasantly as he continued to snap the beans.

"Like a baby," Lila replied. "Janey's still asleep. I just looked in on her."

Bud nodded. "Want another cup of coffee?"

"No, thanks. Do you know where Jeff is?"

"He's using the phone in his study. He said to tell you he'll be out in a few minutes."

Lila sat down in the chair nearest Bud and reached toward the pan of beans. "Here, I'll help you."

"You don't have to do that," Bud protested.

She shrugged. "Might as well. As long as Janey's asleep, I don't have anything else to do. Are these from the garden I noticed outside this morning?"

Bud shook his head. "Too early yet. I bought these at the supermarket. Jeff told me you're Elinor Addison's granddaughter. My wife Martha was good friends with her. Still misses her." He grinned suddenly and added, "She could make the best blackberry jam for a hundred miles around. Martha's is darned good, but nobody could beat Ellie's."

Lila laughed. "I remember it, too. It was out of this world. I wish I knew her secret, but you know how it is— when I was a kid spending summers with her and could have learned such things, I wasn't interested. I was too busy enjoying myself."

The two of them appeared to be getting along like comfortable old friends by the time Jeff joined them. He paused for a second in the doorway while his gaze took in the extraordinarily ordinary scene of Lila helping Bud snap beans. She continually amazed him. Her behavior was the complete opposite of what he expected. Lila did not conform to his mental image of how a sophisticated model from New York would act. It just went to show you never knew about people, he thought. All his preconceived notions were flying out the window.

Lila looked up just then and gave him a welcoming smile that warmed him right through. "I see Bud put you to work," he said lightly as he entered the room.

"That's right," Lila answered. "He said if I was going to hang around and keep eating him out of house and home, I might as well work for my supper."

"I never—!" Bud exclaimed indignantly.

Lila and Jeff burst into laughter. Then Jeff sat down at the table across from Lila.

"I was just talking to the school principal," he said. "I explained the truth about Janey's absence." His expression became tense. "I told him she'd probably be back at school after a couple more days, but I dread having to send her back at all. I'm afraid to let her out of the house."

"You're still shaken by what happened. That's understandable, but it'll get better with time." Lila said gently. "Those men are locked in jail now. It can't possibly happen again."

A shudder ran through Jeff. "I guess it'll just take time for me to get over it. I don't know if I'll ever feel safe about her again."

"Me either," Bud echoed strongly.

The kitchen door opened and Lionel Himes came in from the back yard. "There's a bunch of people down by the gate," he stated without preamble. "Reporters from Tyler and Dallas and TV cameras all over the place. They asked me a lot of questions about the kidnapping, but I told them I only worked here and didn't know any of the details. They want you to come out and talk to them, Jeff."

Jeff grimaced with distaste. "Damn it!" His eyes narrowed as he looked at Lila. "You were right. They don't give up easily."

"You gonna talk to 'em?" Bud asked.

"I don't know how to deal with reporters." Jeff shook his head. "I wouldn't know what to say, and anyway, it's none of their business."

"When something like this happens, the press makes it their business," Lila told him. "They'll only keep pestering you if they aren't given something. Not only that, but they'll say and print wildly speculative things when they aren't given anything factual to report." She hesitated a moment, then offered, "Would you like me to speak to them for you?"

Hope flared in Jeff's eyes. "Would you do that for me?"

"Somebody needs to, or they'll probably stay camped there for hours. First, let's decide what I should tell them."

Ten minutes later, accompanied by Lionel Himes, Lila walked down the driveway to the locked gate. Beyond it were several cars and Minicam vans. A number of people were milling around restlessly.

"Hey, who are you?" shouted the first person who spotted her.

"I'm Lila Addison, a family friend and neighbor of the Chappels," she replied glibly. "I'm here to try to answer some of your questions."

Cameras were suddenly trained in her direction and several microphones were thrust toward her as she went through the gate to join the throng. Lionel stayed behind the gate to make sure no one entered the grounds.

"Where's Mr.Chappel? Why can't we talk with him?"

"Mr. Chappel is getting some much needed sleep right now," Lila said calmly. "So is Janey. I'm sure you understand, considering their long ordeal."

"How is the girl?"

"Fine, thank you." Lila smiled warmly. "Just fine. She's quite a spunky young lady and we're all very proud of the way she's come through this."

"We understand she was held in a farmhouse for four days. Did the kidnappers harm her in anyway?"

"Physically, she's unharmed, but she was kept locked in a closet the entire time. Only a very strong character could emerge from something like that without tipping over the brink, but fortunately Janey *is* strong. She said that to remain calm and to pass the time, she mentally worked out algebra problems and conjugated French verbs. Now can you beat that?"

The journalists chuckled, pleased to be given an anecdote that would make good copy. Lila soon had them eating out of her hand, or rather, Janey's, if she had been present. All the same, when the interview was finally over and she turned to walk back to the house, she was in a dark mood. Unexpectedly, one of the reporters had recognized her, recalling news stories about her involvement in what she mentally termed "The Nick Episode," and had begun asking questions about that. It had been an unpleasant jolt and it took every ounce of self-discipline she had to act seemingly unperturbed. She had dispensed with the subject as quickly as she could without showing her uneasiness and had returned to the discussion at hand.

When she re-entered the house, Bud met her at the door. "How'd it go?"

Lila shrugged. "As well as possible, I suppose. At least they're beginning to leave now."

"Good. Janey's awake now and Jeff's upstairs with her. They want you to join them."

Lila mounted the stairs and went down the hall toward Janey's bedroom. She was still extremely annoyed over having been recognized by that one, sharp-eyed reporter and she paused in the hallway to draw in a deep breath and collect herself.

Janey was sitting up in bed, propped against a mound of pillows, when Lila went inside. Jeff stood at the window, peering out, but he turned when he heard Lila's voice.

"Hey!" Lila exclaimed with a smile directed at Janey. "You look like a different girl already!"

"All I needed was a little sleep," Janey replied with a grin. "I'm ready to dress and go downstairs, but Jeff's being difficult and has ordered me to stay in bed the rest of the day."

"Hmmm. He's an ogre, all right," Lila agreed with mock seriousness. "Still, maybe he has the right idea. It won't hurt you to rest and allow yourself to be pampered for at least one whole day."

"Boring," Janey drawled. "I don't even have a TV. Jeff won't let me have one in my room because he's afraid I'd spend too much time watching it and not enough on my homework."

"He really is the meanest sort," Lila agreed in a commiserating tone. "Jeff, how could you deprive her so?"

Jeff grinned. "It comes naturally. The whole point of my existence is to make life tough for this kid." He moved to the bedside and ruffled Janey's hair. Then he asked Lila, "How'd it go down at the gate?"

"Fine. They're all full of admiration for our girl here. They wanted to meet her, of course, but I said they'd just have to make do with me."

Janey grimaced. "After this morning, I don't ever want anything to do with them. Anyway, they told me at the police station that I shouldn't talk about it in public because of the trial and having to testify. Do you think they'll keep bothering us?"

Lila shook her head. "Maybe for another day or two, but then something else will claim their attention and the outside world will forget you."

Janey appeared satisfied, and changed the subject. "What are you two planning to do, stay cooped up in here and babysit me the rest of the day?"

"What's the matter?" Jeff retorted. "Don't you like our company?"

"Sure, but I can't help feeling a little silly with you just watching me lie in bed."

"Do you want us to go?"

"No!" The word was vehement and sharp. "I don't want that, either. I . . ." Her voice broke abruptly. "I don't think I can . . . handle being all by myself just yet."

Lila became thoughtful. Finally, she ventured, "Janey, do you have a best friend?"

"Sure. Beth Winston. She lives down the road. I was on my way to her house the day . . ." Her voice faded. "You know," she finished lamely.

Lila raised her eyes to Jeff's face. "Why not invite Beth over to visit?" she suggested. "I'll bet that would do Janey a world of good and be a whole lot less boring than having just us old grown-ups for company."

"I didn't say you were boring," Janey quickly disclaimed. "I just said staying in bed is boring. But I would like to see Beth. Does she even know what happened to me, Jeff?"

He shook his head. "We had to keep it a secret, honey. We couldn't take the chance of telling people. It might've made things worse."

"Then can she come? I'd like to tell her myself before it gets on the news."

Jeff laughed, clearly pleased at the interest and eagerness that shone in Janey's eyes. "I'll see what I can do," he declared. Bypassing the telephone next to her bed, he went toward the door. "I'll call her mother from my room and if she agrees, I'll send Lionel down to let Beth through the gate."

Lila remained with Janey for the next half hour, but then the arrival of Beth made her own presence superfluous. Beth was a cute girl with short blond hair and a tiny body clad in the standard teenage uniform of jeans and a T-shirt.

"Janey!" she squealed when she entered the room and rushed toward the bed. "I don't *believe* all this!"

"Oh, Beth, just wait until I *tell* you!"

While the two girls embraced, Lila went quietly toward the door where Jeff stood. He closed the door behind them and together they went downstairs.

"You had a good idea there, inviting Beth over. How did you know?"

Lila shrugged. "Probably because I used to be a teenage girl. At that age, they tell their best friends everything. I just thought Janey could probably use a good talk with a close friend. It might help her to get things off her chest and she needs that right now... to talk it all out of her system instead of leaving it inside to fester."

"I wouldn't have thought about it myself," Jeff admitted. He sighed and went on, "I love that girl dearly, but she can be a handful sometimes and I never know the right way to handle her. I try, but it's not easy. Teenage girls are so temperamental. Sometimes a simple 'good morning' can bring on a flood of tears."

Lila laughed. "It just goes with the territory. I don't think you need to worry too much, though. She seems like a great kid to me."

An hour later Bud served everyone's dinners on trays, the two girls' upstairs in Janey's room, Jeff's and Lila's in the family room where they could watch the evening news on television while they ate.

When the segment about the kidnapping appeared, Jeff put down his fork, leaned forward and concentrated intently upon Lila's image on the screen.

He was impressed by the adroit manner in which she handled the questions. She was so convincing about his being asleep that if he hadn't known better, he'd have believed it himself. When she spoke of Janey she appeared forthright and filled with pride. She was adept at revealing only what she wanted them to know. Her tone was upbeat and admiring as she described how strong a person Janey was; not by even the smallest hint did she allow them to gain a glimpse of a tearful, frightened girl. Lila projected a positive image of his sister and Jeff appreciated that.

"Miss Addison, you're a model from New York. Weren't you involved in that Barrow investment firm scandal a few months ago?" a reporter asked in an abrupt change of subject.

This was all new to Jeff and he listened even more intently. The on-camera Lila registered momentary surprise; the real life Lila beside him was silent, but even though his concentration was on the screen, Jeff sensed her sudden tension.

Smoothly, the Lila on-screen replied, "If by involved you mean was I an innocent victim, yes I was."

"You were engaged to be married to Mr. Barrow, weren't you?"

"That's right. But it's certainly no longer the case."

"After the truth came out, the authorities were unable to locate Mr. Barrow. Do you know his whereabouts now?"

"No, I do not."

"What are you doing here in a small community in Texas?"

"I live here."

"And what's your connection to the Chappel family?"

"I told you before—I'm a family friend. Now..." Lila smiled and it included the other journalists as well "... are there any other questions concerning Janey? I'd like to get back to the house before she wakes up."

"What about the men in custody right now? Will Janey be testifying against them in court? Can she identify them?"

Lila shrugged. "I don't really know the answers to those questions. Janey has been too tired to discuss it and her brother hasn't pressed her about any details. As to what will happen at the trial, you should discuss that with the prosecutor's office." Nodding pleasantly, she terminated the interview. "We're having a wonderful day now that Janey's home safe. I hope you all have a nice day as well." Then she turned her back on the journalists and strode purposely through the gate.

Using the remote control, Jeff switched off the television set. All was silent in the room until he said, "You handled that well." He turned to look at her and saw that she, too, had ceased eating her dinner.

"Thanks." Without warning, she stood up and said quietly, "If you've finished eating, I think it's time I went home."

Her manner was different than earlier, tense somehow, and the tone of her voice, while soft, had a firmness that brooked no argument. Jeff had a feeling the change that had come over her had something to do with the interview, with those enigmatic questions about a financial scandal and a fiancé. He wanted to ask about it, but he sensed that this wasn't the right moment.

He got to his feet, too. "Sure. We'll go now if that's what you want."

Lila said her goodbyes to Janey, Beth and Bud, promising that she would return to visit soon and then she went outside to the car with Jeff.

They were both rather silent and preoccupied on the short drive. Lila was really feeling tired now, physically and emotionally, and she was glad when they reached her house. The sooner she was away from Jeff Chappel, the better, for then she would be able to regain her equilibrium.

But a quick getaway wasn't possible. When she placed her hand on the door handle, about to get out of the car, Jeff's hand on her arm stopped her. Reluctantly, she turned back to face him. It was her undoing.

"I have to thank you," he said huskily. "For everything you've done."

"There's nothing to thank me for."

"Don't be silly," he chided softly as his arms went around her and he drew her close. "Of course there is."

Inexorably, as though Fate itself had decreed it, their lips met. She could blame it all on him, but who was she kidding? A weakness came over Lila. His warmth and gentleness magically softened her resistance, melted the icicle of her heart, and she found herself giving as much as she received.

The kiss grew more intense, their breathing raspy and irregular. Jeff's arms tightened around her and Lila's fingers brushed through his dark hair. An aching longing came over her, strong and insistent.

When his hand moved over her breast, she gasped. It was as though a current of electricity was charging through her veins. The heat within her increased, growing hotter and hotter. Her body was suddenly, acutely alive, sensitive to his slightest touch. Forgotten was her fatigue as she felt herself being submerged in an enveloping flame of desire.

And yet, from somewhere deep inside her, she found strength and drew away from him. "I think we'd better stop," she said breathlessly.

"Why?" Jeff's eyes were glazed with unmistakable passion. "I could go on kissing you like that all day. Do you have any idea just how soft your lips are?" he added whimsically.

"Things are moving too fast," Lila murmured unsteadily. With a firm motion at odds with her voice, she extricated herself from his arms. "Last night...and earlier this afternoon...maybe it was excusable. We were both elated, on an emotional high, thrown off balance because Janey was safe. But now..." Her voice trailed off.

"Now the kisses are all the sweeter because it's just for you and me and not from any outside influence."

"Maybe," she conceded. "All the same, it's still too fast, too unsettling. We barely know each other, Jeff."

"How well do we have to know one another after the night and day we've been through? How long do we have to be acquainted before we demonstrate the undeniable truth that we're attracted to each other?"

Lila shook her head. "I don't know. All I do know for certain is that I'm not ready to get involved with you or anyone at this point in my life."

"Does this have anything to do with the business that reporter was talking about...your ex-fiancé?"

She nodded and lowered her gaze to his shirt collar. "I was stunned when that reporter recognized me. I didn't expect that."

Jeff placed a finger beneath her chin and lifted her face. A teasing smile curved his lips. "When a woman is as lovely as you are, she'd better expect to be remembered. Don't you realize that you're unforgettable?"

The mesmerizing quality of his voice, as well as the words themselves, set Lila's pulses racing. Her throat constricted as his gaze held hers for a long time. The expression in his eyes was as ancient as time, a silent but compelling call from the maleness of him to the counterpart femaleness of her.

Something in her soul stirred and answered the call—a primitive, sweeping truth that the basic foundation of humanity itself is man and woman becoming one. It was as simple as that.

And as complicated and frightening. Lila caught her breath. She felt threatened by all the feelings this man brought forth in her just by a mere look or word. As for his kisses, the sensation of his touch...

She had come to Texas to be free, not to become ensnared by erratic emotions or ungovernable demands from her body. It was time to put a stop to this madness before it went any further.

"I've just come through a relationship that ended badly and I'm not interested in beginning another. I can't face being hurt again."

"And you're so sure I would hurt you?" Jeff asked quietly.

"How do I know?" Lila touched his arm in a beseeching gesture. "Look, I really do need time to get myself together. Let's not start any complications. I...I simply can't handle it. Let's start over and just be friends, okay?" She smiled wistfully. "I'm still new in town and I could use another friend besides Dave and Amy Mathis."

"So that's how you know Dave," Jeff mused. "I wondered about that when he obviously knew you when he came to examine Janey."

"Amy and I became friends when I was a girl and used to spend summers here with my grandmother."

Jeff's lips quirked and he looked wistful now. "How come I never met you back then?"

Lila smiled and said in a light manner, "Oh, I expect I was too young to catch your attention. Or too plain. I was just a bean pole then, all arms and legs and nothing else."

Jeff grinned devilishly. "Well, you're certainly no bean pole now. You're still tall—just right, in fact, to reach my shoulder—and there's plenty else besides." His eyes traveled deliberately down to the swell of her breasts beneath her sweater.

"Stop that!" she ordered with hoarse abruptness. "I asked if we could just be friends, remember?"

To his pleasure, Lila actually blushed. He didn't know any woman beyond puberty who did that anymore, much less a woman who was as beautiful and sophisticated as Lila. It made him more curious about her than ever.

"Friends?" Lila asked again. She extended a hand to him.

Jeff suddenly grinned. "It goes against the grain," he told her, "but friends it is." He took her hand in a firm handshake. "At least," he warned belatedly, "for the time being."

They both fell silent for a moment, just gazing at each other, but then Jeff broke the silence, his tone thoughtful. "I had a feeling all along that a beautiful model, obviously at the height of her career, who comes to bury herself in a place like Cattail must be running away or hiding from something or someone. That reporter spoke about some investment firm scandal, and the fact that you knew exactly how the press would react concerning Janey tells me they must have given you a pretty bad time of it in New York. Did you come here to get away from the unwelcome publicity—or to get away from the man in question?"

Lila shrugged. "The whole situation, really. By the time I left, the publicity had pretty much died down, and as for Nick—he had vanished into thin air. They think he's living out of the country."

"Then why did you leave your life there...your career? What is there for you here?"

She shrugged again and looked away from him, through the windshield. Dusk was falling. It was that time of day when the sky was a special silvery gray, hovering between light and dark and dramatically streaked with bold orange and shimmering pink. Things at a distance such as the neighboring farmer's cornfield were still visible, yet not easily identified, obscured by the gathering night. Crickets were humming and a hushed peacefulness spread over the landscape—the peacefulness from the simplicity of childhood she had come here to recapture.

Slowly, she attempted to explain. "Everything that happened just convinced me that it was time to make a drastic change in my life. I wanted a fresh start in a place where honest values still exist and this was the only place I could think of."

"Do you still love him?" Jeff's voice was soft, but probing. "The fiancé who skipped?"

Lila turned to look at him once more and she answered as honestly as she could. "No. I'll admit I'm still hurt by what he did, by the fool I made of myself for believing in him, but I don't love him anymore. I'm no longer sure I ever really did." She tilted her head and asked curiously, "What about you? Isn't there someone special in your life?"

Even in the growing darkness she could see Jeff's eyes begin to twinkle. "You ask that after the way I just kissed you?"

Lila flushed again, cheering him immensely. But then she squinted her eyes and wrinkled her nose at him. "That's no answer."

Jeff's grin broadened. "If you must know, there is a very special female in my life. We left her back at the house, visiting with Beth."

"That's still no answer," Lila said, plainly aggrieved.

"Tit for tat," Jeff said. "You haven't been exactly forthcoming, either. All you've actually admitted was that the deal soured with your fiancé and now you don't want to make room in your life for any other man. That's not what I call terrifically enlightening."

"It's more than you've told me," Lila said with a slight pout to her luscious lips. It made him want to kiss her again. But before he could make up his mind to try it, she shrugged and went on, "Maybe it's better if we drop the subject altogether."

"Fine with me," Jeff answered. "I don't find it the most pleasant one to discuss."

"Neither do I."

Jeff leaned back against the door frame as though settling in for a long, comfortable chat. "You still haven't told me what you do with your time here. Obviously modeling is out of the question."

"I'm trying to concentrate on establishing a new career in art," she answered. "In the past I've sold a few of my paintings through a gallery in New York, but I've never had the time to get into it as much as I wanted. So I'm going to give it a shot. Meanwhile," she said in a different tone, "I've got a few money problems. I'm trying to find a part-time job that will enable me to keep eating while I try to get some paintings ready to show."

"Thinking of food again," Jeff teased.

Lila didn't smile. "It's a serious matter to me."

Jeff was plainly skeptical. "Is it really that urgent?" he asked. "Finding a job? I always thought models as successful as you were pulled in piles of money."

Lila drew in a deep breath and expelled it slowly. "They do. And I did. But recently I hit a rather crucial financial snag and now I'm back to square one."

Jeff felt slightly sick. Lila somehow had seemed different from other women and her face reflected a seemingly sincere expression as she talked, but basically she was just like all the rest, after all. It seemed as though something precious had been snatched from him. Lila knew he obviously had money, or else the kidnappers would never have bothered taking his sister, and now she was playing on his sympathies. It was the same old game. She was hoping to touch his weak spot and become the recipient of his generosity. Probably she had managed to squander all her own earnings on high living and then when her fiancé had skipped out, she'd been thrown back onto her own resources without a man's wallet to dip into. Suddenly, his former weariness overcame him again.

His mouth twisted cynically. "So you need a job right away to bail you out?"

Lila nodded. "If something doesn't turn up soon, I might be forced to go back to New York and modeling after all. There don't seem to be many jobs available around here, part-time or full time."

"Well, Cattail's not a hotbed of vigorous industry. But I can offer you the job you need."

Lila's green eyes widened in astonishment. "You? Do you have a job opening?"

Jeff noted that she played the game beautifully. She seemed so surprised, but he knew that she'd been fishing for something all along. Well, he'd play the sucker and offer her employment. After all, she had been supportive and helpful to him during the worst moments of his entire life. He supposed he owed her and though he had his share of faults, Jeff didn't welch on his debts.

"Do you know anything about bookkeeping?" he asked.

Lila looked disappointed and shook her head. "Not the first thing."

Jeff shrugged carelessly. "No matter. Clara, my accountant, can teach you. You can start Monday morning if you like. Half-days five days a week. Does that sound okay?"

Lila stared at him for a moment before her eyes narrowed. Her thick lashes concealed what she was thinking.

Jeff wondered why it took her so long to reply. After all, he'd just offered her what she wanted. Or hadn't he? Maybe she'd been expecting a straightforward cash handout instead.

But she surprised him by demanding, "Why haven't I seen an advertisement about the job in the *Cattail Banner*?"

He shrugged again. "We don't always advertise. What difference does it make?"

"The difference," Lila answered slowly, "is that it's just a make-work job, isn't it? You don't really need anyone at all."

Jeff didn't trouble to pretend. "So what? It'll give you the job you want and I'm sure you'll become a big help to Clara."

He was astounded when a soft red color stole into her cheeks, burning them like hot coals.

"No thanks," she said crisply. "I don't need your charity."

"Charity?" Jeff was genuinely amazed at her sudden anger. "All I did was offer you a job!"

"One you only dreamed up this second!"

"What are you getting so steamed about?" he asked mildly. "You did me a big favor and I'm only trying to repay it."

"That's what's so infuriating!" Lila's voice trembled.

"I don't understand."

"Obviously. See you around, Mr. Chappel."

Lila opened the passenger door, got out, slammed the door and ran toward the steps of her house all in one swift, fluid movement.

Jeff sat frozen, wondering what in hell *he'd* done wrong.

Chapter Seven

"Life is just one long frustration," Lila said to the red bird that perched on a branch of the nearby elm. She took a break from her efforts at tilling the ground with a hoe, straightened her aching back and wiped the perspiration from her brow.

Her face was grimy from the dust. Her hair was held away from her face by a dark blue terry cloth stretch band. The back of her neck was sticky and it itched from wisps of damp hair. She wore tan shorts and a blue shirt, and already the sunshine during the warm spring days was turning her skin to a golden brown. Clotilde would have a fit and Lila grinned sardonically at the thought. Certainly nobody in their right mind who happened to see her at this moment would imagine she'd once been an acclaimed fashion model.

The irony fitted her present ill humor.

A week ago she'd had the vegetable garden plot tilled by a handyman from town and now she was chopping weeds that had sprouted in it so that she could prepare the soil for planting. Not that she knew much about gardening—only what little she'd picked up through the years from her grandmother and a few books. But she was determined to try. Around Cattail, everyone had a vegetable garden. She might be a greenhorn, but she would make the effort or die in the attempt. When in Rome...

Besides, she mused grimly as she set to work again, she could certainly use any food that resulted from it. Oh, she wasn't down to starvation level yet, but the day might well come. During the past week, her painting hadn't been coming along as she'd hoped. She'd been turned down for yet another job possibility and this morning when she'd spoken to the realty agent in New York, he'd told her he still hadn't had any serious buyers looking at the condominium.

Lila couldn't help asking herself whether she'd made a grievous mistake by settling here. The people were neighborly and friendly and she'd met several nice individuals this week alone—a sympathetic secretary at an insurance agency who had seemed to understand her acute disappointment at not being able to find a job; the lady who ran the post office; the attendant at the garage where she'd taken her car for an estimate for repairs, who had given her a jar of honey that he had taken from his beehives; a woman at the grocery market who'd invited her to church. But kindness wasn't money in the bank and right now that's what she needed most. If the condo didn't sell soon...Determinedly, she refused to finish the thought.

Most disappointing of all was the severing of the budding friendship with Jeff Chappel. Since that evening when he had brought her home and she'd gotten so furious over his job offer, she had neither seen nor heard from him again. The incident had also effectively cut her off from Janey and Bud Himes, both of whom she would have enjoyed seeing again. But now that was impossible.

There had been a growing attunement with Jeff during the short span of time they'd been together. It was as though they were on the same wavelength and that had filled her with a warm, soft glow. But then he'd offered her a job and that had abruptly brought everything between them to a halt.

Not only had she resented his offering her a job that didn't really need doing, but worse, it had seemed to Lila that his attitude toward her had changed. It was almost as though she was trying to coerce him and he had grudgingly made the offer. Perhaps she was being fanciful and super-sensitive, but that was the impression she'd received and a chill had shivered up her spine. She hadn't wanted their fragile new relationship to be reduced to a matter of cold dollars and cents.

Lila tried to convince herself that there had been nothing between Jeff and herself to miss. Never mind the tender way he had smiled at her; never mind the thrilling warmth of his kisses, or the safe, sheltered feeling she'd had when his arms were around her. She told herself it didn't matter one whit that she'd felt a desire for him unlike any she'd had for any other man. Sure, her flesh had a way of going hot every time she remembered that, but so what? *So what?*

Forget him! It didn't matter. It had only seemed to matter because everything had happened in such a short time. She wasn't interested in starting up a new romance yet, maybe not ever. Nick's treachery had formed a layer of ice around her heart and taught her not to trust anyone.

And yet . . .

And yet, much to her disgust and annoyance, she kept right on remembering Jeff—his kisses and the flame she'd seen flickering in the depths of his eyes. He had clearly wanted her, too. Thoughts of him would pop into her mind at the most inconvenient times, interfering with her concentration on her painting; causing her to lapse into a day-dream instead of gleaning informative tidbits from a gardening book; removing her, mentally, so far from the task at hand that yesterday morning she had let the milk she was pouring into a cereal bowl overflow onto the table. The entire matter aggravated her no end. This obsession was getting entirely out of hand, wreaking havoc with the orderly life she was determined to establish for herself.

When the noonday sun was high over her head and all of nature around her seemed to be nodding off, Lila went into the house for lunch and a well-earned rest. Late in the afternoon, when the air began to cool again she would go back and finish the job. Tomorrow she would broadcast the seeds.

She was relieving her parched throat with a glass of water when the telephone rang.

It was Amy Mathis. "Hi. I'm calling on my lunch break," she said, "just to remind you that you're talking to my class tomorrow afternoon."

Lila was appalled at her failing memory. The day following her accident with Jeff they had rescheduled a time for her to speak to Amy's class and lately, due to her involuntary preoccupation with Jeff, the matter had completely slipped her mind. It was a good thing Amy'd had the foresight to call.

"I'll be there," she said cheerfully, unwilling to admit she'd forgotten all about it. "Barring any new crisis, that is."

Amy chuckled. "Cattail's usually an uneventful place. Hopefully you'll be able to manage it this time. While I've got you on the line, I also wanted to invite you over for dinner Friday night. Dave's tied up with a civic club meeting then, so it'll just be us and another friend I'd like you to meet. We can have a good old-fashioned hen party."

"Sounds great," Lila answered. The idea appealed to her enormously. She'd spent far too much time alone lately and the isolation was getting to her. Maybe if she had a more well-developed social life she wouldn't feel quite so adrift and thoughts of giving up and going back to New York wouldn't plague her so often.

Anything was welcome, she thought in desperation after they'd hung up, anything at all, so long as it helped to get her mind off Jeffrey Chappel.

Late that afternoon Jeff's business with his customer in Houston wound up and he felt well pleased. He had secured a lucrative new contract for the delivery of a considerable amount of lumber. It would keep his mill humming for the next few months.

"Now that we're done with business talk," Wayne Hammond said, "why don't we relax and have a drink?"

"Sounds good to me," Jeff replied. While the other man poured whiskey at his private office bar, Jeff stood and stretched. They'd been sitting for a long time and he felt stiff.

He had been doing business with Wayne Hammond for several years and they had a relatively easygoing relationship. Hammond was in his late fifties, much older than Jeff, but the two of them had the lumber business in common. Both enjoyed fishing and hunting and were avid Dallas Cowboy and Houston Astro fans. Therefore, they had many subjects to choose from as they left business talk and eased into more congenial conversation.

A half hour later, Hammond offered a second drink, but Jeff refused it. "I suppose I ought to be getting out to the airport and heading home," he said.

"The day's still young," Hammond protested. "Why don't you stick around a while? I'll call my wife and we can meet her and my niece at the club for dinner. I'll even spring for champagne to celebrate our new contract."

Jeff came close to refusing. Nowadays he didn't like to be away from Janey any longer than was necessary and besides, ever since that evening when he'd taken Lila home and she'd angrily refused his job offer, he hadn't felt very sociable toward anybody.

But he could tell that Hammond really wanted him to stay and he was too important a customer to offend. They'd had many business luncheons together, but this was the first time Hammond had ever invited him to socialize with his family. Jeff reluctantly decided it was prudent to accept.

"Fine," he said with an easy smile. "I'll call home to let them know, then call my pilot to tell him I'll be running late. I'd enjoy meeting your wife."

Hammond grinned. "I think you'll probably enjoy meeting my niece more. She's a sweetheart."

Jeff hadn't believed him. He'd figured the niece was probably homely and desperate for male companionship since Hammond was selling the idea of an evening with her, but he was wrong. Katherine Willis was indeed a sweetheart. She was lovely, with dark brown hair and soft blue eyes. She also had a lovely personality. Her voice was gentle, her smile was winsome, her conversation intelligent and interesting. She was a nurse at one of Houston's hospitals and she seemed so competent that Jeff felt sure she was a good one. That competence, coupled with her compassionate nature, probably made her an excellent one. Even so, she spoke little about herself. Rather, she asked Jeff questions about himself and his life and she spoke knowledgeably about world events, the latest books and movies.

In short, she was just the sort of woman Jeff had been longing to meet for a long time. Unassuming, sweet natured, charming, one who didn't seem the grasping type—the sort who would probably make some man a fantastic wife.

The only trouble was that he couldn't get Lila Addison out of his head. If he could only forget her, forget how it had felt to have her in his arms, to kiss her soft lips, he might have found it easy to fall for Katherine Willis.

But it was no use and Jeff knew it. He couldn't forget Lila, furious as he still was with her. In no time at all, she had captured his emotions, upset his equilibrium in a way that he resented wholeheartedly, but nevertheless could not deny.

Therefore, when the pleasant evening finally drew to an end, Jeff did not make any arrangements to meet Katherine again. There was no point in it, much as he had enjoyed her company. He felt a genuine regret that he was turning his back on something that probably could have been wonderful, and all on account of a hot-tempered woman he didn't understand and whom he didn't even want to see again.

He didn't understand himself either, and as the pilot flew the Cessna back to the Cattail airstrip through the clear, starry night, Jeff berated himself for his foolishness. Why and how Lila had come to assume a major significance in his life was beyond his understanding. Sure, she'd been kind and helpful to him and Janey, but logic told him most anybody else, given the same circumstances, would also have been as compassionate. So that wasn't it, or at least not all of it. Nor was it just the few kisses they had shared. Oh, sure, he admitted to himself, he had wanted to make love to her. How could a red-blooded man help feeling that way when he was holding such a gorgeous creature in his arms? His blood sizzled even now at the thought of her ripe, luscious body.

Yet somehow it all added up to more than mere sexual desire—powerful as that was—but exactly what, he had no idea. All he knew for certain was that he'd been cut to the quick when she had turned on him like a cat with unsheathed claws after he'd offered the job. Lila couldn't have shocked or hurt him more if she had slapped his face.

He had believed something rare and special was starting to happen between them, but obviously he'd been mistaken. Once the crisis with Janey had been over, Lila had made it perfectly clear that she wanted nothing more to do with him. Well, if that was how she wanted it, that was how it would be. Jeff had better things to do with his time than to pursue a woman who wasn't interested. All he had to do now was learn how to put the thought of her out of his mind. Soon he would overcome those persistent, unrequited feelings he'd developed for her so quickly and when he did, he told himself firmly, he would return to Houston and seek out Katherine. Now wasn't the time, but later, when he was free of all thoughts of Lila...

But somehow Jeff had a disturbing hunch that getting over Lila might take a long, long time. It was annoying and disquieting and made him feel strangely helpless. He'd never felt so threatened and out of control in his life and he didn't like it one bit.

The following day Lila abandoned her original plan to plant her garden and dutifully got dressed for her speech to the high school girls. In truth, she was glad of the altered plans. She was heartily sick of her own company, of brooding about the unsold condo, and her lack of a job.

And Jeff.

Why couldn't she just dismiss the man from her mind as she had so many others? Look at what Nick had done! He'd betrayed her love, or what had passed for love between them, and stolen her money, yet oddly enough, she brooded over him far less than she did over Jeff Chappel, whom she scarcely knew. It was absurd!

Today when she drove toward town and the school, there was no accident to prevent her from keeping her appointment. Lila stopped first at the principal's office where she was warmly received. The school secretary accompanied her to the gym, where the class was to meet.

A lightheartedness came over her as she walked down the hallway. Memories of her own youth came flooding back. It seemed that all schools everywhere had the same scent, the same atmosphere.

In the gym, Amy Mathis, dressed in white shorts and a blue and white T-shirt with a whistle hanging on a string around her neck, came forward to greet her. She wasn't a beauty in the way Lila was, but her lively personality more than made up for looks, in Lila's estimation. She was friendly, fun-loving as well as athletic and Lila privately thought Dave Mathis was one heck of a lucky man to have won her. When they were teenagers themselves, Amy had been very popular with all the local boys.

"I guess you didn't have a car accident today," she said with a pixieish grin. "I'm glad you could make it."

"So am I," Lila responded with a smile. "I'm sorry about the last time."

"What's to be sorry about? It wasn't your fault you got mixed up in a kidnapping. By the way, your biggest fan is in this class."

Lila gave her a puzzled look. "Biggest fan?"

"Janey Chappel. She's been telling all the girls how wonderful and beautiful and interesting you are. You've got a reputation to uphold here, so don't you dare let Janey and me down."

Lila laughed. "I'll do my poor best, but I hope Janey didn't build me up too high."

"Oh, but she did," Amy retorted. "To hear her tell it, you're right up there with the angels."

"I can see I'm in serious trouble already," Lila said with a grimace.

"Well, muddle through as best you can," Amy replied. "Come on over and I'll introduce you." Together they walked across the gym to where the class sat on bleachers.

Lila gave her talk, though she knew the girls weren't hearing exactly what they had expected. Instead of dwelling on the jobs she had done, or expert makeup tricks, she told them the values of not smoking, drinking or eating too much junk food. "Beauty begins within," she told them. "If you eat healthy foods, you'll have a healthy body and that will give your face a glowing beauty that no cosmetic in the world can produce. If you want to maintain a slim, firm body, exercise, eat right and get a lot of rest.''

The girls hung on to her every word as though it were gospel and afterward there was a question and answer period during which Lila did elaborate on her work, dressing with style, and methods of applying makeup.

The visit was a huge hit and when the bell rang the girls were reluctant to leave. They crowded around Lila and told her how much they'd enjoyed her advice and the fact that a "celebrity" like her now lived among them.

Janey hung back until all the other girls finally departed. Lila smiled at her warmly. "How are you, Janey? Fully recovered?"

"I'm fine," Janey replied. There was an odd, hurt expression in her dark eyes as she looked at Lila.

Lila asked sharply, "What's wrong?"

Janey gazed down at her feet, then lifted her chin almost belligerently. "Jeff says you don't want to have anything more to do with us. How come?"

The direct attack surprised Lila. "If he told you that, he was wrong," she responded softly. "I'm delighted to see you again. I've been wondering how you were doing."

"Then how come you didn't come back to visit me? You said you would."

Lila sighed. "Jeff and I didn't see eye to eye on something, that's all. It has nothing to do with you."

"I thought that might be it," Janey said flatly. "I didn't think I'd said anything to make you mad at me."

"Of course you didn't."

"Well, if you won't come back to my house, can I come see you at yours sometime?"

"You'd better!" Lila smiled and touched Janey's arm. "I count you as my friend, Janey. Come visit me anytime you feel like it."

"You really mean it?" Janey's eyes began to sparkle.

"Sure, I mean it. If your brother doesn't mind, that is."

"Okay." Janey flashed a quick smile, then said, "I've gotta run or I'll be late to history class. See you, Lila."

Lila watched as the girl hurried away. Her friend, Beth, waited for her near the door and together they left the gym. Lila then turned to Amy and they said their goodbyes and prepared to go their separate ways.

"Thanks for coming," Amy said. "The girls loved you. I just hope you got through to them about not smoking and drinking. Don't forget dinner tomorrow night."

"I won't," Lila said. "I'm looking forward to it. And I enjoyed talking with your class."

Lila drove straight home and when she arrived, the mail had come. She sifted through it as she entered the house and abruptly, she went still. There was an envelope with the return address of Chappel Mill and Lumber Company on it.

After a moment, she ran a fingernail beneath the flap and opened it. There was no note; only a check for two thousand dollars. Lila stared at it blankly, not understanding until she glanced at the lower left corner where the words, Car Repairs were written.

New anger rolled over her. Why was the man so patronizing toward her? She'd bought the car secondhand in Dallas when she'd first arrived in Texas and the whole thing wasn't even worth much more than two thousand dollars!

Lila dropped the rest of the mail on the nearest table and whirling around, went straight back outside to her car. She glared fiercely at the crumpled passenger side. What evil whim of Fate had placed her in that accident with such an irritating man as Jeffrey Chappel?

Chappel Mill and Lumber was located on the northeast side of town on a vast plot of land. Near the road was a sprawling red brick building which housed the main offices and the retail lumber business. Behind it were metal buildings where the lumber was milled. As Lila turned off the road, she followed a large truck that was hauling logs to the mill.

She found a parking place in front of the main building and went inside. A young clerk approached her with a smile. "Good afternoon. May I help you?"

Lila forced herself to nod pleasantly. Her temper was still on the rise, but there was no reason to take it out on an innocent bystander.

"I'm looking for the offices," she said evenly. "I need to see Mr. Chappel."

"Sure." The young man pointed toward heavy swinging double doors on the right. "Go through there and down the hall. First door on the left."

"Thanks."

Lila followed his directions and easily found the office. A secretary sat at a desk, working with a calculator. She looked up and smiled. "Can I help you?"

"Please. I'm looking for Mr. Chappel."

"May I ask your name?" The secretary's fingers went from the calculator to the intercom button on her telephone.

"Lila Addison."

The other woman repeated her name to Jeff and a moment later Lila was shown into his private office.

For a man of Jeff's means, his office was surprisingly modest. Knotty pine panelled the walls, which were decorated with civic awards and a large photograph of Janey. Otherwise, it was just an ordinary office with a large desk, two comfortable-looking leather chairs for visitors and several file cabinets.

Jeff had risen from behind his desk when she came into the room. He wore dark slacks, a pale blue dress shirt and a striped blue and white tie, but no jacket.

For some reason she didn't analyze, Lila found herself resenting the neat way his shirt fitted his bold, well-developed shoulders and how it emphasized the hard, lean flatness of his midsection. She was annoyed by the enticing way his hair swept to one side of his forehead. She was irritated by the mesmerizing appeal of his deep brown eyes. Most of all she was aggravated by the sheer, intimidating size of him. She'd forgotten just how tall he actually was. Since she, herself, was tall, she was used to men being close to her own height, not towering above her. There was such blatant power and strength in his body, such authority in his very stance that it somehow made her feel small and weak. There was such a potent, masculine sensuality about him that her mouth went dry, and that only heightened her outrage and anger.

She didn't want to be attracted to Jeff Chappel. She simply wouldn't allow it! She wouldn't!

Jeff's voice was unexpectedly husky when he spoke. "Lila, this is a surprise. Won't you sit down?" he invited. One large hand swept toward the leather chairs.

Lila found herself focusing on his hand. It, too, was overwhelming. Long, sturdy fingers stretched out and Lila recalled with what tender gentleness and sensitivity that they had touched her skin and threaded through her hair.

She swallowed with difficulty and forced her gaze back to Jeff's face, but that, too, was a mistake. His sensual lips had parted into a half-smile, welcoming, yet wary. Her eyes traced the outline of his lips and she could almost feel the way they had warmed hers when he had kissed her.

She didn't understand why his very presence was affecting her so badly, and the awareness frightened her. Somehow she was completely losing control over her senses and emotions as far as Jeff was concerned, and that would never do.

Jeff tilted his head, looking at her curiously. He repeated, "Won't you sit down?"

From somewhere deep inside her, came salvation. Lila remembered her anger and now she deliberately fanned the flames of it.

"Thank you," she said stiffly, "but that won't be necessary. What I came to say won't take long." She opened her handbag and extracted the envelope with the check in it. "I came to return this to you."

She held the envelope toward him.

Jeff still stood behind his desk and now he became motionless. He made no move to accept the envelope. "Why would you want to do that?" he asked after a moment's silence. "I owe it to you."

"Don't play dumb," Lila snapped. "I'm not in the mood for it." When he still didn't take it, she defiantly tossed the envelope to the desk. "It's far too generous. Ridiculously so. I don't know why you did it, or what you must think of me to have done it in the first place, but I'm not a person who accepts money I don't have coming to me."

"It's to cover the expenses of repairing your car," Jeff said mildly. "That's what you wanted when you sent the police after me."

"Of course I want that. It's only fair. I can't get my car fixed without it."

Jeff quirked one eyebrow. "Then what's the problem?"

Lila made an exasperated sound. "I told you! It's far too much and you know that as well as I do. I got estimates the other day and it only comes to about four hundred dollars. Write me a check for that amount and I won't bother you anymore."

Jeff picked up the envelope and offered it back to her. "I'd rather you took this one," he said.

Lila put her hands on her hips and stared at him in amazement. "Why, for heaven's sake? Are you so filthy rich that you just enjoy tossing good money away for the heck of it?"

Jeff sighed. "The truth is I felt I owed you for something more than just the car," he finally explained. "You were a big help to me the night they found Janey. We both needed someone and you were there for us. You said you were in financial difficulties and I was simply trying to repay your favor in a practical, concrete way.''

Lila's voice trembled. ''You've cheapened the whole thing!'' she exclaimed indignantly. ''I was merely trying to help two fellow human beings who were under extreme stress. I never expected to be paid for it. I...I did it from the heart, not because I hoped to line my pocketbook, but I guess a man like you can't understand that. You're used to buying whatever you want! Well, let me tell you something, Jeffrey Chappel...I'm not for sale!''

She was so deeply wounded that he was trying to pay her off for simply caring that she feared she might burst into tears. Without another word, she ran from the office and down the hall toward the swinging doors.

She was lucky. She made it all the way to her car before the tears began to streak her face.

Chapter Eight

Jeff left the office fifteen minutes after Lila did. He felt confused, hurt and angry as hell. He could no longer concentrate on business, so he decided he might as well call it a day and go home.

Janey, who was already home from school, was delighted to see him. "I'm glad you came early, Jeff. I wanted to take Toby for a ride, but Lionel's too busy to go with me. Will you come?"

Since the kidnapping, Jeff and Janey both had continued to be shaken. Jeff had asked Janey not to ride her horse, even within the confines of their own property, without someone with her. It was a request to which she had readily acquiesced, because the truth was, she had been too fearful yet to ride alone. Since she'd returned home, she'd been out riding several times, but usually Lionel Himes accompanied her. Today he was busy helping his father repair the tractor and had no time to spare for an outing.

"Sure, I'll go with you," Jeff said. In his present mood, he could use some exercise. Maybe a ride would blow away some of his turbulent feelings.

They passed through the kitchen where Martha was already occupied preparing dinner. Now that she was also back home and Janey was safe, life had taken on a semblance of normality again. It was only when Janey left the house to go somewhere without him that Jeff tensed with anxiety. Since she'd been back, he wouldn't even let her ride the school bus anymore. He had Bud or Lionel drive her back and forth to school when he couldn't do it himself.

"How was school today?" he asked a little later once they were in the saddle and their horses were ambling across a pasture.

"Fine," Janey replied. "Lila Addison came to speak to our gym class about modeling."

Jeff's muscles tightened at the mention of her name. "Did she?" he responded noncommittally. "Was she any good?"

"Terrific. All the girls loved her. Mostly she just told us if we want to look good to eat healthy foods, to exercise and not to take up smoking or drinking."

"She gave you sound advice," Jeff murmured with unwilling approval.

"I guess." Janey fell silent for a moment, then blurted, "Jeff, I talked to her afterwards and she was as nice to me as she could be. You said she didn't want anything to do with us anymore, but she said that's not true."

Jeff shot her a quick glance. "You mean you told her what I said?"

"Well," Janey answered defensively, "I wanted to know if she really felt that way. I like her and I want to be friends with her. You know I want to be a model someday and Lila can give me a lot of tips. She told me I could visit her anytime I liked, if it was okay with you. Is it?"

Annoyance stirred anew inside Jeff. The way he felt about Lila Addison just now, it would be fine with him if he never saw or heard of her again. The last thing he wanted was for his little sister to get in thick with her. He felt trapped and he hesitated a long time before answering. Deep down he knew it would be churlish of him to refuse. Lila *had* been kind to Janey. From that first night at the police station, he had recognized that there was an immediate rapport between the two of them. Moreover, he sensed in an uneasy sort of way that Janey was at an age when she needed the influence of a woman friend. They had Martha, of course, and she loved Janey like her own child, but Martha was getting old. She was far removed from the realities of a modern teenage girl's world. Lila, on the other hand, was young, beautiful and from what he'd seen and heard, she also had an instinctive, common-sense way of dealing with girls. In spite of their own difficulty in getting along, Jeff realized unhappily that it would be very wrong and selfish of him to keep Janey away from Lila. It was possible that she might become a very good influence on his sister.

Concealing his personal hostility toward Lila, he finally said, "I guess it's all right for you to spend some time with her now and then. Just don't overdo it. She's got her own life to lead."

Janey looked at him shrewdly. "You liked her a lot, too, at first. I could tell. What happened to change your mind?"

Jeff shrugged. "It's not important," he said lightly. "We just discovered that we look at things differently, that's all. We don't have anything in common." He grinned, forcing himself to lighten his frozen features. "Except that we both happen to think you're wonderful, of course."

Janey grinned back and to Jeff's relief, she changed the subject. "I'll race you to the foot of the hill," she challenged.

"You're on," Jeff flung back.

But later, after dinner while Janey was upstairs doing homework and he sat with an unread newspaper across his knee, his morose thoughts returned to Lila. Jeff still couldn't understand why she had gotten so angry when he'd offered her that job. And then this afternoon, she had practically thrown his generous check back in his face! He'd done his level best to be good to her in the only way he knew, and instead of appreciating it, she'd become defensive and angry, as though he'd done something terrible. It just didn't make any sense. Never before had anyone turned down his proffered largesse and for the life of him, he couldn't figure out what he'd done wrong.

Lila was certainly the antithesis of Angela Thompson. Jeff smiled grimly to himself, dwelling on the irony of it. When he'd been dating Angela, she had avidly accepted everything he offered, and looking back, he could see that she'd also often hinted for even more. The trouble was that she had been too greedy and now he counted himself lucky to have found out in time. He had come too close for comfort to being taken for a permanent ride.

They had been dating about four months and the relationship had grown serious enough that Jeff had brought Angela from Dallas to spend the Christmas holidays at his home. He had wanted Angela and Janey to get acquainted, to see how well they got along together before he made up his mind to propose, which he had been seriously considering.

Janey, Bud and Martha had all been polite, but reserved with Angela and it had irritated him no end because he had hoped Angela would be accepted by them. Of course, her life-style had been different from theirs. She'd grown up in the city, with all its varied entertainments and she hadn't seemed very enthusiastic about the farm itself, but Jeff had thought it would grow on her once she was living here for good. Angela herself had convinced him that given a little time, she could be charmed by the country as long as she could make frequent visits to the city.

Jeff didn't go so far as to buy her an engagement ring for Christmas, though he had thought about it. But some deep instinct had held him back and had prevented him from making what would have been the most serious error of his life. Instead, he'd presented Angela with diamond and ruby earrings that had set him back a good deal. Angela had been thrilled with his gift and had thanked him appropriately, with warmth and affection.

But later that same day he had accidentally overheard Angela talking on the upstairs telephone. Supposedly, she'd gone to the guest room to rest and he'd followed her upstairs a few minutes later to get something from his room. The guest room door had not been closed completely and when Jeff had heard her voice, he had gone to the door, thinking she was calling to him.

He would never forget the things he had heard her say. There had been references to hayseed country, simpletons and the like. But it was the rest of the conversation that had burnished itself into his mind like a branding iron. Jeff nursed the memory deliberately so that he would never forget, so that he would never again lay himself open to the possibility of being taken for a sucker.

"If I can manage to latch onto Jeff, I'll be able to do as I please and live in style," Angela had told the person on the other end of the line. "He's crazy about me and gives me everything I want. And the first thing I'll do is ship that sister of his off to a boarding school. The little brat doesn't like me and I don't like her and I'm not about to be saddled with the responsibility of raising her. I'm sure I'll be able to convince Jeff that it'll be for the best." She had laughed then and added, "Oh, yes. I'm willing to bet I'll have an engagement ring on my finger by Valentine's Day."

The only satisfaction Jeff had from the situation was the horrified expression on Angela's face when he pushed open the bedroom door and walked inside and she realized that he had overheard her conversation.

He shook his head, ridding himself of the unpleasant memory for now. Since Angela he'd dated a lot of women, but never seriously. The old adage, "Once burned, twice shy," applied to him. No other young woman of his acquaintance had so much as crossed the threshold of his door until Lila had come.

Jeff wished earnestly that he had never met Lila. For some inexplicable reason, she was firmly lodged in his mind, refusing to be dislodged. The memory of the softness of her skin, the sweet warmth of her lips moving on his sent vibrations of new desire pulsating through his body.

Jeff resented the feelings and after a moment, he got up and turned on the television. Maybe that would distract him from his uncomfortable thoughts.

Lila enjoyed dining on Friday evening with Amy Mathis and her friend, Jerri Dickson. Jerri was an English teacher at the high school, unmarried, but engaged. Her wedding was set for next month when school was out and the three of them talked a great deal about gowns, flowers and decorations. Amy was to be the matron of honor. The conversation was a good way to break the ice between strangers and soon Lila was as caught up in Jerri's excited plans as Jerri was herself.

Amy served lasagna, a large green salad and red wine. They spent a long time over the simple meal, mostly doing more talking than eating.

"I still need someone to preside over the guest book," Jerri told Lila. "Would you like to do it?"

"I'd love to," Lila replied swiftly. She was pleased that Jerri liked her enough to include her in that most special day. She felt that she had indeed made a new friend.

"Have you decided on who will be your ushers yet?" Amy asked as she refilled their wine glasses.

Jerri named several men Lila didn't know, and then she named the groomsmen. They included Jeff Chappel. Lila gave a little start and her heart lodged in her throat. She hastily took a sip of wine to ease her discomfort but the wine was difficult to swallow. She had never even considered seeing Jeff at the wedding, which just went to show how dense she was. Of course, in a town this small, just about everybody for miles around would be there, if not in the wedding party itself, then certainly as guests. It would be difficult for her to face him again after the temper tantrum she'd thrown in his office yesterday.

Lila was ashamed of the way she had lost control when she'd confronted him. She had meant to coolly set him straight and leave with dignity. Instead, she'd behaved like an idiot. Jeff must despise her and feel nothing but scorn toward her.

Amy somehow picked up on her thoughts of Jeff. She said, "It's still hard to believe Janey Chappel was actually kidnapped. I'll bet Jeff hasn't gotten over the shock of it yet."

Jerri nodded. "Rob," she said, referring to her fiancé, "saw him a couple of days ago and he said Jeff told him he's anxious all the time now when she's at school. He's afraid it'll happen again."

Amy looked thoughtful. "Actually, Janey seems to be handling herself pretty well after the ordeal she went through. She laughs and giggles with the other students just as she always did, but I have noticed that between classes she won't walk down the corridors alone. She always has a friend with her, and she doesn't venture outside the building at the end of the day until Lionel or Bud Himes comes inside to get her."

"Who can blame the poor kid?" Lila murmured. "Is she getting any psychiatric help? I'd think she needs it."

Jerri nodded. "Jeff's been driving her to Tyler two afternoons a week to see a psychiatrist." She paused, then went on, "He's a good brother to her. He really loves that girl."

"Well, Jeff is a lovable guy." There was a sudden twinkle in Amy's eyes. "He's also good-looking and eligible. Lila," she told Jerri, "was in on the rescue excitement with Jeff. Have there been any further developments between the two of you, Lila?"

Lila grimaced, wishing Amy had not brought up the subject. "That night was just an extraordinary, accidental thing," she said carefully. "There's no reason for us to see each other now that it's over."

"Come on now," Jerri teased, "don't tell us you didn't find Jeff attractive. We all have at one time or another, from the time *we* were in high school ourselves."

Lila twirled the stem of her wineglass in her hand, gazing at it intently to avoid the other women's eyes. "Sure," she admitted at last, "I think he's attractive, but I'm not attracted *to* him." Which, she admitted to herself, was probably the biggest whopper ever told. But she couldn't bring herself to glibly admit to Amy and Jerri how she really felt about Jeff. The pain was too new, too raw. She wanted to allow it time to heal, not to keep widening the wound by probing it more deeply.

"Still carrying the torch for Nick after what he did to you?" Amy demanded indignantly.

"Are you kidding?" Lila retorted. "The torch flickered out and died the minute I found out what a two-faced scoundrel he really was. What he did leave me with is a total and complete lack of interest in men. I don't trust any of them, and I'm certainly not about to get involved with another one. I've sworn off men for good."

"With your looks?" Jerri laughed and shook her head. "Not a chance. You may think you've sworn off men, but I can tell you for sure they're not about to swear off you. I can't imagine men ever leaving you alone. One of these days you'll have to marry one just to ward off the rest of the horde."

Lila grinned. "Maybe I could join a nunnery?"

Amy chuckled. "You may be nice enough by the standards of this wicked world, Lila, but pious you're not. I remember the time when we were kids and you tossed a water balloon from my bedroom window onto my brother's head."

Lila laughed. "I'd forgotten all about that. Has he ever forgiven me?"

"Probably not. I also remember another time when you snitched that..."

Lila held up her hands. "Enough! Enough! Don't rehash my sordid past, will you? You've convinced me I'm not qualified for sainthood, but you don't have to rub it in."

"Well," Jerri put in, returning to the original subject, "I think you and Jeff would be perfect for each other. After Rob and I are married, we'll have you both to dinner some evening."

"That's a good idea," Amy seconded. "Maybe I ought to do that sometime soon myself... have Rob and Jerri and you and Jeff over for a barbecue. It would be fun."

"Don't you dare!" Lila breathed. "Either one of you! Really, girls, just drop it, please, will you? The truth is Jeff and I don't like each other very much."

Amy looked puzzled. "Why is that?"

Lila shrugged. "Who knows? Chemistry, I suppose. Some people just don't hit it off and this is one of those times. Now," she said, getting to her feet and picking up her plate, "let me help clear the table."

Saturday morning was bright and clear and warm. The birds were singing cheerfully and Lila couldn't blame them. It was a perfect day, too perfect to remain indoors.

Without bothering to take time to wash up her breakfast dishes, she dressed in shorts and a T-shirt and tied her hair back at the nape of her neck. Then she headed outdoors to the small tool shed in the backyard and got the supplies she needed. This morning she would work on the rose beds in the front of the house. During the afternoon she would drive into town to the nursery and pick up some flower seeds for the backyard.

She'd been working steadily for perhaps an hour when she heard the sound of a car coming up the driveway. She paused, straightened and glanced in the direction of the sound.

A moment later Jeff's car came into view.

Lila froze as the car pulled up in front of the house and stopped. Her heart began pounding and her nerves clamored with sudden alarm. Had he come to resume the hostilities of the other day? To get back at her in some way? To have the last word? Her heart sank to her toes at the idea of another angry confrontation with him.

And yet when Jeff got out of the car and slowly strode toward her, as though he had all the time in the world to spare, her heart lurched with a different sort of nervousness. Her mouth went dry and a tingling warmth raced through her veins.

He looked magnificent. He was a specimen of manhood at prime. His height, as always, was impressive and today, instead of the neat dress clothes he wore on workdays, he was attired in faded jeans, cowboy boots and a short-sleeve polo shirt. A straw western-style hat topped his head, casting his face into shadows. His arms swung freely at his sides as he came toward her and she couldn't help but notice the incredible strength of them, the well-developed muscles that stood out beneath the healthy browned color of his skin.

Lila was speechless and when he reached her and stood just inches away, she was surprised to see a smile crooking his lips to one side. It was most engaging and she inhaled sharply, trying to quell her fluttering heart.

"Nice day," Jeff said.

Lila found her tongue and inclined her head. "Yes. Lovely."

"I see it's inspired you to do some yard work."

She nodded again. "Yes. These beds haven't been worked in so long that it's hard going, but I'm determined to get them into shape. I love plants and I was never able to indulge in anything more than a few houseplants in New York, so I'm trying to make up for lost time. Besides, these rosebushes Gran planted are desperate for a bit of care."

"Want some help?" Jeff offered impulsively. "I've been known to be pretty handy with a shovel and a spade."

Lila's eyes widened with surprise. "Why should you bother?"

Jeff shrugged and answered with a question of his own. "How about as a friendly gesture between neighbors?"

She shook her head. "Thanks, but I couldn't possibly let you do that."

"Don't be silly." With lightning speed, he removed the shovel handle from her grasp. "I could do with a bit of exercise, anyway. While I loosen the soil, you can spread the mulch. That way we can have the job done in an hour, tops."

Lila knotted both fists and placed them on her hips. She tilted her head and gazed at him curiously. "Why should you help me?" she demanded. "We weren't exactly on the friendliest of terms the last time we met. Anyway, you didn't come here to work flower beds. Why did you come?"

"Good thing you reminded me." Jeff reached inside his shirt pocket and pulled out a blue piece of paper. "Here's the revised check you demanded for your car repairs. Four hundred and not a cent more. Does that suit you?"

Lila took it from him, unfolded the check and looked at it to make sure he was telling the truth. He was. "Fine," she said at last, without looking at him. "Thanks."

"No call for thanks," Jeff said shortly. "It's what I owed you. Now," he said, turning to glance over the flower beds just as she looked toward him once more, "where do you want me to begin?"

"I don't," Lila said firmly. "I told you, I don't expect you to do my chores."

"Oh, I know how independent you are," Jeff replied. He swung back to look at her again. His eyes were dark and stern, forbidding her to make any further objections. "But I'm not here trying to 'buy' you or overburden you with unwanted generosity. I'm just offering a little neighborly help and you can't refuse that. Everybody in Cattail helps each other in one way or another, so you might as well get used to it. Maybe it's not how they do things in New York, but it's how we do things here, and if you want to fit in, you'll stop taking offense over every little favor someone does for you."

Lila sighed. It was the truth. People here did do little things for each other all the time. That was one of Cattail's greatest charms. The friendly, cheerful way people lent helping hands to each other or shared the bounty of their gardens, as though they were all one big, extended family.

"All right," she said at last. "If you really don't mind, I'd be glad of your help. The soil's packed so solid, I was having a difficult time of it."

"See," Jeff said with a teasing grin, "that wasn't so hard, was it? Accepting a neighborly gesture for what it is?" He stepped over to the flower bed and with one booted foot on it's top ridge, thrust the shovel deep into the soil and turned it.

Lila watched him in uncertain silence for a few moments. Finally she worked up her courage enough to step to his side. When she spoke her voice was soft and shy. "Jeff?"

He rested one bronzed arm across the handle of the shovel and paused to look at her. "Yes?"

"I'm . . . I'm really sorry about the way I blew up in your office the other day. I know you were just trying to be kind to me, and I took it the wrong way. I apologize."

Jeff flashed a quick smile that heartened her.

"Apology accepted."

That was all that was said about the incident and after that they worked in virtual silence for the next half hour. Yet somehow, Lila felt that it was a friendly, companionable silence. Jeff turned the soil and Lila walked behind him, spreading mulch, then working it into the broken soil with a spade. A fresh new happiness spread over her. It seemed to her that the already beautiful morning had turned into a brilliant, spectacular day. She was glad, truly glad, that their enmity was at an end, and her spirits rose while her heart sang with a strange, unfamiliar elation.

Jeff only nodded without speaking when, after another half hour passed, Lila said she was going into the house to get them some cold drinks.

He watched as she went toward the porch steps. Her long, bare legs were smooth, honey-toned, and her movements were graceful. Her narrow hips swung gently from side to side in a magnetic, sensual rhythm that stirred his blood. Like the other times he'd been with her, an unwilling, but undeniable desire for her flared in Jeff. He wanted to hold her, embrace her, touch her lovely body everywhere. In short, he wanted to make passionate love to her. The feeling was so overwhelming that he bit hard on his lip as he fought to stifle the wild sensations that ran rampant through his veins.

By the time Lila returned with glasses of iced cola and he joined her on the porch, Jeff's feelings were under lock and key. He still wasn't certain exactly why he had come here today instead of just mailing the check to her. Maybe it was that he'd wanted to prove to himself that he didn't want her. If that was the case, he had failed dismally. All the same, he was careful not to allow her even a glimpse of his true feelings. Their relationship with each other was so tenuous, so fragile that he didn't dare. At least they were on speaking terms again, without the hostility. He would have to be content with that small beginning.

As they relaxed in the two old rocking chairs on the front porch, enjoying the slight breeze that gently feathered their moist skin, they talked of inconsequential things, neutral subjects far removed from themselves. Jeff sensed that Lila was as wary as he was, that she, too, was struggling to keep the atmosphere light and free of tension.

Fifteen minutes later he drained his glass and decided it was time to leave. They'd about exhausted their stock of small talk, and he wasn't quite sure where to go from there. It might be dangerous to stay much longer because the more he looked at Lila, the more he longed to touch her.

He swung to his feet and said prosaically, "I'd better shove off now. I've got a few errands to run."

Lila got to her feet, also. Her voice was soft and polite as she tilted her head to look up at him. "Thanks for your help with the rose beds. It would've taken me the better part of a week to do it alone."

"It was my pleasure," he answered with a tiny smile.

For a moment they stood gazing quietly at each other. Though she was tall herself, Lila seemed to him very small and ultrafeminine. The T-shirt she wore, though loose, could not conceal the lovely roundness of her breasts; her shorts, though modest and not too tight, could not hide her exquisitely shaped hips. And then there was that smudge of soil trailing down her cheek. Jeff was sorely tempted to brush it away. In fact, he actually half-raised his right hand to do it before he realized what he was doing and let the hand fall back limply at his side.

He was suddenly, acutely aware that if he so much as lightly touched her, all his hard-won restraint would be gone in a flash. Then he wouldn't be able to stop himself from kissing her, from claiming her for his own, from making love to her.

It would be disastrous if he tried. Sure, Lila was being friendly enough now, but there was still a barrier between them. He could feel it. She had shown him more than once that though she might respond to his kisses, she disliked and disapproved of him in some fundamental way. He wasn't about to risk being rejected again. Not now.

"Well," he said at last, breaking the small, but tense silence that had arisen. "Be seeing you."

"Yes," Lila echoed in a subdued voice. "See you."

Her spirits, which had risen so high with hope, though she wasn't entirely certain what she had hoped for, collapsed like a deflated balloon as she watched Jeff get into his car. He'd been friendly, neighborly, helpful, but nothing more.

There had been no mention of seeing her again, either specifically or generally, and Lila discovered, as he drove away with a casual wave, that her disappointment ran deep, to the very core of her being.

The interview was over. The heavy-set man behind the desk rose to his feet and Lila followed suit.

"I wish I could hire you, Miss Addison, I really do, but ... you understand?"

"Of course I do, Mr. Stryker." She smiled to mask her keen disappointment and chagrin. "Maybe I ought to go to Tyler and investigate taking a course in computers."

"It wouldn't hurt," he answered seriously. "Like it or not, those things are here to stay and we need trained people to operate them, even in a place like Cattail."

"Yes. Well, thank you for your time."

Lila left the tiny realty office and got behind the wheel of her car, grateful to be alone.

She felt like such a fool...a useless fool who was good for nothing of practical value. All she had going for her was a pretty face, and that didn't seem to go for much in Cattail. Here, skills were needed. If you couldn't type, do short-

Chapter Nine

FIRST-CLASS ROMANCE

Mail This Heart TODAY!

And We'll Deliver:

**4 FREE BOOKS
A FREE PEN & WATCH SET
PLUS
A SURPRISE MYSTERY BONUS
TO YOUR DOOR!**

See Inside For More Details

SILHOUETTE DELIVERS FIRST-CLASS ROMANCE—DIRECT TO YOUR DOOR

Mail the Heart sticker on the postpaid order card today and you'll receive:

— **4 new Silhouette Special Edition novels—FREE**
— **an elegant pen & watch set—FREE**
— **and a surprise mystery bonus—FREE**

But that's not all. You'll also get:

Money-Saving Home Delivery
When you subscribe to Silhouette Special Editions the excitement, romance and faraway adventures of these novels can be yours for previewing in the convenience of your own home at less than retail prices. Every month we'll deliver 6 new books right to your door. If you decide to keep them, they'll be yours for only $2.49 each. That's 26¢ less per book than what you pay in stores. And there is no extra charge for shipping and handling!

Free Monthly Newsletter
It's the indispensable insider's look at our most popular writers and their upcoming novels. Now you can have a behind-the-scenes look at the fascinating world of Silhouette! It's an added bonus you'll look forward to every month!

Special Extras—FREE
Because our home subscribers are our most valued readers, we'll be sending you additional free gifts from time to time as a token of our appreciation.

OPEN YOUR MAILBOX TO A WORLD OF LOVE AND ROMANCE EACH MONTH. JUST COMPLETE, DETACH AND MAIL YOUR FREE OFFER CARD TODAY!

Remember! To receive your free books, pen and watch set and mystery gift, return the postpaid card below. But don't delay!

DETACH AND MAIL CARD TODAY.

If offer card has been removed, write to:
Silhouette Books, 901 Fuhrmann Blvd., P.O. Box 1867, Buffalo, NY 14269-1867

MAIL THE POSTPAID CARD TODAY!

BUSINESS REPLY CARD

First Class   Permit No. 717   Buffalo, NY

Postage will be paid by addressee

Silhouette Books®
901 Fuhrmann Blvd.
P.O. Box 1867
Buffalo, NY 14240-9952

NO POSTAGE
NECESSARY
IF MAILED
IN THE
UNITED STATES

order cooking, juggle accounts or run a tractor, you were more of a liability than an asset.

When she got back home and stood before the current painting underway on the easel, she sighed in utter despair. Maybe it was time, after all, to throw in the towel. Nothing, but nothing, seemed to be going her way. Not only could she not find a job, but she was far from satisfied with the way her paintings were shaping up. She gazed critically at the one in front of her. The sky coloring was okay, but the clouds just weren't quite right. It was the same with every painting she'd done recently. They were *almost* there, but almost wasn't good enough. She didn't dare send them off to the gallery. They'd be sure to reject them, and as it was, her self-esteem was already in tatters. Who would've thought she couldn't find *some* kind of job?

And money was still flooding out at an alarming rate. She hadn't heard from the realty agent about her condo in some time. She decided she'd better check on that matter at once and turning her back on the unsatisfactory painting, she went to the phone and placed a call to New York.

The news wasn't good. Still no buyers in sight. The agent ran several excuses by her as to his viewpoint on why the apartment hadn't yet sold and Lila listened in growing consternation. It was simply impossible to hang on forever and in the meantime she was pouring money down a rat hole.

"Try to lease it," she instructed now.

"If you do that, you won't be able to sell it for the duration of the lease."

"I know," Lila answered with a heavy heart, "but at least it won't be gobbling up money the way it is now. Lease it."

"Whatever you say."

Lila hung up the telephone and grimaced. Just one more thing, she thought bitterly, to top an already miserable day.

She went into the bedroom to remove the dress she'd worn for the job interview and as she stood in slip and stockings, she caught a glimpse of herself in the dresser mirror.

"Face it," she snapped at her reflection. "Nothing has essentially changed over the past few days. What you're really unhappy about is Jeff."

It was a hard truth. Four days had passed since he'd arrived unexpectedly and helped her with her gardening. Four long days during which she'd hoped against hope that he would return, or at least call, but it hadn't happened. She had apologized for losing her temper that day in his office and he had gracefully accepted it. The rest of the time he had been friendly in the casual sort of way a neighbor is friendly, nothing more. He had left without mentioning seeing her again. Apparently whatever interest he'd had in her in the beginning was dead.

Jeff's change of heart hurt more than she liked to admit, but there was nothing she could do about it. If a man wasn't interested, he just wasn't. He had found her wanting in some way and she had to accept that.

And anyway, she asked herself harshly, why was she pining over him? Did she really want to get involved with Jeff? No; the answer was a firm, unequivocal no. The very thought of getting seriously entangled with any man gave her the shivers.

It was only that she felt a weakness whenever she recalled those few tender moments she'd spent in Jeff's arms, but given time and a lot of self-discipline, she'd get over it.

She filled the remainder of the week with as much activity as she could squeeze in. She found that on the whole, when she worked to the point of exhaustion, she slept easier, thought of Jeff less. Mornings, while the air was still cool, she spent outdoors working in the garden or the yard; afternoons and evenings were spent painting, sometimes until one or two in the morning.

On Saturday, she gave herself a break. She slept late, cooked herself a large breakfast and then drove into town for groceries. She bought a couple of paperbacks and magazines and intended to spend the afternoon doing nothing more stringent than flipping pages or lifting a cool drink to her lips.

That afternoon, while she sat on the porch, glancing through the latest issue of *Vogue*, in which her image appeared in a cosmetic advertisement, Lila received a pleasant surprise. Bud Himes drove up, bringing Janey Chappel and another girl by for a visit.

Lila invited Bud to stay, but he said he had other things to do. "I'll be back for them in a couple of hours, if it's okay with you for them to stay that long."

"Of course it is. I'm glad of the company."

Janey's friend was named Tina and at first she was shy and quiet, but before long Lila had drawn her out and she was chattering away as much as Janey.

"It must be so exciting to be a model . . . all those beautiful clothes and jewelry and men admiring you."

Lila laughed. "If working under hot lights ten hours a day is exciting, I suppose modeling is. As for the glamorous clothes, that aspect is not always what it's cracked up to be. If you're doing a magazine layout, you're wearing bathing suits in December and fur coats in August."

"Yeah, but look at all the money you can make, not to mention being on magazine covers and in television commercials. Doesn't it give you a thrill every time you see yourself?" Janey asked.

The thrill had long since faded for Lila, but as she looked at the two eager faces, she remembered how she had once felt, glowing with anticipation and youthful optimism.

She chose her words carefully. "That part is nice, Janey, but modeling isn't an easy life. You pay dearly for every bit of success you get. In the first place, it's very hard to break into the business. Luck, as well as looks, plays a big part. For every person who makes it, there are hundreds more who start out just as full of hope, only to see their dreams dashed to pieces. There's a lot of knocking on doors, a lot of competition, a lot of rejection. You have to be tough inside to be able to handle the stress.''

''I'm tough,'' Janey declared. ''I'll be able to take it.''

Yes, Lila thought silently. *You probably can.* Her bet was riding on anyone who could go through a terrifying kidnapping ordeal and come through it so emotionally and mentally intact. All the same, she refused to paint a rosy picture of modeling. She didn't want to make the life sound so bleak as to be absolutely hopeless, but she didn't want to give out a false impression of it as being all icing on the cake, either. She tried hard to be truthful and informative about both the pros and cons of the profession.

Jeff normally didn't go to his office on Saturdays, but today there had been a few things he needed to work on, so he went in for a couple of hours.

When he returned home and pulled into the driveway, he met Bud, who was just about to get into his pickup truck.

''Where are you headed?'' Jeff asked as he got out of his car.

''Janey and Tina wanted to visit Lila Addison for a while, so I dropped them off. I was just going back for them.''

''I'll do it,'' Jeff offered promptly. ''You go on home.''

''Are you sure?'' Bud quizzed. Since the kidnapping, if Jeff had to be somewhere else, either Bud or Martha stayed at the house with Janey until his return. Nobody, including Janey, wanted her to stay alone.

''I'm sure,'' Jeff replied. ''Have a good weekend, Bud.''

Bud nodded and climbed into the cab of his truck. Jeff got back into his car.

He was delighted to have a legitimate excuse to see Lila again. All week he'd wanted to call her, but he'd fought the urge. He wanted more than friendship from her, but since she wasn't interested in him, it was better all around if they didn't see much of each other. While that still held true, now he allowed himself pleasure over the fact that he was going to see her.

When he arrived at the Addison place, he found Lila and the two girls sitting on the shady front porch. Janey was perched on the ledge while Lila and Tina occupied the rocking chairs.

He mounted the steps and his gaze went straight to Lila. She looked refreshingly beautiful, yet utterly casual. Her long, slender jean-clad legs were tucked beneath her; she wore a bright red cotton shirt and clips held back her hair. She wasn't wearing any makeup at all as far as he could tell and somehow the utter simplicity of her appearance enchanted him.

Nicest of all was the genuine, welcoming smile she gave him. Her eyes glowed and there was unmistakable happiness in her expression. It filled him with satisfaction.

"Been having a good visit?" he asked.

Lila nodded. "I was thoroughly bored with my own company, so the girls couldn't have come at a more perfect time."

"Lila's been telling us a lot about what it's like to be a model."

"And they've been filling me in about all the cute teenage boys in town," she said with a twinkle glittering in her eyes.

"I'll bet they have." Jeff grinned. "Janey has a thing for a boy in her algebra class named Pete."

Janey giggled and shook her head. "Wrong. That was last week."

"This week it's Doug Hampton," Tina said, clasping her hands, rolling her eyes and pretending to swoon.

"The basketball star?" Jeff asked.

"Yes," Janey admitted.

"No! No!" Jeff protested. "He's a senior. He's too old for you."

Janey sighed. "Unfortunately for me, you don't have a thing to worry about. Doug doesn't even know I'm alive."

"Good," Jeff replied heartily.

Lila laughed. "You sound like a father."

"I know. It sort of ruins my image as a carefree playboy, doesn't it?"

Her eyes met his and they were both remembering the first evening he'd come here to her house and she had given him a tongue-lashing for being rich and irresponsible. She hadn't taken offense at his words now because she laughed again, and Jeff thoroughly enjoyed the sound. It was warm and liquid and spread right through him like melted butter. Maybe she was unaware of it, but she was charming him all over again, filling him with a quiet happiness and an illogical yet stubborn optimism that refused to be subdued.

With lithe grace, Lila got to her feet. "How about something cold to drink, Jeff?" she offered. "I've got soft drinks or tea."

Jeff glanced at his watch and shook his head. "I have a better idea. It's getting on toward dinner time and I'm hungry. How about if I take you three girls into town for a hamburger?"

"Great!" Janey seconded the idea.

"I'll just call my mom and make sure it's okay," Tina said, vacating her chair. "I told her you'd probably take me home by six." She went toward the door.

Jeff nodded, but his gaze never left Lila's face. She still hadn't agreed or disagreed to the plan. Now he tilted his head slightly and asked, "Well?"

Suddenly, she grinned. "Can I have a chocolate malt as well?"

Jeff chuckled. "Always thinking about your stomach! Now I know the real reason you left your career...so you could eat all you want."

"Precisely! I may never look another salad in the face as long as I live."

"Are you taking notes, Janey?" he asked good-humoredly. "See what modeling does to a woman? It eventually turns her into a food fanatic."

"No problem," Janey replied breezily. "I always eat whatever I want and I never gain extra weight." She opened the screen door of the house and said, "I'm going inside with Tina."

Lila laughed softly as the girl vanished. "Spoken with the supreme confidence of a fifteen-year-old who's convinced her body will always behave and look as if it's fifteen."

Jeff nodded. "Only time itself will teach her differently."

"Will it ever!" Lila sighed. "*Especially* if she does go into the modeling profession."

Just then the two girls returned to the porch to join them. "Ready?" Jeff asked.

"Ready," Tina replied.

On the drive to town, Janey told Jeff, "Tina's mother said it's okay if I spend the night with her tonight. All right with you, Jeff?"

Jeff's fingers tightened around the steering wheel. "I'd rather you didn't, honey," he said as calmly as he could. "How about if Tina stays at our house instead?"

"She asked me first, and her mother agreed," Janey argued.

"I know, but I'd feel better if you were home."

"Give me one good reason!" Janey demanded hotly.

"You know the reason."

"Yes, and it's silly. It's not like I'm asking to go to the moon! Besides, Tina's mom and dad will both be there!"

Jeff sighed. "Janey, let's not argue about this."

"Then let me go! I'm tired of staying at home. Anyway, you know her parents. I'll be as safe at Tina's house as I would at ours!"

He was silent for a time, considering the matter. Reluctantly, he concluded that Janey was right. Tina's parents were responsible people and as long as they were on the premises, his sister would be as safe in their care as she would be in his.

"All right," he said reluctantly. "Just promise me one thing...that you won't go off somewhere with anybody else."

"Such as?" Janey's voice was challenging.

"You know. Such as if some other kids come by in a car and want you girls to go riding around or something."

"Jeff, you're not being fair!"

"Take it or leave it," he said firmly.

"We'll take it," Tina chimed in. Turning to Janey, she added, "You know my folks. They won't let us go off in a car with any of the kids anyway."

"Well...okay," Janey conceded grudgingly. "But I still think you're getting all bent out of shape over nothing, Jeff. I've got a right to *some* freedom."

"I know," he answered softly. "It's just that I don't want anything to happen to you."

"I know," Janey replied in a slightly mollified tone. "And nothing will, I promise."

By the time they arrived at the fast-food restaurant, Janey was completely out of her ill humor and Jeff seemed to have made peace with himself about allowing her to spend the night away from home. The four of them sat in a booth, exchanging jokes and satirical comments about one another. It became a fun outing for everyone and Lila was glad she had come.

Later, after depositing the two girls at Tina's house, Jeff drove Lila home at a leisurely pace. Whatever constraint there'd been between them a week ago, after this evening the tension had evaporated. Lila felt comfortable and content to be alone in Jeff's company.

"Have you had a good week?" he asked with idle curiosity as they reached the edge of town and the open highway spread before them.

"Actually, it's been a rotten week," she admitted.

"That so? What happened?"

Lila shrugged and told him about the job interview, her troubles with her painting, the still unsold condominium. "I feel as though someone attached a faucet to my bank account and all my savings are running right down the drain."

"What are you going to do about it?"

"I told the realty agent to try to lease the apartment. It's about the only thing I can do."

"Hmmm. In spite of the risk of getting my head bitten off, my job offer still stands."

Lila smiled wryly. "Thanks, Jeff, but my problems aren't yours, and I can't accept a job that doesn't really need doing."

"Well, you can always change your mind."

"Thanks, but I won't."

He shook his head. "Stubborn."

"Principled," she countered.

"Obstinate."

"Scrupulous."

"Stiff-necked."

"Ethical."

They both began to laugh at once. Finally Jeff said, "I think it's a subject we're never likely to agree on."

"I think you're right." Lila smiled. "All the same, I'm pleased we're friends again."

"Hmmm," he answered noncommittally. They had reached her driveway and Jeff turned into it and a moment later stopped before the house.

Like that other evening when he'd brought her home, dusk was falling. The sky was silver, spangled by a few early stars. The air was soft as satin and through the dusky stillness came the sweet scent of roses.

"Would you like to come inside?" she asked.

"I won't be keeping you from anything? Your painting?"

"Not tonight. I gave myself the day off. Come on, I'll make some coffee if you like."

But in the end, the coffee was never made, never even thought of again. When they stepped inside the house, Lila flipped on a light in the living room. She turned around to face Jeff, saying, "Why don't you make yourself at . . ."

The remainder of the sentence was left unsaid, for the expression in Jeff's dark eyes silenced her. She caught her breath and then his arms went around her and he bent his head to kiss her. Completely off guard, she did nothing to stop it from happening.

The kiss seemed to last a long, long time. After a moment, Lila's hands went to his chest, as though she might push him away, but she didn't. Instead, she responded honestly from the heart, and her lips parted beneath the growing pressure of his. She felt his arms tightening around her and when they finally looked at one another, Lila was filled with wonder.

"You said in the car," Jeff uttered thickly, "that you were glad we were friends again. You know simple friendship's not going to be enough for us, don't you?"

Lila understood him perfectly and she felt emotion swell in her throat. She was bemused by the fire of his gaze. "Yes," she whispered after a moment. "I know."

A smile began to play about his lips. Jeff raised one hand and ran it down her cheek. "I think you must already know I'm absolutely crazy about you. I haven't been able to get you out of my mind since that night you let me sleep on your sofa. I tried to dislike you after you flew into a rage when I offered you that job, not to mention the time you threw the check back in my face, but I'm afraid I didn't succeed. There's something about you . . ." He shook his head as though unable to figure it out.

Impulsively Lila captured his finger and kissed it. She was smiling, too. "I've been busy telling myself how much I disliked you, too, but somehow I was never quite convinced."

"And now?" he asked quietly.

"Now I'm glad you're here...that we're together. It's what I'd been hoping for," she confessed.

Jeff pulled her closer and pressed his face to hers. "I want to make love to you, Lila," he whispered. "I've been wanting to ever since that night you were so good to me. I don't know how you feel, but..."

She cut him off by teasing softly, "I guess you're just going to stand here talking about it all night, aren't you?"

Jeff grinned and for an answer, he surprised her by scooping her up into his strong arms. The light of passion and playfulness danced in his eyes. "Never let it be said that Jeffrey Chappel allows anyone to get by with taunts like that! You're going to pay, woman!" he growled ferociously. "You're going to pay!"

In the bedroom, he placed her on the bed and before she could roll away, he came down to cover her, pinning her with his arms on either side of her. His eyes smouldered as he gazed at her and Lila laughed breathlessly.

"I've changed my mind," she said huskily. "Why don't we have that coffee?"

"Not even for the last drop in Texas," he retorted. "I've got you now and I'm not letting you go!"

His kiss followed his words and all at once both of them forgot everything as they became wrapped up in the thrilling wonder of each other. Their lips met willingly, with warmth and promise and with the exhilaration of discovery. Lila felt herself going soft inside as the pressure of Jeff's firm, well-shaped mouth on hers became even more demanding. Moment by moment, his passion grew and the flame inside her flared to match it.

Next, Jeff's kisses inched down to her throat. She felt gently, exquisitely tortured, and the rest of her body, yet untouched, quivered with expectation. He was taking his time with her, determined to rouse her fully. He was a man who would accept nothing less than everything, a man who would give nothing less than everything. The realization made her shamelessly glad that she was a woman—a woman in his arms.

At long last, Jeff raised himself up so that he could work free the buttons on her shirt. Lila did the same for him with trembling, yet bold fingers.

Little by little, they undressed, pausing in between each task to share a kiss or to caress each other with light, sensitive strokes.

"You're as lovely as I knew you would be," Jeff whispered raggedly when there were finally no more barriers between them. He touched a breast, tracing its contour, then slowly he bent his head to it.

Lila inhaled sharply and touched his hair. She didn't understand how so large a man had the capacity for such grace and tenderness, yet he did. Warm, sensual pleasure filled her and then her heart began beating rapidly as a sense of urgency swept over her.

As his gentle hands traveled the terrain of her body, becoming intimately acquainted with all her secret places, her fingers ventured over his body as well. His broad back was silky soft beneath her fingertips, like a baby's skin, but his chest was hard, muscled and roughened with crisp dark swirls of hair.

Jeff continued to take his time, savoring each moment, allowing her to savor it as well. There was all the time in the world and though he was growing impatient and eager, he tempered his desire. He wanted this night with Lila to be memorable and special for them both in every way.

So he contented himself in learning every inch of her delectable body with his hands before possessing it. Her skin was creamy white, delicate and fine. He loved its softness beneath his firm, large fingers. Her curves were tantalizing and it pleased him the way she fit so well to him, nestled against his hard male body. Above all, he loved her eagerness for him.

Everything about Lila was femininely appealing and at last Jeff lifted himself up so that he could see her again. When he did, her expression brought an ache to his throat. Her eyes were closed and her thick dark lashes fanned downward to brush her skin, but it was the smile on her lips that arrested him. Silently, but eloquently, it spoke of untapped desires mingled with the gratification of the moment.

When Lila realized he had ceased to stroke her body, which had been raised to a feverish pitch of sensitivity as it responded to his every touch, she cried out softly in unconscious protest. Her eyes flew open and she found Jeff watching her with such a loving expression that she almost couldn't bear to see it.

"You stopped," she accused in a clearly unhappy voice.

Her disappointment thrilled Jeff. "I only wanted to look at you again," he replied hoarsely. He threaded his fingers through the tumbling mass of her fiery red-gold waves and leaning closer, captured her lips once more.

"I want you," she whispered unsteadily when they stopped to gaze at each other again. She never thought she could be so brave, so open about her own needs, but she found somehow that it was easy to tell Jeff exactly how she felt.

The smile he gave her in return made her pulse race. "You have me," he answered softly. "Oh, Lila, darling, you have all of me."

They came together, became one, and as the raging storm of their rising passion reached toward its zenith, all else receded. There was only the oneness of them . . . here, now, together.

When the moment of completion arrived, Lila gasped at the same time Jeff moaned. Slowly, she became herself again; she breathed hard and erratically and her body was damp and glistening. Her eyes had been closed again and now she opened them to look up into Jeff's eyes.

The afterglow that burned in his gaze sent a new tremor through her. There was such a depth of tender caring in his eyes. It made her feel special and wonderful; yet at the same time the intensity of it was almost frightening. She wondered if he saw the same thing reflected in her eyes.

They lay together for a long time afterward, side by side, fingers lightly intertwined. At first they were both too spent to talk, but later the words came, caressing them with sound and nuance that, for the moment, in their pleasant fatigue, satisfactorily replaced the excitement of physical sensation.

"It was perfect," Jeff said softly. "*We* were perfect . . . as though we've always belonged together. As though we've always known how to fulfill each other."

"Yes," Lila answered in a voice full of surprise. "I felt that, too. As though it was somehow inevitable, meant to be."

Jeff's fingers tightened around hers. "I don't think I could have kept my sanity much longer if we hadn't resolved this between us."

Lila felt languid and contented as she smiled. "Me, too. This . . . now . . . our being together," she explained slowly, "feels so comfortable, so right."

Jeff rolled over onto his side and looked at her fully. His dark gaze was earnest. "What does it all mean, Lila?" he asked. "The sexual desire I understand perfectly. How could I help desiring you when you're so lovely? But . . ."

"But?"

"It's more than just that."

"You sound worried."

Jeff shook his head. "Confused is more like it. I thought I was in love once, a while back. It turned out I was wrong. I told myself afterward I wasn't ever going to get seriously involved with anyone again. Yet here you are . . . here *we* are, and I'm not quite sure where we go from here."

Lila felt as though she'd been slapped in the face. After what had just happened, he had doubts about them, didn't want to become involved with her! For him, it had been a mere one night stand! It made her feel cheap and dirty.

Yet his words did even more than that. They also jarred her back to her own truth. Apparently Jeff had an ugly romance behind him; she'd had her moment of truth with Nick, a real loser if ever there was one. She hadn't intended to allow herself to become vulnerable where another man was concerned, yet look where she was now!

She must have gone completely crazy to have allowed things to go this far with Jeff! She was appalled to realize she'd more than allowed it to happen...she had actually encouraged it! What an idiot she was. In that moment, she wasn't sure who she detested most...Jeff or herself! Bitterly she wished with all her heart that she'd never met him, that this night had never come to pass.

"Let me reassure you," she said in a cold, calm tone, "we don't have to go anywhere from here."

In one swift motion, Lila snatched her hand away from Jeff's, grabbed her robe from the foot of the bed, tossed it around her shoulders and slid out of bed. She slipped into the robe and knotted the belt firmly and only then did she turn to confront him with anger glittering in her eyes. "This whole thing was a mistake, a terrible mistake that I deeply regret. Now, if you would be so kind...I'd like you to leave."

Jeff sat upright in the bed, still half-covered by the bed sheets, and stared at her in total astonishment. "What's come over you? We were just having a conversation! Nothing was a mistake!"

"You're wrong," she answered in a voice that vibrated with hostility. "It was a mistake and one I don't intend to ever repeat!"

"For God's sake!" Jeff exclaimed, raising his own voice. "What did I say wrong? Maybe I put things badly, but all I was doing was trying to figure out where our relationship is headed . . . how we feel about each other.''

"There's no relationship and we're headed nowhere. Period.'' Lila started for the bedroom door. "I'm going to take a shower now,'' she announced. "I expect you to be gone by the time I'm finished.''

Chapter Ten

Sitting on the bride's side of the church, Lila was afforded an excellent view of Jeff's profile as he stood at the altar during the wedding ceremony. His face was pensive and somber and he appeared almost as pale as the groom. Despite that, she found him unbearably attractive in his black tuxedo and pleated white shirt. A pink rose adorned his lapel.

Lila sighed inwardly and attempted to pay attention to what the minister was saying. They were beautiful words of love and promise and forever. Everything was beautiful, in fact, from the altar flowers to the bride's attendants in their pink organdy and lace dresses to the bride herself. Jerri was glowing, as a bride properly should be, as she joined hands with her Rob.

But despite her best efforts, Lila's attention continued to stray to Jeff's profile. What was he thinking? she wondered. What was he feeling as he listened to the words that bound a couple together for a lifetime?

This was the first time she had seen him since the night they had made love. That was two weeks ago. Two agonizingly long weeks during which Lila had lost all the weight she had gained since moving to Cattail.

When she'd finished her shower that evening, Jeff had been gone just as she had demanded. The utter pain of it all was still heavy on her heart. She had given all of herself to him and then he had let her know he wasn't interested in a serious involvement. The hurt still burned like fire. What a fool she'd been!

Yet as she watched him now, she knew that try as she might, she still wasn't over him. He might have taken her heart and stomped on it, but she still cared. Dear God, yes, she still cared; much good it did her!

With a jolt, she returned to the present and heard the minister say, "I now pronounce you man and wife." He motioned for the couple to turn and face their well-wishers as he added buoyantly, "Now, I'm happy to introduce to you Mr. and Mrs. Robert Ward."

There was applause, the organ swelled majestically and the newlyweds, wreathed in smiles, moved up the aisle. When the remainder of the wedding party followed, Lila lowered her eyes so that she wouldn't accidentally meet Jeff's as he passed by her pew.

It was a shame she'd committed herself to attend the wedding, she thought sadly as she slowly made her way out of the church with the other guests. She would never have done so if she'd known Jeff was to be there, but once she gave her word, she didn't want to go back on it. Somehow she would just have to get through the reception and seeing Jeff, but as soon as she completed her task of presiding over the guest book she would quietly take her leave.

Meanwhile, she braced herself for the forthcoming face-to-face meeting with Jeff in the receiving line. She dreaded it for both their sakes, but there was no way to escape it.

Inside the church reception hall, she inched her way down the receiving line with a pounding heart. When she finally reached Jeff, their hands barely touched. Were his fingers icy cold, or were hers? She forced herself to look up into his face. His features were rigid and expressionless. Without a word, he merely inclined his head toward her and Lila followed his lead. A moment later the encounter was over and she was shaking hands with Dave Mathis, the best man.

It was easier after that. Jerri embraced her, happily introduced Lila to her new husband, who smiled and shook her hand and then she was greeting Amy Mathis, the matron of honor. The meeting with the other members of the wedding party passed in a blur for Lila and when it was over she moved away quickly and took up her post at the table with the guest book.

The single most fortunate thing was that, as one of the groomsmen, Jeff was occupied with his own duties. There were photographs to pose for; later there were toasts to be made, the cake to be cut and all the rest.

Except for the strain of Jeff's presence, Lila actually managed to enjoy herself somewhat. She had gradually become acquainted with quite a few local residents and this afternoon she exchanged small talk with many of them as they signed the guest book. Others whom she hadn't known introduced themselves to her and paused to share a few words. They all made her feel welcome and wanted in the community and the attention was good for her battered morale.

Later, when the refreshments were being served, Janey approached. She carried a plate and a cup of punch. "Hi. I brought you some goodies in case you can't leave your spot. Although," she went on as she glanced around, "I think your job must be about over."

"I was thinking the same thing," Lila said. "I'm sure everyone has signed in by now. Actually, I was trying to get up the nerve to leave."

"So soon?"

Lila shrugged. "Well, I don't know everyone in town as well as you do. They've all been very nice to me, but I figured it was time for me to go. Now that you're here, I'll wait a bit. Pull up a chair while I eat some of this."

Janey reached for a nearby folding chair and placed it beside Lila's. "How's your painting going?" she asked as she sat down.

Lila wrinkled her nose. "Don't ask. I guess you're glad now that school is out, hmm?"

Janey nodded. "Jeff and I are going to Europe at the end of this month."

"Are you? That sounds fantastic. You must be looking forward to it."

"What I'm not looking forward to is getting back. The trial for those men starts in the middle of August."

Lila touched her hand sympathetically. "You'll do fine, kiddo. Just fine."

"That's what Jeff says, but I'll be glad when it's over, all the same."

"I know. You—"

Lila was interrupted by another teenager coming up to talk with Janey. Janey introduced them and then soon moved off with a casual, "See you soon, Lila."

Left by herself again, Lila felt her solitude more keenly than before. She looked across the crowded room and saw Jeff laughing as he carried on a conversation with one of the bridesmaids. All at once she lost her appetite for the loaded plate of finger sandwiches, nuts, candies and cake that Janey had brought to her. She felt as though her throat was closing and without further hesitation, she grabbed her purse and left the festivities.

Jeff watched Lila go and didn't know whether he felt relief or disappointment. All he knew for sure was that suddenly, though the reception hall was crammed with people, it seemed empty, a desert, a wasteland. He wanted to leave himself, but he couldn't. He had to remain until after the newlyweds departed.

The bridesmaid next to him still chattered away inanely about her series of minor disasters earlier as she had dressed for the wedding. Jeff continued to tune her out while expertly maintaining an interested expression on his face.

He had made no attempt to approach Lila while she'd been present. What would've been the point? She had dumped him good and proper the evening he'd attempted, with such disastrous results, to examine his feelings for her.

But though he might have made no move toward her, he had been intensely aware of her from the moment he'd first entered the church with the rest of the wedding party. He'd spotted her right away—sixth pew, second person on the bride's side. It had been a shock to see her there.

And painful. In one swift glance he'd absorbed every detail about her, from the glorious waves of her hair to the sheer, delicate shell-pink dress she wore. She had been a vision of beauty, so lovely that she might have been a bride herself.

What had gone so wrong that evening together? Everything had been wonderful until that moment he'd tried to tell her how much she had come to mean to him. Somehow he'd bungled it badly and abruptly, without warning, she had turned to ice and ordered him out of her house.

He tried to comfort himself that it didn't matter, that it had been just a brief, unimportant fling without meaning, a fling that he could be glad was over. Life would go on as it had before and, given time, he'd be able to view Lila from a position of detachment.

Meantime, he forced himself once more to focus his attention on the happenings at hand. Excitement was stirring in the room. The bride was about to toss her bouquet. Next it would be the garter. Grimly, Jeff set what he hoped was a pleasant smile on his face. He would play the game as though he was enjoying himself as much as everyone else. He owed it to Rob and Jerri.

By Monday morning when he arrived at his office, Jeff's head felt battered and bruised as though a ton of logs had fallen on him. After seeing Lila at the wedding, he hadn't slept well all weekend. Something about her had woven itself insidiously through his mind. He was obsessed with the thought of her, taunted by the erotic memory of their night of lovemaking and tormented by the way it had ended so senselessly.

He dealt with routine business matters most of the morning, but when he finally had a moment to rest, he leaned back in his chair and tried to relax by flipping through the brochures and other material the travel agent in Tyler had sent to him concerning his proposed trip to Europe.

Jeff glanced at the enticing photographs of Rhine vineyards, a cabaret in Paris, canals and gondolas in Venice and sighed. He'd decided to set the trip for two reasons—one, to give Janey and himself a break from all cares before she had to face her abductors in court and second, to give him the opportunity to get away from Lila, to give him time to cool off, a chance to regain his perspective.

But as he stared morosely at the brightly colored pictures, it occurred to him that perhaps he was doing exactly the wrong thing as far as Lila was concerned.

Jeff tossed the brochures on the desk and stood up. Restlessly he paced the room, deep in thought, debating the pros and cons of the sudden, breathtaking idea that had come to him. The more he thought about it, the better he liked it, and he wondered why it had taken him so long to think of it.

Once he had made up his mind, he decided to waste no time. He went to the door and flung it open. Mary, at her desk, looked up, startled at his abrupt entrance.

"There's someone I need to see," he told her. "I'll probably be gone a couple of hours."

"Do you want to leave a number where I can reach you?"

Jeff thought for a moment and then decided against leaving Lila's phone number. He didn't want to be interrupted by any distractions, business or otherwise. "No. No number. If I'm not back in two hours, I'll call you."

In the car, his heart raced as fast as the engine. He was tense, yet exhilarated. Lila felt something for him, too, despite her about-face that night. Otherwise she couldn't have been so receptive earlier, as eager for him as he had been for her. Whether either of them liked it or not, there was some magnetic attraction that drew them, compellingly and relentlessly, toward each other. They owed it to themselves to work through the confusion and the doubts until they could be certain where they stood.

Only as he turned off the road and into the long driveway that led to her house did he entertain misgivings. Maybe he should've thought the idea through more thoroughly, given it time to gel, slept on it. But he was here now, and there was no turning back. Lila's Volkswagen was parked at the end of the driveway, so that meant she was at home. Good or bad, he would follow up on the impulse that had brought him here. He would say what he had come to say.

Lila was about to apply more blue-gray shadow to the water in her painting when she heard the sound of a car in the driveway. Grimacing with slight annoyance over the interruption, just when, for a nice change, the work was going so well, she hastily dabbed her brush in turpentine and wiped it clean. As for herself, she thought ruefully, there wasn't time to spruce up. She wore a paint-stained pair of jeans and a T-shirt and her hair was caught back in a ponytail. She hadn't bothered with makeup since she'd known she'd be working. Anyway, she hadn't been expecting company.

She left the sun-porch studio and went through the living room to the front door. When she opened it and saw Jeff standing there, her mouth went dry. Not only had she not expected company, the last person she had expected to see at her door ever again was Jeff.

For a long time they simply gazed at each other. Lila's heart thudded as her eyes took in the sight of him. He wore a tan dress shirt with the sleeves rolled almost to the elbow. A dark brown tie matched his slacks. He looked neat and fresh and she could even catch the faint scent of after-shave lotion. His expression was somber, his eyes dark and unfathomable. Light and shadow played across his immobile features and the sunlight at his back cast gold and russet highlights on his hair.

Finally Jeff broke the lengthy silence with a quiet and simple, "Hello."

Lila managed to respond in kind.

Another silence fell and then he asked, "May I come in? I'd like to talk to you."

Lila hesitated momentarily, wondering why he had come, a part of her curious, but another part of her not wanting to know. He didn't act as though this was a mere social call, but on the other hand, he didn't appear angry or hostile, either. His expression was serious, but otherwise unreadable.

At last she nodded her assent and stepped back and allowed him to enter.

Once they were facing each other in the living room, Jeff's gaze flickered briefly over her paint-stained clothes. "It looks like I interrupted you at work. I'm sorry."

"It's all right. It was time for a break anyway."

"May I see it?" he asked unexpectedly. "What you're working on?"

Lila shrugged indifferently. "Why not?"

Turning, she led the way toward the sun porch. She was far more nervous about his presence, about the purpose of his visit, than she was about his opinion of her painting. Maybe it would be a good way to break the ice between them.

The room had been completely converted into a studio. Sunlight flowed in through the windows unhampered by curtains or shades. Against one wall was a stack of canvasses, some containing paintings already completed, some blank, awaiting use. A small cluttered desk stood against another wall and it was covered by sketches and business papers. Near the windows stood the easel. A small table next to it held a palette, tubes of paint and brushes. The room was heavily scented of turpentine and linseed oil.

Jeff went to stand before the nearly finished work on the easel. The painting depicted a lake with a background of pine and oak trees. He recognized the site immediately.

"Cattail Lake," he murmured.

"Yes. I'm pleased you recognized it."

"It's very good." Jeff continued to study the canvas for some time. "The sunlight just beginning to light the sky behind the trees and touch the lake is a scene I've witnessed a thousand mornings when I've gone fishing. I like the painting very much."

"Thanks." Lila drew a deep breath and decided they had postponed the inevitable long enough. "You didn't make a trip out here to look at paintings, though."

Slowly, Jeff turned to face her. "No. I didn't."

When he didn't go on, Lila tilted her head. "Then?"

Instead of elaborating right away, he walked to one of the windows and looked out. Lila wasn't certain, but it seemed to her that he was uneasy, tense. She started to speak, but thought better of it. She would keep her silence and wait.

"That night..." Jeff began at last. His voice was low, without any particular inflection. "That night we were together, I'm still not too sure what happened. I was trying to tell you that I'd come to care for you a great deal, but somehow it went wrong. You took what I said the wrong way or got upset about something entirely different, I don't know. But if it's my fault, then I apologize."

"It isn't necessary," Lila answered quietly. "I did get upset, but I think perhaps I overreacted. I apologize, too."

Jeff turned to look at her. "So—where does that leave us now?"

Lila spread her hands. "I don't know," she replied honestly. "I . . . I think things happened between us a little too fast. I'm just not ready for that yet."

Jeff nodded. "I thought that might be it. It's sort of how I feel, too. I was trying to tell you that night that while I cared for you very much, I had my doubts, too, but I guess I shouldn't have said it. At least not just then." He moved toward her then, slowly, and he paused when he was only a pace away from her. "I do feel something for you that's very strong, that's undeniable, and I can't simply dismiss it, Lila. I don't want to. I'm not looking for just an affair with you, in spite of the fact that I loved making love to you, but I'm not quite ready to commit myself to anything binding. I had a bad relationship before, and apparently you did, too, so that makes us both somewhat cautious."

Lila gave a tiny smile. "Then what have we been at odds about? Those are my feelings exactly."

"Then I have a suggestion . . . a way for us to have the chance to be together for a while without any pressure. A way to find out more about each other, to discover how we really feel, but without demands or assumptions."

Lila's eyes darkened. "Surely you're not suggesting I move in with you? There's Janey!"

Jeff's lips curved and his voice was wry. "Precisely. There's Janey. No, I'm not suggesting that, but in a way, my idea is similar. In three weeks Janey and I are leaving for a vacation in Europe."

"Yes, I know. Janey told me at Jerri and Rob's wedding reception."

"We'll be gone a month." Jeff paused before asking, "Why don't you come with us?"

Lila stared at him blankly, so Jeff hurriedly elaborated. "Like I said, there'd be no pressures or demands. You'd share a room with Janey, or have your own if you like. We'd simply be together in a relaxed atmosphere and..."

"And how would you explain all this to Janey?" Lila interrupted brusquely.

He shrugged. "That you'd come along as her chaperon, or as her traveling companion. She could use some feminine company on the trip, and this would be ideal. She already likes you." He smiled. "So do I. It's a way we could all be together and enjoy ourselves. You and I would have time to get to know each other without any complicated expectations. You'd simply be doing a job. Of course I'll pay all your expenses, as well as a salary and—"

"No."

"No?" He was taken aback at her flat refusal. "Just like that? No?"

"Just like that! My God, Jeff, don't you see, you're trying to 'buy' me again? You've just come up with another make-work proposal. Well, I'm having no part of it! Janey doesn't need my companionship, paid or otherwise, on a vacation trip. She has you!"

Jeff sighed. "You're just being difficult again!"

"Am I? Well, you're being obnoxious and overbearing! If I took you up on your offer, I'd feel like a kept woman!"

"How can you say that? I've already told you you'd be Janey's com—"

"Like heck! I'd be *your* companion, your bought-and-paid-for companion. You said that was the reason you wanted me to go...so we could be together, not because Janey needs me. That would only be a cover-up of the real reason for her sake! But I'm having no part of it."

"Why are you so unreasonable?" Jeff flared. "I told you I wouldn't be making any demands on you of a romantic nature. How could I with Janey right there? We could just have a good time together, nothing more."

"No?" Lila sneered. "Maybe not at the time, but with you footing the bill for me, the time would come when you'd expect me to pay up. The whole idea makes me feel cheap. Get out, Jeff! Go peddle your proposition someplace else!"

"You're misinterpreting my intentions. It wasn't meant to make you feel cheap! It was meant to give us a stress-free opportunity to get to know each other well, but now you've ruined any possibility of that. You've made me out to be crass and calculating and manipulative and I didn't mean it that way at all! You're the damnedest woman I ever met, Lila Addison! You take everything I say or do and turn it into something ugly. Right now I wouldn't take you across the road if you begged me, much less on a trip that could have been wonderful for all of us!"

Two weeks later Lila went into town to the hardware store. She wanted to hang some shelves on a wall in her studio so she bought shelf boards and brackets.

The owner, Mr. Sutton, carried the boards outside and placed them in the back seat of her car. When he was finished, Lila thanked him and was about to go around the Volks and get in behind the wheel when she heard someone call her name.

Coming toward her on the sidewalk was Janey Chappel, followed more slowly by a lady with gray hair.

"Hi," Lila said when Janey reached her. "Where'd you come from?"

"The dress shop next door." She held up a bulging white paper bag with blue lettering. "I needed a few things for..."

"Your trip to Europe," Lila finished for her, laughing.

"Right." Janey grinned. "Of course Jeff will think I was being extravagant again, but honestly, I needed every single thing I bought."

"Sure, you did," Lila teased. The older woman joined them and Lila smiled and introduced herself. "Hello. I'm Lila Addison."

The woman extended her hand. "I'm Martha Himes. Janey and Bud have told me how you helped out when Janey was found. I'm glad to finally meet you."

"Thanks. I'm happy to meet you, too."

Janey spotted the boards on the back seat of Lila's car. "What're you going to do with those?"

"Hang some shelves in the studio," Lila replied. Impulsively, she added, "You wouldn't want to come home with me and help, would you? I could use an extra hand."

Janey looked at Martha questioningly. "Okay with you?"

Martha smiled and nodded indulgently. "You might as well. If you go with me to the grocery store, you'll just nag me to buy all the wrong things."

Lila laughed. "That bad, is she? Thanks, Martha. I'll drive her home later to save you or Bud a trip."

A few minutes later they were on their way. Janey chattered happily about the clothes she'd just bought and a movie she'd seen the previous week while Lila listened with amusement.

Back at the house Janey helped her carry in the boards and soon they were busy at their task of measuring the wall and putting up the brackets. It took them about a half an hour and Janey proved during that time that she could be serious and intent about a job when it was called for.

After they'd finished, Lila went into the kitchen and poured two glasses of cola and they carried them out to the front porch.

"So," Lila asked after they were comfortably seated in the rocking chairs, "how's life been treating you since school got out?"

"Life is fine, or it might be, if my brother would only give me a break," Janey said in frustration.

"What do you mean?"

Janey sighed heavily. "Oh, the same old thing. Ever since the kidnapping, he won't let me out of his sight unless an adult is with me. You saw how he gave me a hard time about staying overnight with Tina. Well, he's still just as bad. Yesterday a whole bunch of my friends were going out to Cattail Lake for a picnic and swimming, but he wouldn't let me go along because nobody's parents were going. I'm almost sixteen years old and he makes me feel like a baby!"

"Was he this way before the kidnapping?" Lila asked.

Janey shook her head. "No, that's what makes it so aggravating! He was always strict to a certain degree, but not like this."

"How was he strict?"

"Oh, like not letting me go out on car dates until I'm sixteen, even though most of my friends are dating, or driving all the way to Tyler with a bunch of kids to a movie. Stuff like that. But he would usually let me hang out with my friends when something like this came up. I mean, he was never totally unreasonable before. You know?"

Lila nodded sympathetically. "He's had a bad scare, Janey. You're just going to have to be patient with him. I'm sure he'll come around after a while."

"Yeah," Janey said morosely. "If I'm lucky, I might be allowed to go out on a date when I'm eighty."

Lila chuckled. "Poor, decrepit old lady! You'll be ready for a nursing home soon, won't you? Anyway, you just said that even before the kidnapping, Jeff set a rule that you couldn't date until you're sixteen, so who's being unreasonable now?''

Janey grinned wryly. "Okay, okay. I understand he was frightened; what do you think I was? I still get nervous going to my bedroom alone at night, but I don't want to turn into a hermit. I need to get out and stop always being afraid someone's out to get me. And I need freedom to be with my friends."

"Give him time," Lila repeated. "I'm sure he'll come around eventually. Your vacation trip will probably do a lot to make you both feel more at ease."

"I hope you're right." Janey brightened at the mention of the trip. "I'm saving my allowance to buy a Gucci bag when we get to Italy. All my girlfriends are going to just die with envy!"

Lila laughed and while the girl talked of the sights she hoped to see in Europe, she kept her own thoughts about the trip concealed. It was obvious Janey didn't know of Jeff's invitation, and it was best to keep it that way.

For the remainder of the month, Lila kept as busy as possible, following a relentless routine as though her very life depended upon it. Since there still seemed to be no job openings in town, she stopped wasting her time looking and concentrated on her painting. In the mornings she tended the garden or the lawn; afternoons she worked in the studio; evenings she did whatever chores needed doing in the house. By the time she fell into bed around eleven, she was always so tired that she went to sleep without thinking about anything or anyone, and that was what she was trying to achieve. As long as she didn't have the time or the energy to think about Jeff, she was content.

The only breaks in her routine were a couple of visits from Amy, who had time to socialize now that school was out, or an occasional brief trip into town to run errands.

In short, her life was dull, boring, work-filled and without balance. And because of the boredom, inevitably, thoughts of Jeff came despite her best efforts to avoid them.

On the day Jeff and Janey were to leave for Dallas and their overseas flight, Lila awoke feeling listless and drained, as though she were coming down with something. Her heart was heavy, she ached all over and strangely, she felt close to tears.

She carried her morning coffee out to the front porch and even the sight of two young squirrels scampering along the branches of the big pecan tree failed to cheer her.

I could be on my way to London this very minute, she told herself plaintively. *I could be with Jeff and Janey and having a wonderful time.* Instead, she was alone, lonely and more unhappy than she'd been in a long time. Maybe she'd been a fool to be so cautious about an involvement with Jeff. In spite of her anger at the way he was always trying to pay her for doing nothing, almost as though he wanted to mark her and keep her as a mistress, she couldn't quite despise him or dismiss him from her mind the way she wished she could do. She was strongly attracted to him, like it or not, and she couldn't forget their night of lovemaking. At the time she had felt so warm and free, and her response to him had been spontaneous and true. Now, in the aftermath, she was left vulnerable, hurt, and dissatisfied.

Yet she knew she'd made the right decision. Above all, she had to maintain her self-respect. If she ever lost that, she would have lost herself. If she'd given in, what would she have gained? Jeff had only been angry because he'd wanted everything his own way. He was attracted to her, too...that went without saying, but if she had given in to his suggestion, he might soon have grown tired of her, lost respect for her, seen her as a clinger and a taker, and then what? Right back to square one. No, she had to make it or break it on her own, depend on no one except herself. She had trusted and depended on Nick, had believed him when he'd said he loved her and wanted to marry her and look what had happened there.

She was convinced she'd made the right decision where Jeff was concerned. All the same, as she went back inside the house, determined to get to work as usual, as though this day was the same as all the others, the dull ache of the loss of something beautiful persisted.

Chapter Eleven

Jeff stood on his hotel balcony overlooking the Seine. The soft, moist air caressed his face as gently as a woman's hands. Below, a few lights twinkled here and there, but the river and most of the city were shrouded in the predawn darkness, for at three a.m. even Paris slept.

Jeff wished he were as lucky.

He had returned to his room about one-thirty, but he had been unable to sleep despite the considerable amount of champagne he'd indulged in during the evening.

They had been touring Europe for two and a half weeks and for the past three days they had been visiting Paris. Over all, he could find fault with nothing. The weather had been idyllic, the hotel service impeccable, the food, of course, incomparable. Some old family friends lived here and on the first evening he and Janey had been invited to dine in their lovely apartment in the fashionable seventh arrondissement. The couple had a daughter about Janey's age and last night she had stayed overnight with the other girl.

Jeff had allowed it without protest, much to Janey's surprise and his own amusement, but he hadn't forgotten the tussle they'd had at home when she'd wanted to spend the night with her friend Tina. He was trying, earnestly trying, to let go, to give her a bit more of the freedom she craved. It wasn't easy on his nerves, but he knew he had to deal with the problem. He couldn't keep her by his side and under his watchful eye forever.

Back at the hotel alone, he was free to make plans of his own for the evening. The first day he'd met a young woman from Australia and last night the two of them had dinner together in a cosy little bistro. Later they had gone dancing. Again, he could find fault with nothing. It had been a pleasant evening, his companion had been lively and fun and he had enjoyed himself as much as it was possible to enjoy anything these days. When the evening drew to a close, his date had made it quite plain that she wouldn't be averse to spending the rest of the night with him as well, but Jeff pretended to misread her signals and soon afterward pleaded fatigue and an early morning departure for Brussels.

The fatigue had been a fabrication; the early departure was not. Jeff knew if he didn't get some shut-eye soon he was going to feel like hell in the morning.

He returned to his room and the wide empty bed and now he berated himself for being such a fool as to have turned down his date's charms. He was behaving like a monk—in Paris, no less—and for what? For what?

The answer he sought didn't please him one bit when it came. He had tossed away the opportunity for a night of carefree pleasure with an attractive, willing woman all because he couldn't get Lila out of his system. That's how hopelessly ensnared he was, mooning around over her like a lovesick calf instead of seizing the moment and thanking the gods for what he was offered. He was thoroughly fed up with himself.

Tomorrow, he told himself as he crawled back into bed, things would be different.

But a tiny voice in the faint recesses of his mind whispered that nothing would change, tomorrow, the next day or the one after that. Jeff turned over onto his side and pounded the unused pillow next to him.

"How's the job going?" Amy asked as she piled her groceries onto the conveyer belt.

Lila shrugged. "It's paying the bills. That's what counts." She reached for a gallon of milk and rang it up on the cash register.

"Why don't you come have dinner with us tonight? Dave's cooking those steaks on the grill," she said, nodding at the packages of meat Lila was ringing up.

"Thanks, but I'd better take a rain check. I'm working until seven this evening and the truth is, by the time I get off, I'll be dog tired."

"Umm. Then how about coffee and doughnuts in the morning?"

Lila shook her head. "Sorry. I need to go to Tyler and pick up some art supplies. I'm running low. I have to do it in the morning because I'm scheduled to come in to work at two tomorrow afternoon."

"You *would* land a job in the summer while I'm out of school and have time to play," Amy complained.

Lila grinned and reached for a box of cereal. "That's life. I'm just relieved I finally found something."

"You have a good point." Lila rang up the total amount of her purchases and Amy began filling out a check. "Well, stop by on Sunday afternoon if you feel like company."

"I just might do that," Lila answered.

It was her second week as a cashier in the local grocery store. The pay wasn't great, but any amount of income was better than none. It couldn't possibly help her out with the condo, but at least it covered her modest living expenses.

She tried not to think of the pitifully small size of her paycheck when compared to the handsome sums she'd been paid as a model. If she did, she might just throw up her hands in disgust and rush back to the rat race of New York.

By the time she drove home that evening, as she had predicted to Amy, Lila was exhausted. She had thought she was used to working for long hours standing on her feet; modeling had required a lot of that, but somehow this was different. Here she had to stand in one place for hours on end while loading and lifting heavy grocery bags into baskets for carryout. Her back, legs, feet and arms weren't used to the abuse and she ached everywhere. Even her head and eyes hurt from the constant strain of checking prices and making certain she rang them up correctly on the register.

Too tired to cook for herself when she got home, she put a frozen dinner into the oven and while it was heating, went to take a long, luxuriously hot bath.

Gradually the water eased her aching muscles. Afterward, clad in a nightshirt, she went into the kitchen to eat, but by then she'd lost her appetite. She was too tired to eat and after only a few bites, she gave up the effort and went into the bedroom.

Even as exhausted as she was, she knew she wouldn't fall asleep this early, so she flipped on the television before stretching out on the bed.

There was a spy thriller on and Lila watched it mechanically, not really absorbing the plot. Inertia had overtaken her and she felt too relaxed and lazy to get up and switch the channel.

But then a scene of London flashed on the screen and it jerked her thoughts toward Jeff.

Where was he now? she wondered. What was he doing? Was he enjoying himself? Did he still wish she had accompanied them?

Lila sighed. He was probably having the time of his life with a bevy of European beauties and hadn't given her another thought. Who could blame him if he did become involved with other women? *She* sure hadn't given him any encouragement.

She wasn't really sorry she'd turned down the trip. She still thought she had made the right decision. Besides, if she had gone, she would've missed out on getting this job. No, what she was sorry about was the angry way she'd turned Jeff down. He had come to her to try to straighten things out between them and she hadn't let it happen. Once again, she had overreacted. She had let her defensiveness spoil the nicest thing that had come along in her life in a long, long while.

Her fingers fanned out across the bed sheets to the side of the bed where Jeff had lain that night they'd been together. Lila swallowed hard at the memory of that evening. It had been so wonderful. Jeff had seemed to be more intent on giving her pleasure than he had been on his own. And his smile... how endearing that tender smile had been! As though she were the most perfect woman ever born! He had made her feel so special, so desirable, as though she were the only woman who could ever make him happy.

She had adored him that night, until the end. Did she still? Or was it just her loneliness that made her think of him so yearningly?

But that excuse didn't wash anymore and she knew it. Since school had been out, she'd spent a lot of her free time with Amy. Since she'd gotten her job two weeks ago, she'd met a lot of friendly people. One of the other checkers had invited her to lunch yesterday and they had hit it off well. The assistant manager of the store had even asked her out. His name was Marty, he was about her age and he was divorced. He seemed nice enough, but Lila hadn't been interested and she had turned him down as kindly as possible with the explanation that she didn't want to date someone she worked with.

The point was that now she could socialize as much as she liked. She had begun to fit into the community. In addition, her job and her painting kept her more than busy. Loneliness was no longer a factor.

So, her depression had nothing to do with spending too much time by herself. The reason was painfully clear. She missed Jeff.

It was late July when Jeff and Janey returned home. The summer heat was stifling, the grasses dry and tinged with brown and the crops in the fields looked stunted and wilted. Bud told Jeff it hadn't rained a drop since they'd left. That was sad news to come back to, but all the same, home sure looked good.

Janey seemed to have had a grand time in Europe, so for her sake he was glad they had gone. For himself, the trip had lasted far too long. He'd visited enough cathedrals to last a lifetime; he'd tasted enough wine to turn a man either into a drunk or a confirmed teetotaler, and he was heartily sick of living out of a suitcase, not to mention calculating foreign currency against the dollar. But he wasn't about to admit any of it to Bud. That would just be giving the old man ammunition to berate him for having been so foolish as to leave the comforts of home in the first place.

During the following week Jeff worked hard, catching up on business matters and most evenings he didn't even get home from the office before eight or nine o'clock. Staying so busy was good because it kept him too occupied to brood much over personal matters. He had little free time to think about Lila and that was the way he liked it.

The only time that he couldn't avoid thinking of her was whenever he happened to be coming or going from home on the country road that passed the turnoff to her place. Then he couldn't stop himself from glancing down that narrow lane, of wondering if she was home, how she was doing, or thinking of how much he wanted to see her in spite of everything.

In Rome he had bought a gift for her. At the time he'd felt absurd for doing it. He still did. Now he wondered whether the day would ever come when he would present it to her.

There was nothing to stop him from going to see her, of course. Nothing except his wounded pride. But that was a powerful deterrent and as much as he longed to be with her, he couldn't bring himself to force a meeting. That would be showing her just how much he still cared, even after her rejection of him. All the same, his heart still beat a little faster every time he was in the vicinity of her house.

On Friday evening when he got home and looked over his mail, he found an invitation to a barbecue scheduled for a week from Saturday. It was a birthday bash for his old college roommate. Scribbled below the pertinent details were the words "Bring a date if you like."

Jeff leaned back in his chair and closed his eyes. He would have to attend, of course. He and Charlie had been great friends and nowadays they didn't get to see each other very often. As for taking along a date, maybe he would invite that nurse he'd met in Houston—Wayne Hammond's niece Katherine. This was probably just what he needed—an excuse to force him into seeing someone else. He hadn't spent time with another woman since that one evening in Paris with the Australian. It was high time to get back into the swing of things and make a concerted effort to forget about Lila Addison.

But though he told himself that was definitely what he would do, he made no effort to contact the nurse over the weekend.

By Monday morning when he returned to the office, he still couldn't bring himself to the point of calling Katherine Willis in Houston. She had been a lovely person, but deep down inside, Jeff knew it would be a mistake to call her. He had no desire to get involved with her or anyone else. He would, he decided finally, simply go to the party alone.

At eleven he left the office to drive to his lawyer's office. There were a couple of new business contracts in the works that he needed to go over before the deals were wrapped up.

The meeting took only about half an hour and when they were done, it was nearly noon. "How about some lunch, Gary?" Jeff suggested.

Gary Langford shook his head. "Wish I could, but I'll have to take a raincheck. I've got an appointment with the dentist in Tyler at one-thirty, so I'm going to have to shove off in a few minutes."

"Ouch." Jeff grinned and stood up to leave. "Good luck."

"Thanks. I need it."

Since he still had a pile of paperwork on his desk back at his own office, when Jeff went outside toward his car, he decided impulsively to walk across the street to the grocery store. He'd grab a deli sandwich and a cola and carry them back to his office to eat.

Inside the store, he went straight toward the back to the small deli section. There he chose a couple of ham and cheese sandwiches, then moved farther down to the cooler where the soft drinks were stored.

He carried his purchases to the front of the store, nodding once or twice at other shoppers with whom he was acquainted.

At the checkout, another customer was just finishing up. Jeff paused behind him and killed the waiting time by scanning the lurid headlines on the front cover of a tabloid on the rack.

"Here's your change, sir. Thank you."

The familiar voice penetrated through Jeff's distracted thoughts. He hadn't bothered to look toward the checker before, but now he did and an electrical shock jolted through him.

Lila smiled at the middle-aged customer before he moved away. Still with the smile in place, she turned to greet her next customer.

Shock rippled through her. It was Jeff and the unexpected encounter knocked her breath away.

He looked so wonderful that she could not draw her gaze away from him. The sky blue shirt he wore enhanced his healthy, bronzed color. His hair seemed darker than usual and instantly she wished she had the right to touch it. His face was endearingly arresting, and his eyes . . . His gaze appeared to burn right into her skin as he stared at her, obviously as taken aback at seeing her as she was to see him.

Jeff studied her for a long while, caught once again by her beauty. She wore the store's standard, unremarkable uniform, a brown and ripe-orange polyester dress, but somehow Lila managed to make the outfit seem attractive. It fit her neither too tightly nor too loosely, and it actually looked becoming on her trim figure. Her hair, as always, was stunning. It swirled about her face and shoulders with bewitching appeal. As for her face, though she wore very subdued makeup, her face glowed with compelling loveliness.

Lila found her voice first. "Hello, Jeff," she said softly.

Jeff inclined his head slightly. "Lila."

He made no move to place his purchases on the counter, nor did she make a suggestion that he do so. They continued to gaze at one another, their eyes eloquently speaking things neither could express.

After a long moment, Lila broke the silence again. Her voice held a husky quality as she asked, "Did you . . . did you and Janey have a nice trip?"

"Very nice."

"I'm glad."

"Are you?"

"Yes." Lila drew in a deep breath, then stunned herself by saying in a rush, "I missed you."

She saw something flare in Jeff's eyes. He remained silent for endless seconds, his expression unrevealing. At last he asked, "Did you? You didn't have to."

Lila lowered her gaze to her hands. "I know. In a way, I've regretted it. But," she added brightly as she brought herself to look at him again, "on the other hand, I wouldn't have gotten this job if I'd been away."

Jeff put his sandwiches and drink on the counter now. "How long have you been working here?"

"Three weeks."

"Do you like it? Is it really better than my offer?" There was an underlying bitterness in the question.

Lila's eyes were earnest as they met his. "At least it's honest work, Jeff. Please don't be angry with me anymore."

The sincerity, the pleading in her voice did something to Jeff. He felt himself softening inside and smiling at her for the first time. "I missed you, too," he finally admitted.

Lila tilted her head and her gaze was searching. "Truly?"

"Truly. Look, can you get away from here? Take a break, so we can go someplace and talk?"

Lila shook her head and reached for the packaged sandwiches. "No." Her answer sounded genuinely regretful. "I just got back from my break."

"Then can I see you tonight?" he asked as she began punching numbers on the cash register.

She shook her head again and turned to face him. "I'm sorry, Jeff, but I'm working until nine every night this week, and by the time I get home I'm so tired I just fall into bed."

"You shouldn't be doing this," he said gruffly. "It's too hard on you."

"Don't be silly. Other people manage. I'm lucky to have gotten this job. I am off on Saturday, though."

A tingle of pure happiness surged through Jeff. She wasn't trying to put him off. She really did want to see him. His spirits soared and suddenly he grinned. "Saturday?

That's even better. I've been invited to a birthday barbecue party that day and I was told I could bring along a date. How about it?''

Lila nodded and her smile was warm and flatteringly eager. "I'd love it."

"Good." Jeff dropped money on the counter for his purchases. "I'll pick you up around ten."

"In the morning?" Lila looked astonished. "Isn't that awfully early for a party to begin?"

"It's an all-day affair and anyway, we'll have a bit of a way to go to get there."

"Really? Where is it going to be?"

He shook his head. "Nope. You'll find out Saturday when I pick you up." Another customer was now waiting behind him, so Jeff had no choice but to leave. He picked up his sandwiches and soft drink, shook his head when Lila held out a paper bag and added, "Wear jeans or shorts. It's definitely an informal event."

"All right. I'll see you Saturday." Reluctantly, Lila turned to greet her next customer.

By Saturday morning Lila could scarcely contain her excitement over the prospects of the day ahead. She tingled all over with anticipation and her heart was singing with elation. Janey Chappel herself, she thought with a chuckle, couldn't possibly get more excited when the time came to go out on her first date. That was how Lila felt—all fluster and delight and warmth mingled together in an emotional soup. She felt as though she'd never been on a proper date before. Certainly she never had with Jeff.

Following his instructions, she dressed casually in a red and white Hawaiian print shirt, white shorts and sandals.

At a quarter of ten, she heard the Porsche coming up the lane. In the few moments remaining to her, she hastily checked her hair and lipstick. Casual or not, she wanted Jeff to find her beautiful.

When she opened the door to him, her stomach was knotted with nervous tension. Maybe she expected too much of this day. Maybe she expected too much of Jeff and of herself. And yet, she couldn't seem to help it. She was glad to see him and she knew it showed on her face and sparkled in her eyes.

Jeff was dressed as informally as she was—he wore Levis, a blue western-style shirt, boots and a wide-brimmed Stetson-type summer straw hat. One hand was thrust casually into a hip pocket and he looked utterly relaxed.

"Good morning." His smile came slowly, intensely sensual.

Lila's heart skipped a beat. "Good morning. Would you like to come in?"

Jeff started to take her up on the invitation, but then he thought better of it. She looked as tempting and delicious as homemade strawberry-vanilla ice cream and if they were alone together inside, he wasn't too sure he'd be able to resist sweeping her into his arms right here and now.

"No thanks," he answered with the hint of a smile. "You look far too delectable. You'll be much safer in the car where I have to keep my hands otherwise occupied."

Lila's throat went dry. He still wanted her after all! It was there in his flashing eyes and his teasing words. A thrill trembled through her. All at once she became daring and coquettish. A provocative smile tugged at her mouth. "How do you know I want to be safe?"

Jeff groaned and his eyes narrowed. "I guess you know you're playing with fire! If you want me to come in, I will, but I'm pretty sure if I do we won't ever make it to the party."

"Hmmm. That would be a shame." Lila pretended indecision, then stepped out onto the porch and firmly shut the door behind her. "Let's go."

Jeff's eyes twinkled. "You still have time to change your mind. I'm really not all that keen on going."

Lila laughed. "Well, I am! You invited me to a party and I'm not about to let you renege. I haven't been to one in ages."

Jeff sighed. "I was afraid you'd hold me to it. It's the prospect of food, isn't it?"

"Right. I've been daydreaming about it all week."

He shook his head. "You and your appetite! Next thing you're going to tell me is that that's the only reason you accepted my invitation."

"W-e-l-l," she drawled, "I *could* say that, but if I did, I'd be lying."

Abruptly she was caught in the tight vise of his arms. "Lila, you drive me crazy. I never know how you're going to react to me from one minute to the next. Why do I keep coming back for more?"

"You tell me," she breathed softly. Her fingers clung to his arms and she felt almost light-headed at his nearness. A feverish warmth spread through her and her limbs became weak. His effect on her was powerful and unsettling.

"It's a complete mystery to me." Another smile flitted across his mouth. "What do you say we stay here today? I'm not so sure I want to share you with others."

Lila was sorely tempted to give in to his suggestion. Her self-control was slipping badly. She had an overwhelming desire to surrender to her clamoring emotional response to Jeff, to take his hand and go inside the house and close out the rest of the world. At the same time, some deeper, inner strength disciplined her. Their troubles from the beginning had stemmed from a physical attraction that had dominated their relationship too quickly, before they'd had time to get to know each other properly. Finally, in a rather unsteady voice, she said, "Maybe it'll be good for us to be with other people, at least for a while. Whenever we're alone, things get awfully intense."

"And is that so bad?"

"Not bad," she answered thoughtfully. "Just... unnerving. Let's take things slowly today."

"And tonight?" His voice was deep and husky.

She smiled. "Why don't we let tonight take care of itself?"

Jeff dropped his arms to his sides and said, "I don't like it, but somehow, in a weird sort of way, you make sense." He grabbed her hand and swung her around, pulling her willy-nilly alongside him. "Come on, then. We'd better get going."

Lila was surprised when Jeff drove to the airstrip just outside town. A small blue and white private plane was waiting there.

"You didn't tell me we were flying!" she exclaimed. "Where *is* this party, anyhow?"

"About fifty miles on the other side of Austin. Still want to go?"

She shrugged. "Sure. I'm game." Lila opened her door and got out of the car.

The flight was pleasant, the weather sunny and clear and almost before she knew it, the plane landed on a private airstrip at a ranch. A ranch hand met them in a Jeep and drove them to the house.

Their hosts were Charlie and Diane Green. Charlie, Jeff explained as he made the introductions, had been his college roommate. The birthday celebration was in his honor. "He just turned thirty-one," Jeff told Lila. "Poor old Charlie. Something happened to him back in college. I'd think he hit the books too hard, except that I know for a fact he never cracked a book. Anyway, he turned into an old man while I stayed the same."

"Don't you wish!" Charlie responded. "He's the old man here, Lila. He's three months older than me."

Lila grinned and scrutinized Jeff. "You do look a bit decrepit around the edges, come to think of it."

"'Atta girl!'" Charlie patted her shoulder. "You can visit us anytime!"

Diane chuckled at their nonsense. "Come on, Lila," she offered. "I'll introduce you around. These two will be stabbing each other in the back for the next half hour. They always do whenever they get together."

The day was thoroughly enjoyable. There were perhaps a hundred and fifty guests, counting the children, and everyone was friendly. Early in the day there were games for the children and adults alike—sack races, horseshoes, softball. There was a swimming pool for anyone who wished to use it, and horseback riding. Some took advantage of the tennis court while others sat beneath canopies on the lawn and played bridge or poker. In the evening there would be dancing to the music of a country-western band that had been hired for the occasion.

There was a mass of food—barbecued ribs, chicken, steaks, brisket, accompanied by pinto beans, potato salad and cold watermelon.

Throughout the day Jeff scarcely left Lila's side, but whenever he did she felt his gaze following her. It was evident by his look and his manner that he had staked his claim. Far from objecting to his possessiveness, Lila thrived on it. It made her feel very, very special.

During the afternoon, Jeff went with Charlie and several other men to a pasture to see Charlie's new prize bull. Others were dozing in chair by the pool or on the shady patio. Diane, having learned that Lila painted, invited her inside the house to see the works of art she had acquired.

Lila admired the paintings Diane had chosen, as well as her tastefully decorated home. Everything was ultramodern, but with a touch of classic elegance. "You're an artist, too," Lila told her. "I can tell by the way you've put your home together."

"Thanks. I'd like to see your work sometime."

"Look me up if you're ever in Cattail," Lila said easily.

"At the Chappel house, no doubt. I'm so happy for Jeff. You're just perfect for him."

Lila's eyes widened in surprise. "What on earth are you talking about?"

Diane answered with a question of her own. "Aren't wedding bells in the picture?"

"W-wedding?!" Lila gasped. She was so taken aback she couldn't think, much less answer coherently.

Diane flushed. "Now look what I've done! Charlie would be furious at me for being nosy and jumping to conclusions. It's only that I couldn't help noticing the way the two of you are together. You're obviously so much in love."

Lila caught her breath and stared blankly at the other woman. She had fought the idea from the first minute she had been drawn to Jeff; had refused to face the unalterable truth. She had acknowledged all along that she was attracted to him, that she cared about him far too much for comfort, but she had never let herself put her feelings into words. The closest she had come was the night they had made love, but she had withdrawn when she'd seen his own doubts.

Now she silently accepted the truth. She loved Jeff, but somehow the knowledge brought no comfort. Sure, he had been attentive today, perhaps even adoring, but she recalled his exact words to her the day he'd invited her to go to Europe with him. Then he had admitted he felt something for her, that he didn't merely want to have an affair with her, and yet he'd also said he wasn't ready to commit himself to anything binding.

So where did that leave her? she wondered with a bittersweet ache in her heart.

Chapter Twelve

It was nearing midnight when Jeff drove Lila home from the airstrip. All evening she'd been subdued and he couldn't quite figure out the reason for the change that had come over her. He wasn't sure if it was boredom, sheer fatigue because the party had gone on all day long or that she had come to regret spending an entire day in his company. She didn't seem to be exactly unhappy. Rather, she'd simply grown increasingly silent and introspective.

At her door, Lila turned toward him. The porch light cast shadows on her face, emphasizing the inexplicable somberness in her eyes. "It's been a marvelous day," she said softly.

Jeff felt a stabbing disappointment. "Are you saying goodnight?"

An odd uncertainty came into her eyes. She shook her head. "Not . . . if you don't want me to."

"I don't," he answered emphatically.

Lila turned hurriedly and unlocked the door. When they were inside and she'd flipped on a lamp, she became all motion, as though she were uneasy being alone with him. She dropped her purse on a nearby table and took a few steps in the direction of the kitchen. "I'll make some coffee. If you'd like something to eat, I can—"

Jeff caught up with her and gripped her arm. "I don't want anything." When she hesitated to meet his gaze, he added gruffly, "Let's just sit down and talk."

"All right." Her voice was subdued.

When they were seated on the sofa, Jeff took her hand. "Okay, now, what's going on? You're acting like you're afraid of me."

"Of course I'm not afraid of you," she protested at once.

"Then what's the matter?"

"I'm not sure I can put it into words."

"Then I'll do it for you. You think I'm going to pressure you to go to bed with me and you're not sure that's what you want; isn't that it?"

"I just..." Something caught in her throat and Lila swallowed and started again. "I just don't want to make another mistake in my life, Jeff, and I'm not sure where we're going. That one night between us was lovely, but it *was* a mistake. I don't want it to happen again unless it's really right for both of us. I just can't be casual about it."

"I won't deny that I'd like to make love to you this minute," Jeff said slowly. "But I won't insist. I want you to be sure, too. Even so," he continued with a smile, "I refuse to admit that night was a mistake. It just made me adore you more than ever."

Lila made a small sound that might have been a gasp or a groan. All Jeff knew for sure was that he had to kiss her. Slowly, he bent his head toward her.

When the kiss ended, he said huskily, "I still adore you."

"Oh, Jeff," Lila sighed. Of her own accord, she lifted her arms and intertwined them around his neck. "I just don't know what to think about you. About us. I'm thoroughly confused."

His smile widened. "Maybe that's the trouble. Maybe we both think too much. Maybe we ought to stop analyzing the situation and just accept our feelings for each other."

Lila smiled back. "Maybe," she conceded.

He kissed her again and this time it was deeper, more intense. Lila became all feeling. Every part of her became exquisitely, painfully alive. A rampaging fire spread through her, consuming, relentless, engulfing her totally, without mercy. Finally she rested her head in the crook of his neck.

Jeff's breath was soft against her forehead, where he planted warm, gentle kisses. The scent of him, the strength and virility of him was intoxicating. His hands, which moved with infinite tenderness across her back and up to caress her neck, offered her both healing balm and erotic tingles.

She wanted him. She ached with wanting. Despite her reservations, he had only to touch her with the lightest stroke and her body throbbed with a need only he could satisfy. His nearness seemed to trigger some ancient memory, as though every caress was dearly familiar, as though they'd been lovers in some other existence. It felt right to be where she was, wrapped in his arms, enveloped by his warmth, and she ceased to think of right or wrong, of a later time when regrets would surely come.

The sadness that had briefly washed over her earlier in the day when she had squarely faced the fact that she was hopelessly in love with him was fading. It was replaced by a glowing happiness. She didn't want to doubt anymore. She wanted to believe, to hope that he might love her, too.

Jeff lifted his head and, brushing her hair away from her face, sighed contentedly. "I've been dying to kiss you like that all day. I was beginning to think the moment would never come."

"I know," she whispered. "I was feeling the same way."

"Were you, now?" he teased softly.

All at once, Lila stopped fighting logic and surrendered to the urgings of her heart. She looked up into his eyes and stated with quiet certainty, "I'm tired of being afraid, of whether we're making a mistake or not. Jeff," she drew in a deep breath, then said in a rush, "I want you to make love to me tonight."

Jeff's eyes darkened with an echoing desire. "Are you sure?"

Lila nodded and managed a smile. "Very sure."

He drew her to him and pressed his cheek to hers. "Except for Janey, you're the dearest thing in the world to me, Lila. All I want is to show you just how much I care."

He released her and surprised her by pulling a small box from his pocket. Placing it in her hand, he said in a low voice, "This is for you."

It was a long, narrow velvet jeweler's box. Lila stared at it without comprehension. "What is it?"

Jeff's lips curved into a soft smile. "Open it and find out. I got it for you in Rome."

Lila opened the box, then gasped. It was an exquisite necklace of patterned gold flowers centered with precious stones. It must have cost a fortune.

Her hand shook as she closed the box and handed it back to him. "I can't take it, Jeff."

His smile was instantly wiped away. "What do you mean, you can't? Of course you can."

"No."

Jeff sighed and asked in a tone of long-suffering, "Now what? Don't you like it?"

"What's not to like?" she retorted. "It's the most beautiful thing I've ever seen."

"But?"

"But it must have been wildly expensive. I can't accept it."

"Don't be ridiculous. Of course you can."

Lila shook her head. "You're trying to buy me again, Jeff. Why do you keep on doing that?"

"That's crazy! It's just a gift. If I'd brought you a T-shirt or one of those ugly little ceramic replicas of the leaning tower of Pisa, you'd have accepted that, wouldn't you?"

"That's different."

"It's not."

"How is it different?"

"A souvenir doesn't have strings attached."

Jeff made an exasperated sound. "Neither does this necklace."

"Yes it does. A man gives a gift like this to his wife . . . or his bought-and-paid-for-mistress. I'm neither."

"You're the most unreasonable woman I ever met!"

"And you're the most insufferable man *I* ever met! Why can't you stop trying to gain some kind of hold over me?"

Jeff's face turned a dull red. "Is that what you think I'm doing? Trying to get control over you somehow?"

"That's what it looks like from where I sit," she answered stiffly.

"You know, you sure have one hell of a warped way of seeing things." In one swift movement, he was on his feet. A moment later he had walked out of the house.

For a long time Lila remained where she was, and she wondered bitterly who was truly at fault.

She came to no conclusion, and finally, wearily, she got up to lock the door and go to bed. Hot tears burned her eyes as she went toward her bedroom. She was intensely aware of how very alone she was.

The trial had drawn national interest and the courtroom was packed. It was two o'clock on a rainy August afternoon and everyone had just returned to their seats to hear the jury's verdict.

Jeff and Janey sat in the front row directly behind the prosecutor's table. The courtroom was silent with electrified tension.

The members of the jury filed in and took their seats. Jeff scanned the individual faces, but their expressions were impassive, giving no clue as to the decision that had been reached. Next, he glanced toward the defendants. One of them sat stiffly, his gaze rigidly focused on the wall behind the judge's platform. He did not so much as glance toward the jury box. The second man slouched in his chair in a feigned attitude of indifference, but he, too, did not look at the jurors. His head was slightly inclined and he appeared to be calmly scrutinizing his fingernails.

When the judge entered the courtroom, everyone rose. Jeff looked down at Janey next to him. Her young face was tense and pale. He clasped her hand and it was icy.

Altogether it had been a terrible week and a half. Except for the weekend, he and Janey had attended the trial every day. Janey had been called to testify and that had been a traumatic experience for her. The defense attorney had attempted to tear her story to shreds. Since she'd been riding a horse when the kidnappers had approached her, he'd intimated that she'd had the means to escape them, that she hadn't because she'd been giving them the come-on. Janey tried to explain that the car had stopped ahead of her, that both men had walked back toward her and had begun asking directions to a nearby community. That was why she hadn't run away. By the time she'd realized something was wrong, one of the men had grabbed the horse's reins while the other grabbed her. The defense attorney was very good at playing with words, twisting everything she said, and in the end Janey had left the stand sobbing her heart out. Jeff had felt like murdering the attorney and now he waited with coiled nerves to learn whether the jury was going to send the scum who'd kidnapped her to prison or whether they had bought the defense's argument that Janey had seduced the men, that they'd merely taken her with them for some fun and only as an afterthought, when they'd learned her brother had money, had they attempted to blackmail him. The fact that Janey had come through the ordeal physically unscathed, the attorney had stated, demonstrated that the men had never had any intent to harm her.

The judge read the verdict, handed it back to the bailiff and instructed the jury foreman to announce it to the courtroom. Janey's hand tightened around Jeff's fingers. He held his breath.

"The jury finds the defendants guilty, Your Honor."

An immediate clamor arose. Jeff wrapped his arms around Janey, then looked beyond her to the defendants. The one who had appeared indifferent earlier suddenly turned and looked directly at him. The look of hatred burning in his eyes sent a chill through Jeff.

A few minutes later they left the courthouse. Sentencing would be in two days. The ordeal was almost over. For Janey, it *was* over; Jeff had no intention of bringing her back for the sentencing. He would attend alone. He never wanted her breathing the same air as those two men again. With a protective arm around her, he burrowed their way through the army of reporters trying to get a word with them.

They drove directly home after leaving the courthouse. It had rained hard all day, but now it had settled down to a constant drizzle. The dark sky reflected Jeff's mood. He was relieved the jury had convicted those men, but there was little room for rejoicing. Janey's character had been dragged through the mud by that cunning defense attorney, they'd had enough unpleasant dealings with the press to last a lifetime and he knew that as long as he lived, he would never forget the look of merciless hostility that one man had given him.

At home, Janey went to her room to call her friends and tell them the verdict. Jeff went to the kitchen to tell Bud and Martha the news.

A while later, as Martha poured him a second cup of coffee, she said, "I almost forgot! I was in the grocery store this morning and Lila Addison asked to have someone call and tell her the news once the trial was over."

Jeff's stomach tightened at the mere mention of her name. He spooned sugar into his cup, tasted the coffee and made a face because it was far too sweet. Abruptly, he shoved back his chair and stood up. "Call her yourself if you want," he said indifferently as he went toward the door. "Right now I'm going upstairs to change out of this damp suit."

When he got to the top of the stairs, Janey came out of her bedroom. "I was just coming to find you." Her voice sounded eager and excited, in stark contrast to her listless, moody behavior ever since the trial had started.

"What's up?"

"Beth says Pete and Matt want to take us a movie tonight to celebrate the verdict."

"Kinda gruesome, isn't it?" Jeff asked wryly. "Wanting to celebrate the fact that two men are going to prison."

Janey wrinkled her nose. "You know what I mean. To celebrate the trial being over."

Jeff grinned and ruffled Janey's hair. "Yeah, kid. I do know what you mean.

Janey looked hopeful. "Then I can go?"

Jeff shook his head. "Not a chance."

"But..." Janey sputtered.

"No buts. You know you can't date yet."

"But it's not a date!" Janey protested. "It's just a bunch of us going to a movie together, that's all."

"Two boys and two girls sounds like a date to me," Jeff argued. "Or at least a double date. Not to mention that one of those boys would be driving and you'd be going all the way to Tyler to the movie. Sorry, Janey. You know the rules."

"You never let me do anything! You don't want me to have any fun!"

"You know better than that," he answered mildly. "Tell you what, why don't you invite Beth and the boys here tonight? We'll rent a couple of video movies."

"It's not the same!"

"Nearest thing to it. That's my best offer. Take it or leave it."

"Then I leave it!" Janey cried. "What do you think would happen if I went, anyway? Those men are locked up in jail. They can't get me again!"

"Maybe not, but there are other things that could happen, and anyway, you're still too young."

"I'll be sixteen in only a couple more months."

"Fine," Jeff said wearily. "We'll renew this discussion then."

He turned the knob on the door and went into his bedroom. Before he could close the door he heard Janey's furious, "I hate you, Jeff! I hate you!"

Jeff rolled his eyes toward the ceiling. Why did it seem they were always arguing these days? Two nights ago some kids had come by to visit Janey. He'd been perfectly genial and while they had all milled around the patio, he'd even carried soft drinks and chips out to them, then had promptly gone back inside. But even that hadn't been enough for her. When, nearing eleven-thirty, they were still there, he'd gone back out and politely asked them to leave since he and Janey had to get up early the next morning to attend the trial. After they'd left, Janey had called him rude and interfering.

He sighed and, pulling off his jacket, draped it over the back of a chair. Sometimes he wished he could wave a magic wand and Janey would suddenly be a mature, responsible adult he no longer had to worry about.

His tie joined his jacket and Jeff went into the bathroom, peeling off the remainder of his clothes and dropping them wherever he went. Then he stepped into the shower and ran the water hot.

It seemed as if life were caving in on him from every angle these days. There'd been the ordeal of the trial, the almost constant strife of living with a teenager, and only this week the loss of a prospective lumber contract he'd thought his company had sewn up, only to learn another wholesaler had underbid him by selling at less than cost.

And then, of course there was Lila.

Jeff soaped himself, then fiercely scrubbed the soap off beneath the hot spray of water as though he was trying to wash away some particularly loathsome germs.

Forget her, he growled at himself through gritted teeth. *Forget you ever met her.*

Forget you love her.

There was simply no pleasing the woman. One minute she was baby soft and cuddly, asking him to make love to her after putting aside her hesitation, but the next moment she'd turned into a viper. And why? Because he'd bought her the loveliest gift he could find on the entire continental map!

As far as he was concerned, she'd truly ruined things with him this time. Every single time he'd tried to do something generous for her, tried to show her how much he cared, she had accused him of having sinister motives!

Trying to buy her regard indeed!

Jeff snorted indignantly, turned off the water and grabbed a thick towel. He was better off without a woman who was that suspicious and mistrustful. Why, she'd even questioned his simple offer to help work up some flower beds! Who the hell needed it?

He sure could pick women, he thought with disgust. Angela had wanted everything she could get her hands on and more! Lila saw a hidden trap in every thoughtful gesture! Well, she could keep her treasured independence. He was through, plain and simple.

The pain of loss throbbed in him like a relentless drum, but Jeff refused to recognize it for what it was. He told himself it was anger and outrage over Lila's unforgivable assault on his integrity. There would come a day, he solemnly swore, when he would be able to see Lila Addison without feeling so much as a twinge for her.

Sure, sure, taunted a voice from a dark corner of his mind. *Maybe if you say it often enough, you'll live to believe it. Like in a million years or so.*

Thursday was Lila's day off from her job, and because she dreaded being alone with all that free time, she planned a busy day. Before it got too hot, she would pick vegetables in the garden. Next, she would set to work canning tomatoes. When that was done, she would clean out her closet, do a bit of laundry and in the afternoon she would settle down to work in the studio. Fortunately her evening, too, would be occupied. The town was trying to get a library established and Lila had promised Amy she would go with her to a meeting concerning it.

Ever since Jeff had walked out her door that night almost two weeks ago, she had kept frantically busy. It was the only antidote she knew for her aching heart. It didn't stop her from thinking about him, but it did give her a brief respite from it. Last week when another checker at the store called in sick, Lila had volunteered to work on her day off in the other woman's place. As long as she could keep herself occupied, she managed to forget Jeff. It was only whenever she allowed herself to stop and rest that her throat choked with unshed tears and she hurt all over from the desolate void she now felt in her life.

She realized now that Jeff had been deeply hurt by her accusation. She had seen it in his eyes just before he left. She longed to go to him and apologize, but somehow she knew it was too late for that. There had been something final in his eyes; a wall had been erected that couldn't be surmounted.

Yet she'd been hurt, too. It *did* seem as though he was constantly trying to purchase her regard with gifts or trips or offers of jobs. Since it was abundantly apparent that she cared for him without those things, what other explanation could there be except that he felt as long as he paid for her affection in some manner, then he'd remain free from any pressures about forming a more meaningful relationship. If you bought and paid for something, then you had the right to dispose of it whenever it pleased you without any regard to someone else's feelings.

Jeff was as bad as Nick. Nick had pretended to love her so he could get his hands on her money; Jeff wanted to pay for her love so that he could walk away without guilt whenever he was ready.

The difference was that this time it hurt a thousand times more than when Nick had exited her life. The difference was that this time she was genuinely, wholeheartedly, unreservedly in love and she had a sinking suspicion that this love was something she was going to suffer from for the rest of her days.

At mid-morning Janey Chappel telephoned. Lila could tell by the girl's cheery voice that she knew nothing about the latest parting between Lila and Jeff.

"Hi. What're you doing?"

"Canning tomatoes. Martha called me yesterday afternoon to say the trial was over. You must be relieved."

"I am. It was awful."

"So, what are you up to now?"

"Nothing much. I was planning to spend the afternoon with Beth, but she called to say she was driving over to Kilgore with her mom to visit her grandparents. I was invited, but I didn't want to go."

Lila took the hint with amusement. "If you're at loose ends, why don't you come over here for a while?"

"You sound awfully busy."

"I can always put you to work, too," Lila teased. "Actually, I'm almost finished. You know I've been wanting to start a portrait of you for a long time. If you'll pose for me this afternoon, I'll even throw in lunch if you come early."

Janey laughed. "Okay. I've never had a real portrait done before. It ought to be fun. I'll be over in half an hour."

It was strange, Lila thought after they hung up, how she and Jeff could continually be at odds and yet she and Janey had gone right ahead and made friends. For that, Lila was grateful to Jeff. Out of pique, he could have forbidden Janey to visit her, but he'd never done that and she admired his forbearance.

By the time Janey arrived, the jars of freshly canned tomatoes had already been removed from the water bath on the stove and were cooling on the window ledge. Lila had begun preparing a cold lunch of sliced ham, wedges of cheese and fruit.

Janey came in and deposited a small brown paper bag on the table. "For you," she announced. "Fig preserves and tomato relish. Martha sent them."

Lila extracted the jars from the bag. "Did she put them up herself?"

Janey nodded. "I don't know why she goes to so much trouble. Every year she works all summer canning and freezing, making jellies, jams and pickles, and we never eat even half of her preserves when it's time for her to start again."

Lila laughed and made room on a shelf for the two jars. "So she can keep people like me stocked with goodies, I guess. Be sure to thank her for me, will you?"

"Sure. Next week you'll probably get some bread and butter pickles. That's what she was making today."

Lila grinned. "I'd send her a couple of jars of my tomatoes, but I guess she must already have a pantry full."

"She does."

"I know!" Lila exclaimed with sudden inspiration. "Maybe I'll get Bud to come sit for a portrait and give it to her for Christmas."

"She'd love that! Is that what you're planning to do with mine? Give it to Jeff?"

Lila's light mood burst. But she hid her sudden tension at the mention of Jeff's name and said with studied casualness, "I'll wait and see how it turns out before I decide. All the same, I'd appreciate it if you wouldn't tell him I'm doing it."

Janey ran her fingers across her lips. "They're sealed," she promised.

The girl thought it was a terrific secret, especially if Lila ended up presenting it to Jeff, but Lila couldn't imagine that day ever coming. How did you give a gift to someone who wanted nothing to do with you? If the painting turned out well, she'd most likely try to sell it through the gallery or perhaps offer it to Janey herself.

Over lunch, Janey spoke of school starting in a few more weeks, of cheerleader practice and, of course, her ever-favorite topic—boys.

She was helping Lila clear the table when she launched into a recital of her most recent quarrel with Jeff. "We were just going to see a movie, but Jeff wouldn't let me go. You'd think we were planning a trip to Mars instead of only Tyler!"

"Didn't you tell me once that you couldn't go on dates until you were sixteen?"

"Yes, but this wasn't a date! I tried to tell Jeff that, but he wouldn't listen. Sure, it would've been two boys and two girls, but we're all just *friends* and each of us was going to pay our own way."

Lila grinned. "Trying to justify it on a technicality, hmmm? Paying your own way doesn't make it less of a date, Janey. That's just called Dutch treat. Lots of kids do it because usually the boys aren't overloaded with money. I went on a few of those myself."

"You see!" Janey exclaimed triumphantly. "You were allowed to go out!"

Lila shook her head. "You're deliberately missing the point, which is that it was a date whether you admit it or not, and it would've involved a long drive to Tyler and back at night, and to top it all off, you're still not sixteen."

"What difference does a couple of months make, anyway?" Janey asked sullenly. "I had to endure that miserable trial and face those creeps again and you'd think Jeff would be willing to bend the rules a little and let me have some fun after it was over."

"I agree you deserved a little fun, but couldn't you have had it at home? Maybe invited some kids over for the evening?"

"You sound like Jeff," Janey pouted.

"Ah-hah! So, the monster who doesn't want you to have any fun offered that, did he? And did you take him up on it?"

"No way! I thought you'd understand, Lila. Jeff treats me like a baby!"

Lila sighed. "Try to put yourself in his shoes. Jeff didn't have the chance to grow into the role of caring for you the way parents do. They start from scratch and sort of ease into the thing. Your brother was thrust into being a full-time guardian of a young girl. He had no experience or qualifications. It's not easy on him, either. I'm sure he makes mistakes and is unreasonable at times, but he's doing his best. He loves you and he doesn't want any harm to come to you. The kidnapping made him feel even more protective. Surely you can understand that! Janey, if you'd seen his face the way I did the night he told me you were missing—before they called to say they'd found you—you'd be a little more tolerant. I've never seen any person suffering such anguish as he was then, and I hope to God I never do again.''

Janey flushed. ''I know he loves me,'' she said at last in a muffled voice. ''But I'm growing up and he doesn't seem to realize that.''

Lila smiled and her voice was gentle. ''From what I hear, most older brothers are that way. Fathers, too. It's hard for them to let go of the little girl they love. Your best approach is to sit down and have a calm, mature discussion with him about your changing needs. Show him how grown-up you are by your behavior. If you throw temper tantrums, that only reinforces his opinion that you're still too young and irresponsible to make rational decisions.

''Calm and mature, huh?''

''Umhmm.''

Janey grinned. ''I guess it's worth a try.''

''Good. Now,'' Lila added briskly, ''come into the studio so I can start to work. I'll see to these dishes later.''

For the next couple of hours Lila's fingers flew over the sketch pad as she drew Janey in a variety of poses. While they were thus engaged, Janey talked about the trial and of the crass intimations the defense attorney had made about her.

As she listened, Lila's temper rose at the thought of such an ugly verbal attack on an innocent girl who had already endured so much. It seemed indecent, so grossly unfair—yet done in the name of justice! It made no sense whatsoever. Janey seemed hurt rather than angry, but Lila had a hunch that her own anger was but a pale imitation of what Jeff must be experiencing.

Not that she was ever likely to know, she thought with sudden pain. She pushed the thought of him aside and concentrated on his sister.

At four, they called it quits when Bud came for Janey. She promised to return on Monday to sit for the actual painting.

Janey had no sooner left than Lila received two pieces of startling news by telephone, both from New York. The first call was from her real estate agent saying the condominium had been sold at last. Lila was elated. It was like having a load of bricks knocked off her shoulders.

Her feelings were more ambivalent about the second call. It came from her attorney. "I though you'd want to know that Nick Barrows reentered the country yesterday and was apprehended at Kennedy Airport. He's being held in jail without bond."

Lila caught her breath. "Now there'll be a trial. What will happen to him? Will I have to testify against him?" The thought made her blood run cold.

"I understand he's cooperating with authorities in an attempt to make partial restitution to the people he swindled, so that should make things go easier on him. As to your testimony, I doubt it'll be required since there are so many other victims available as witnesses right here. I'll let you know."

"Thanks," Lila said slowly. "I appreciate your calling."

When she hung up, she discovered that she had absolutely no feeling whatsoever about Nick except deep pity that he had squandered so much potential, so many advantages in life, by taking the wrong track.

She glanced at the clock and saw that it was already a quarter of five. She needed to get a move on if she was going to make the meeting tonight. She still had to eat supper, bathe and dress and leave early enough to stop by Amy's and pick her up in time to get to the civic hall before seven.

When Lila arrived at Amy's, with ample time to spare, she saw Jerri Ward coming out of the house with Amy. It was the first time Lila had seen Jerri since the wedding. "What is this," she teased, "a library project only for women, or what?"

"In our families, it is. Dave and Rob preferred to go visit a friend tonight who's in the hospital in Tyler. How are you, Lila?" Jerri asked.

"Fine. You're looking good. Married life must suit you."

Jerri grinned. "It sure does. You ought to try it."

"Maybe I will someday," Lila responded lightly.

The words returned to haunt her a half hour later. In the meeting hall she spotted Jeff across the room and the sight of him caused her heart to race. *Marriage?* she thought miserably. Not a chance. She knew now that the only man in the world with whom it might have been not only tolerable, but perhaps even blissful, would never ask her.

The certainty of that was reinforced an hour later. When the meeting formally ended, all those attending mingled while they enjoyed refreshments. Lila wished she could escape the moment the meeting was over, but Amy and Jerri were both already engrossed in conversations with others. She had no option but to stay.

She saw that Jeff, too, was socializing with his neighbors. He stood not far from her, though his back was turned. Lila didn't think he had seen her. She hoped he wouldn't.

She decided to get a cup of coffee while she waited for Amy and Jerri, mainly because the refreshment table was as far away as she could get from Jeff's vicinity.

But just as she was turning to leave the table, coffee in hand, there was Jeff. He was talking with another couple, again with his back to her. Lila's heart thudded. With a little luck, she might still manage to move away before he saw her.

But her luck ran out. Jeff turned at that instant and suddenly they were face to face. Lila felt weak when she saw the coldness in his eyes.

For a split second, though it seemed like an eon, he stared at her in that hard, distant way, and then he nodded curtly.

"Evening."

"Good evening." The words were like sawdust in her dry throat.

"Good turn out, wasn't it?" His voice was chillingly polite.

"Y-yes. Very. It's encouraging as far as getting a library established is concerned."

"Yes. Well, if you'll excuse me now, I'm going to get a cup of coffee. I see a friend across the room and I want to speak to him."

"Certainly."

Lila stepped away, blinded by hot tears. Jeff had cut her to the quick and she couldn't get away from him fast enough. She had known somehow, deep in her soul, that the next time they met it would be bad, but the actual encounter had been worse, far worse, than she could ever have imagined.

Chapter Thirteen

Though she'd handed in her two week's notice at the store, Lila was actually able to leave the job within the first week. There were several other applicants eager for work, so the manager saw no reason to prolong her stay. They parted company amicably with the understanding that she would be happy to return and help out from time to time on a temporary basis should he be shorthanded.

She knew she was rushing things a bit, quitting the job before the condominium sale was finalized, but Lila was eager to begin painting on a full-time basis and since her financial affairs were definitely looking up, she decided to take the chance. Besides the sale of the condo, her attorney had called to tell her the amount of restitution she could expect out of the settlement Nick was making to his former clients, and while it was a small percentage of the total he had taken, it still came to a tidy sum. In addition, the gallery owner who handled her work had been very enthusiastic about the last three paintings she'd shipped to him a couple of weeks ago and had assured her he would have no trouble selling them. She hoped fervently that he was right. Meantime, she wanted to concentrate on completing more.

She was happy with the way the portrait of Janey was shaping up. The girl had come back twice to pose for the actual painting and this afternoon she would come again. Lila hoped today she would be able to complete it. It was a subdued piece, with soft sunlight streaming from behind the subject, highlighting the beautiful, flowing dark hair that framed the exquisitely youthful face. The background melded with the antique gold lace collar that Janey wore at her throat over a creamy white dress and the whole thing was done in a delicate, not-quite-in-focus, other-world manner. Lila sensed that it was the best work she had ever done and she felt justifiably proud.

When Janey arrived, though she wore shorts and a T-shirt, she brought with her the dress and collar she was modeling for the portrait. The dress had belonged to her mother; the fragile collar had been made and worn by her grandmother.

While Lila busied herself getting set up in the studio, Janey changed in the bedroom. When she returned, wearing the dress, she perched on the high stool a few feet from the easel. But today she was restless and couldn't seem to settle down into the correct pose.

Lila attempted to position her, but when that was finally accomplished, the girl's face was tense, the expression sullen rather than peaceful, and the chin, set defiantly, was lifted too high.

Lila sighed in defeat. "Okay, out with it. Something's bothering you and it's spoiling the mood I need. What's wrong?"

Janey shrugged. "Jeff and I had another big fight last night, that's all. Honestly, I can't wait until I'm old enough to leave home and move to New York to be a model. Then he won't be able to tell me what to do anymore!''

"No. Then photographers and clients and the head of the modeling agency will be your bosses. Not to mention the bathroom scale. That's one of the strictest tyrants of all. Life is never completely free of authority, Janey, in one form or another.''

"I know that. But at least then I'll be in charge of my personal life. I won't have a big brother always saying 'no' to everything.''

"What was the argument about this time?'' Lila didn't really want to know. It was none of her business and she preferred to be able to get on with the portrait, but she knew the only way she was ever going to get Janey to settle down for the sitting was by letting her get whatever was bothering her off her chest.

"A girlfriend of mine, who has her own car and is a safe driver, is going to Houston to spend a week with her cousins before school starts. She invited me to go with her, but as usual, Jeff said I can't.''

"Is she going alone or is an adult going along, too?''

"Alone. But her mom *trusts* her! Jeff doesn't trust me.''

"I don't think trust is really the issue, Janey. Not the only one, anyway. It's more a matter of safety. It's not very wise for two pretty teenage girls to get out on the highway alone and drive that far. Too many things could happen.''

"Nothing would happen! Jeff's just paranoid that somebody might try to kidnap me again! Even the psychiatrist I've been seeing these past few months said I have to venture out sometime, that I can't live the rest of my life in constant fear that every stranger I see is going to kidnap me. Jeff's smothering me!''

"Maybe he needs to ease up a little,'' Lila conceded with cautious sympathy, "but to tell you the truth, if I were in his shoes in this instance, I'd have forbidden you to go to Houston, too."

"You're kidding!" Janey's eyes widened with disbelief. "I thought you were my friend. I thought you understood."

Lila nodded. "I am your friend and I do understand. But I think Jeff is right. Even if you'd never been kidnapped, I wouldn't let you make that trip, period. It's too far and too dangerous."

"Grown-ups!" Janey snapped in disgust. "You're all in cahoots!"

Chuckling, Lila patted her shoulder. "If we are, why do you think that is? Be honest, now, Janey. Is it because we really want to oppress you and ruin your life or because we care about your welfare?"

"Maybe you do care, but there is such a thing as being too strict."

"True, but there's also such a thing as being too lenient. Has your friend found someone else to go with her since Jeff said you couldn't?"

Grinning ruefully, Janey shook her head. "She asked two other girls after me, but their parents won't let them go either."

Lila laughed. "So Jeff's not the only killjoy in the bunch, after all!"

Janey laughed and her expression lightened. "All right, all right! Forget it! Can we get on with the sitting now?"

"With pleasure," Lila answered. "Remember...a serene expression on that puss of yours, if you please."

For the next hour Lila worked steadily as Janey relaxed and chatted about less emotional issues. But after a while she returned to the original subject. "I guess I can accept Jeff not wanting me to make that trip, although I still think it's unreasonable, but it seems like all we ever do these days is fight about every single thing. I tried to have a calm discussion with him like you suggested, but all we ended up doing was shouting at each other. Could you talk to him for me, Lila? Try to smooth things over, so that he won't be so negative about *everything?* I bet he'd listen to you."

Lila still hadn't recovered from the withering look Jeff had given her that evening at the library meeting. Therefore, Janey's request was laughable except for the fact that it was far from amusing to Lila.

Nibbling at her lip, she shook her head. "I'm sorry, Janey, but Jeff isn't likely to listen to anything I have to say. I wish I could help you, but believe me, if I meddled, it would only make things worse."

Janey's eyes were shrewd. "You two had a fight, didn't you?"

"Something like that," Lila conceded.

"See?" Janey exclaimed. "Jeff can't get along with anyone these days!"

Lila swallowed painfully. "The fault doesn't lie with Jeff. I said something pretty cruel to him and I've come to the conclusion that if I were him, I wouldn't ever speak to me again."

"Honest?" Janey's brown eyes were huge with interest. "What did you say?"

Lila shook her head. "I'd rather not get into that."

"Whatever it was," Janey mused, "it must've been pretty awful. I was sure Jeff was crazy about you."

Lila's mouth twisted, but she made no response.

Janey was thoughtful for a moment, but then she asked bluntly, "And how do you feel, Lila? About my brother, I mean?"

I love him with all my heart, Lila cried silently. But she wasn't about to admit it to his sister. Fond as she was of Janey, she didn't trust the teenager's ability to keep quiet about a confidence of that magnitude.

"Some things are private, Janey," she said softly.

She was grateful when the girl didn't continue to press her, but before she dropped the matter, Janey said with a sigh, "I was hoping you two would hit it off. I think the reason Jeff's never married is that I'm in the way. I guess most people wouldn't want a teenager in the house when they first get married. When you came along and seemed to like me, I thought maybe if you fell for each other, he wouldn't have to hold back on my account. I'm not the reason you broke off seeing each other, am I?" A sudden vulnerability crept into her voice.

"You had absolutely nothing to do with it," Lila declared. "Get that out of your head this minute! Some things just weren't meant to be, you know? This was one of them."

Janey sighed again. "You'd have made a good sister-in-law."

Lila smiled wryly. "Believe me, matters never got that far between Jeff and me, so don't waste your time daydreaming about something that won't ever happen. You and I can always be friends, and that's the main thing, isn't it?"

"I suppose. Time out," Janey said abruptly as she raised a hand to her face. "My nose itches. How much longer do I have to sit here, anyway?"

It had been one of those days and Jeff was worn out and bad-tempered by the time he got home that evening. One of his trucks had suffered a breakdown on the highway a few miles outside of Longview, so two of his men were still there, getting it fixed. Another employee had been absent today because his wife was having a baby, so that had left them short on help at the mill yard. Jeff had gone out himself and had helped load another truck with logs to take the place of the one that needed repairs so that the delivery to the buyer in Longview could still be made on time. And if that wasn't enough, the office had problems of its own—the telephone system was on the blink and it had been hours before it was repaired. They'd endured a day of phone calls abruptly cut off when the line went dead and had gotten busy signals when they attempted to dial out.

He had thought he would get a chance to relax and unwind by watching the evening news on TV while Martha put dinner on the table, but he wasn't allowed even that.

Janey came into the room almost the moment he stretched out in the recliner. "Good, you're home. I want to talk to you about something."

Jeff sighed. *Here we go again,* he thought. He could tell he was in for another unpleasant scene by the stubborn jut of Janey's chin.

"If it's about that Houston trip again, the answer's still no."

"It's not. It's something else."

"Okay. Shoot."

Janey sat down on the edge of the sofa and leaned toward him. "Linda Frye is having an end-of-summer slumber party Friday night and I'm invited. I can go, can't I?" There was a challenge in the question.

Jeff's eyes narrowed. "Isn't that the girl whose parents are divorced and her mother works at that all-night service station?"

It seemed to him Janey hesitated a fraction before she answered. "Well, yes, but it'll be all right. We'll be inside the house and . . ."

Jeff shook his head. "Not this time, honey."

Janey jumped to her feet and her face was red with anger. "Not anytime! All you want to do is keep me locked up! You're making me a prisoner just as much as those kidnappers did, Jeff, and I'm not going to take it anymore! You don't give me any freedom at all!"

"That's untrue and you know it!" he snapped. "Last week I let you go to Dallas for two nights on that shopping trip with Beth and her mother."

"Yeah! With her mother! But you won't let me go anywhere without an adult along."

"That's not true, either." Jeff sucked in a deep breath, trying to calm himself. "I let you go places here in town with your friends all the time. I give you plenty of freedom."

"But not about the things I really want to do. Give me one good reason I can't go to this slumber party? Everyone else is going."

"I don't care if the rest of the world goes, you're not. With no adult there to supervise, all kinds of things could happen that you girls wouldn't be able to handle. All it would take is for a carload of boys to show up, bringing booze or maybe even drugs into the house, and there wouldn't be a thing you could do about it. Or some of the girls might decide to sneak out and go off someplace, God alone knows where. Even if you didn't intend to go along with anything like that, you'd be pressured about it. No, Janey, it's out of the question, and if you'd stop being furious at me long enough to think it through, you'd know I'm right about this. Just as I was about the Houston thing."

"I say you're wrong!" she cried vehemently. "Lila can agree with you all day long, but you're both still dead wrong! What it really boils down to is that you just don't trust me!"

"I do trust you," Jeff insisted. "It's the circumstances you keep presenting to me that I don't trust." He leaned forward and asked, "Anyway, what has Lila got to do with this?"

Janey shrugged with impatience. "Nothing! Just that I told her about the Houston trip and she agreed with you. The trouble is you've both just forgotten what it's like to be young! I bet Mom and Dad weren't so hard on you when you were my age! I'd give anything if they were still here." She ended on a sob.

"Amen to that!" Jeff agreed. "But since they aren't, I have to do what I think is best for you, Janey. In a couple more years you'll be off to college and making your own decisions. Let's try to get along until then, okay?"

"That's another thing! I keep telling you I'm not going to college, but do you ever listen to me? No! I'm going to be a model just like Lila, and I don't need a college education for that!"

"We'll discuss that when the time comes," Jeff replied. "And if that's what you really want then, I promise I'll give you my blessing. But for now we've got to tolerate each other, and we both need to try harder. I don't want to make things rough on you, honey. I just want to take good care of you. I wish you could see that."

"Well, I don't!" she answered hotly. "I bet I've got less freedom than any girl my age in the whole country! Let me go to this slumber party, Jeff. That'll prove you trust me."

Jeff was fast losing his patience as he shook his head

"Yes." Martha's footsteps brought her into the room. "She's at a trying age, Jeff. Just bear with her. Eventually she'll grow out of it."

Jeff smiled grimly. "Yes, but they may have to put me in a mental institution before that happens." He sighed, then added, "Go on home, Martha. I'll see to the cleaning up after I eat."

"All right. You haven't forgotten that none of us will be in tomorrow, have you?"

"Oh, that's right. I had forgotten. Lionel's taking you and Bud to see an eye doctor in Tyler." He shoved himself up from the chair. "I'd better go tell Janey before I forget and see what she wants to do while you're gone."

"She could come with us if you want us to take her."

He shook his head. "No, no. That's not necessary. She can spend the day with me at the office or go over to Beth's or something. Don't worry about it. Goodnight, Martha. I'll see you Friday."

While Martha went ░░░░░░░░░░░░ tchen, Jeff went up-

and said, "We're just going around in circles here. You are not going to that slumber party unless the girl's mother calls me herself and assures me she's going to be present, and that's final. I don't want to hear one more word about it."

Janey's eyes, already swimming in tears, now spilled over. Yet through the tears her anger and hostility gleamed. Then, abruptly, she ran from the room.

Jeff leaned back in the chair, all possibility of peace gone for now. He closed his eyes and drew a deep, cleansing breath. If disagreements and ugly scenes kept up at this rate, he didn't see how either of them would survive until Janey finished high school.

Martha came to the door. "Dinner's on the table."

Jeff nodded without opening his eyes. "I suppose you heard everything?"

stairs and knocked on Janey's door.

"Go away," came the muffled reply.

"It's time to eat."

"I'm not hungry."

Jeff opened the door just a crack. Janey sat cross-legged in the center of her bed with red eyes, tumbled hair and her anger and resentment not one whit less than when she'd run from the den a few minutes ago.

"Please come down." He smiled whimsically. "You know how I hate to eat alone."

"I don't want to eat. Can't you just leave me alone?"

Jeff held up his hands in a gesture of conciliation. "Fine. Okay. I'll leave you alone. But I do have to tell you something before I go."

"What?" she asked sullenly.

"Lionel, Martha and Bud have to spend tomorrow in Tyler, so the house will be empty all day. Do you want to come into town with me or see if you can stay with Beth?"

"Neither," Janey answered promptly. "I want to stay here."

Jeff hesitated. "Are you sure? You know you haven't been all alone since the kidnapping."

"I'm sure." Janey tilted her head and glared at him defiantly. "Or am I not allowed to stay home by myself, either?"

He sighed. "Don't be sarcastic. You know it's just that I don't want you to be alone before you're ready for it. I'd hate for you to be afraid."

"I won't. I'll be fine."

"All right, if that's what you want." Jeff backed out the door and closed it again.

He wasn't thrilled with the idea of leaving her alone. Admittedly, it was partly because he was still jumpy with anxiety that some other criminal might attack her; but it was also a genuine concern that she might not yet be emotionally ready to be left entirely alone. It wasn't as though they lived in town with next-door neighbors close by. Here they were miles from anyone. If something happened, there would be no one to hear a cry for help.

Yet logic told him that for both their sakes he had to allow her to try this when she felt ready. On the surface of things, it seemed absurd to have someone stay twenty-four hours a day with a girl almost sixteen years old. There had to come a day when she dealt with being utterly alone again and he supposed the sooner the better, despite his mother hen complex. Maybe after she'd gotten through one day alone, they would both begin to relax.

The next morning, Janey was still sleeping when Jeff looked in on her before he left for the office. His heart melted with the love he had for his little sister. He wanted desperately for her to be healthy, safe, successful and happy—in short, he wanted all the things for her that their parents would have wanted. It pained him deeply that they seemed to constantly lock horns these days. He hated quarreling with her, seeing her in tears, not being able to grant her every wish, yet he knew he had to stand his ground whenever her unwise desires conflicted with what he knew was in her true best interests. He could only hope that, given time, they would work through this difficult period, that one day she would be able to understand and appreciate why he hadn't taken the easy way out and always let her do as she pleased.

He started to wake her to say goodbye, thought better of it and softly closed the door again.

At mid-morning, though, he decided to call home and he was intensely grateful that the telephone system had been repaired.

Janey answered almost at once. "Hi. How're things going?" Jeff asked.

"Are you calling to check up on me?" Janey asked suspiciously.

Jeff sighed. "Come on, honey, don't be like that. I just called to make sure you're all right."

"I'm fine," she said brusquely. "Really, Jeff, I *am* capable of taking care of myself without somebody watching me every minute!"

"I know that," he snapped back with exasperation. "I just thought you might be a little lonely. If you like, I'll come pick you up at noon and bring you into town for a burger. I'll even give you some spending money so you can do a little bit more shopping for school clothes during the afternoon."

"No, thanks." Janey's voice was milder now, as though the brief spurt of anger was gone. "Beth's coming to spend the day with me. We'll just make some sandwiches here. We're going to try out some new hairstyles and watch a couple of video movies she's bringing with her."

"Sounds like a good plan." Jeff was relieved to know she wouldn't be completely alone all day after all. It removed the nagging anxiety he'd been feeling, that he'd known he would suffer until he could return home that evening. "Okay, I'll let you go for now. If you need anything, call me. See you tonight."

"Okay." There was a tiny silence, and then Janey spoke in an oddly different tone. "Jeff?"

"Hmmm?"

There was another pause and then she said softly, "I love you."

Jeff grinned at the receiver. This was more like it! This was his old Janey. "I love you, too, sweetheart," he answered.

He felt vastly better when he hung up the phone. Maybe Janey had calmed down enough already to realize that when he came down hard on her, he was only doing his utmost to take good care of her.

The abrupt change in Janey's attitude cheered him immensely for the remainder of the morning and it dissolved his defenses, not only toward her, but in another direction as well. Last night Janey had shocked him when she'd blurted out that Lila had reinforced his objection to her wanting to go to Houston with that other girl. He knew he owed her a vote of thanks.

At noon, as he drove toward Lila's house, he told himself that he had absolutely no expectations of anything as far as she was concerned. He was merely going to thank her for her unexpected moral support, and that would be that. As to anything else that might once have been promising, he had no illusions. He knew exactly what Lila really thought of him and that left no room for compromise, no room for any sort of relationship to exist between them. If a man couldn't have respect from the woman he loved, then they had nothing together. He couldn't respect himself if he tried.

When Lila answered the door, she looked surprised and wary to see him standing there. She didn't smile, but neither did she appear displeased. Merely cautious. He supposed he couldn't blame her. He'd been pretty cold to her that night at the library meeting.

"Hello," he said at last.

Lila nodded her head. "Hi." She made no move to say more, to invite him in.

Jeff felt foolish just standing there outside her door while she continued to wait for him to speak. At last, he asked, "Do you suppose I could come in for minute?"

Lila appeared to ponder the request, and for a time he thought she was actually going to refuse, but finally, without enthusiasm, she said, "I suppose."

Once he was inside the house, his eyes adjusted to the dim light that filtered in through the windows and he was able to see her clearly. *Lord,* he groaned inwardly, *why did she have to be so damned beautiful?* She was dressed with the utmost casual comfort in a pair of khaki-colored shorts and a green cotton shirt that hung loose. Her feet were bare and her glorious red-gold hair was tied at the nape of her neck with a white ribbon. She wore no makeup whatsoever, no jewelry, and as far as he could tell, no perfume, yet she was just as enticing to him now as she'd ever been decked out in formal finery for an alluring magazine cover. He supposed bitterly that that just went to show how hopelessly in love he was.

He carefully masked his feelings, however, and asked, "How've you been?"

"Fine." She paused and when he didn't go on, she said with a hint of impatience, "You'll have to excuse me a minute. I have a cobbler in the oven and it's time for it to come out." Without waiting for a response, she went past him and into the kitchen.

Jeff followed slowly and paused in the doorway as his gaze swept over the sensual sight of Lila bending over the oven. A second later she was upright once more, setting the steaming dish on top of the stove and then bending again briefly to close the oven door.

When she turned around, she looked startled to see him standing there.

Jeff smiled and leaned against the door frame. "It smells fantastic. Dewberry?"

"Yes."

"Umm. My favorite." He moved into the room and went to the stove where he sniffed the air. "You know a cobbler isn't complete unless it's eaten warm with vanilla ice cream melting on top, don't you?"

For the first time, Lila smiled. In fact, she actually laughed and the sound was genuine and friendly. "So my grandmother taught me." She opened the freezer compartment of the refrigerator and took out a carton of ice cream. "See. I'm all prepared." She put it back in its place and shut the door.

Jeff stepped even closer to the stove and bent his head. "The crust is beautiful. I've never seen Martha make better and she's been cooking for at least fifty years. You know," he went on conversationally, "that's an awful lot of cobbler there for just one person to have to eat all by herself." He turned slowly to meet her gaze.

He felt heartened when he saw amusement dancing in her eyes. Then her grin widened. "I won't have any trouble at all," she told him. "I'm the girl who likes to eat all the time, remember?"

Jeff grinned back. "I remember. But really, a delicacy like this has to be shared to be truly appreciated."

Lila tossed back her head and laughed again. "Okay, okay, you win. I'll share, as long as you don't get too greedy."

"Thanks." Jeff tried to look humble and his expression made Lila laugh again. He hadn't heard a sweeter sound in weeks and it sent a little wave of happiness right down to his toes.

Lila tilted her head to one side and gave him a speculative look. "Have you eaten lunch yet?"

He shook his head.

"The cobbler's still too hot to eat," she said. "You might as well have lunch with me, too, if you don't mind tuna sandwiches."

"I love tuna sandwiches," he said quickly. "What can I do to help?"

"Sit down at the table and stay out of the way," Lila said tartly.

"Whatever you say, ma'am."

"Umm. You don't fool me any with that meek attitude. You're just afraid to get on my wrong side before you get the cobbler."

"True." Jeff exaggerated a sigh as he pulled out a chair and sat down. "You know me better than I thought."

Lila's back had been turned as she took the bowl of tuna salad from the refrigerator and set it on the counter. Now she went very still before slowly turning to face him. Her expression was no longer teasing or amused.

"No," she said softly. "I realize now that I never knew you at all. I accused you of being callous, manipulative and calculating when all you ever tried to do was be good to me. I projected another man's faults onto you. I'm sorry, Jeff. I don't know whether you can ever forgive me, but I hope you'll try."

He caught his breath. She had taken him completely by surprise, jerking the rug out from beneath the long weeks of resentment he'd had toward her. Jeff's heart thudded.

"Lila..." He started to stand up, but she held up a hand, motioning him to remain still.

"No, please. Let me finish. I know I hurt you a lot when I said all those hateful things to you. I know, too, that I ruined any chance of anything developing between us and I accept that. I accept that we can't even really be friends. I...I guess what I'm trying to ask now is if we can at least be cordial to one another whenever we meet."

Jeff was silent for a long time, as cautious and wary now as she had been when he'd first arrived. She'd just said words that he'd been longing to hear, but some little part of him still held back. He didn't want to set himself up for still more pain and rejection in the future. And yet she'd just given him an unexpected opening, fresh hope, and he knew he had to do his part before the opening closed once more...for good.

At last he spoke. "I suppose we could even be more than cordial, more than friends, if we wanted it badly enough. If we were willing to take our time and start over again on a completely different footing."

"I'm willing," Lila said quietly.

His gaze was somber as it met hers. There was sincerity in her eyes. "So am I," he told her at last.

After that optimistic beginning the simple lunch they shared seemed to become a banquet. Pleasure in each other's company hung in the air like a brilliant evening star come to cast added light on an already bright, sunlit day. The sandwiches, the garden-fresh sliced tomatoes and cucumbers tasted far more savory than was warranted and the berry cobbler and ice cream was like ambrosia to their taste buds. Jeff rejoiced with Lila over selling the condominium and being able to quit her job, listened closely as she told him, for the first time, all about Nick and what he had done and ending with the news that he now faced a trial for his crime. In turn, she sympathized with him over his problems with Janey, brushed aside his thanks for backing him up when the girl had complained about him, and fell thoughtfully silent as he told her about the grasping, greedy Angela.

"So you can see," he ended wryly, "how your objections to my doing anything for you or giving you anything sort of threw me for a loop. I thought that's what all women wanted...to get, get, get. I couldn't understand your standoffish independence."

"No, but then you couldn't have known why I was so suspicious every time you tried to be generous to me. You see, Nick was that way, too, in the beginning. He showered me with gifts. But after he gained my trust, he betrayed me."

Jeff smiled. "Maybe we're beginning to finally understand each other."

Lila returned the smile. "Maybe we should've had this conversation a long time ago."

"It would've saved a lot of hard feelings," Jeff conceded. He glanced at his watch, then shook his head with genuine regret. "I hate to eat and run, but I have a business appointment at two and if I don't leave soon, I'll miss it."

"That's all right," Lila said, rising from the table. "I promised myself I'd give the studio a good cleaning this afternoon."

Jeff rose, too. "Mind if I take a peek at what you've been working on lately?"

"Be my guest. Actually, it's something I'd very much like you to see."

In the studio, Jeff went directly to the easel and when he saw Janey's likeness there, he drew in a sharp breath. He gazed at it in mute silence for a full two minutes before he finally turned to Lila.

"It's the most beautiful painting I've ever seen," he said, almost in awe. "When did you do it?"

"I finished it yesterday. She's been sitting for me a couple of afternoons a week."

Jeff swung back to look at the portrait once more. "It's wonderful. An incredible likeness. Would you please sell it to me?"

"No."

The flat refusal shocked him and he jerked around to stare at her incredulously. "No? But you must! Surely you can see that. I'll pay whatever you want for it."

Lila shook her head and said again, implacably, "No."

"Why, for God's sake?" Jeff exploded.

He realized that he'd missed the twinkle in her eyes until she actually began to smile. "Because," she said gently, "it's not for sale. But it's yours. I give it to you as a gift."

"Oh, no!" Jeff shook his head and before he knew he was doing it, he'd scooped her into his arms. "Oh, no you don't! I can't accept such a valuable gift from you unless you take something in return!"

Lila laughed at him and he was enchanted by her nearness, by her teasing spirits. His caution and hesitation about getting mixed up with her again was instantly forgotten and abandoned.

"Touché." Lila pretended to consider the matter. "A necklace might be nice," she said at last. "A delicate gold-worked necklace from Italy with beautiful gems. Would you happen to have one like that just lying about? Or . . . what would you rather give me in exchange?"

"The necklace will be fine for starters," Jeff said huskily. "But there's something else I'd like to give you even more."

Lila's eyes widened with curiosity. "Yes? What?"

"Myself," Jeff heard himself saying. "My name. My love. My children. Damn it all, woman, I'm crazy in love with you. Will you please marry me and be done with it?"

Lila's eyes darkened to a deep sea green as she searched his face. Jeff tensed as he waited in an agony of suspense for her reply.

But before he had the time to grow really alarmed, a gorgeous smile lit up her entire face. She lifted her arms and curled them around his neck as she snuggled closer to him.

"Damn it all, man," she parodied, "I thought you'd never get around to asking."

Chapter Fourteen

They stood at the front door, entwined in each other's arms, whispering the words that are universal to lovers. They touched, they smiled and they trembled with intense emotion.

Jeff cupped Lila's face in his hands. "Say it again," he commanded gruffly.

"I love you," she obeyed readily. "I love you, I love you, I love you."

Jeff moaned as he pulled her to him again and buried his face in her hair. His hands slid down her back, stroking her hips, traveling back up to caress her breasts. "I can't bear to leave you," he whispered. "I want to make love with you."

Lila ached with desire. "I want that, too," she answered raggedly. "In the worst way." She sighed, then asked, "Can't you postpone your meeting?"

Jeff lifted his head so that his gaze could meet hers. He saw the love he felt reflected in her eyes. "I wish I could," he answered fervently. "But this customer is from out of town, so I have to meet with him."

Lila smiled lovingly at him as she raised a hand to touch his lips with his fingertips. "Then I'll just have to share you," she said unsteadily, "even though I want to be thoroughly selfish."

"I'll be back tonight," Jeff assured her as he bent to brush his lips against hers once more.

"I'll be waiting."

"Wear something grand. We'll go to Tyler for dinner to celebrate."

"Must we?" she asked wistfully. "Can't we just dine here and stay in all evening?"

Jeff's mouth curved into a smile. "A girl after my own heart," he murmured approvingly. "I'd much rather stay here. I'll bring a bottle of champagne."

"Then it's settled."

Jeff lowered his arms and clasped both her hands. "Walk out to the car with me?"

Hand in hand they went outside into the bright sunshine. At the car, Jeff embraced and kissed her again and held her as though he never wanted to let her go. Lila felt dizzy with joy. It was almost like a dream—a dream from which she never wanted to awaken. Jeff loved her and wanted to marry her! The black times of misunderstandings and loneliness were over. Forever lay ahead!

Before he let her go, Jeff asked somberly, "Are you sure you really want to marry me, Lila? Remember, I still have Janey to raise. Most women wouldn't want to begin married life with—"

Lila laughed at his anxieties, covered his mouth with her hand and said, "Of course I want to marry you, and I'm not about to let you back out of the deal for such a silly reason!

Besides, Janey told me only yesterday that she thought I'd make a good sister-in-law!"

"Did she now?" Jeff's eyes twinkled. "So the two of you were already plotting all this, were you?"

"No," Lila answered seriously. "Janey was only wishing. I couldn't even bring myself to do that. I didn't think there was a chance in a million of it ever happening."

"Neither did I. I'm still not sure it's happening."

Lila hugged him fiercely, and said, "You'd better go or you'll miss your meeting. Tonight, maybe we'll both really realize it's true."

Jeff reluctantly got in the car and started the motor, but before he drove away, he leaned out the window and said, "By the time I get here tonight I want you to have a wedding date set, and make it soon!"

She laughed and nodded. "Very soon," she seconded, "as long as you don't expect a huge, formal ceremony."

"The simplest will be fine with me," Jeff said gruffly. "It's not the trappings I want. It's you."

With those words he left her. Lila stood and watched as he drove away, turned onto the highway and out of sight. Only then did she slowly return to the house.

The afternoon passed in a haze of euphoria. Lila cleaned the studio as she had originally planned, but she found herself pausing often to think of Jeff, of the momentous change that had suddenly turned her life upside down. She touched her lips as though to hold his warm kisses there and she quivered as she dreamed of what the night would bring. It seemed so far away, the moment when she could be in his arms once more, when they could make love without any barriers coming between them, when she could fully realize that she belonged to him and he to her.

And yet the time sped by and surprisingly, there didn't seem enough of it to accomplish everything she wanted to do before Jeff returned. There was dinner to prepare. She put a roast in the oven; she'd later add vegetables to it. And of course she had to take the time to bathe and dress and make herself as beautiful for him as she possibly could.

At mid-afternoon, topping an already untoppable day, the telephone rang and it was the New York art gallery owner. Two of her most recent paintings had sold, fetching respectable prices. Lila was jubilant. She felt that nothing, but nothing could go awry.

She was wrong.

When the afternoon meeting with his client ended at last, Jeff tried to call home. This time his intent wasn't to check up on Janey's welfare, but rather to suggest she see if it would be all right with Beth's mother if Janey spent the night at Beth's house tonight. Normally when he was away in the evenings, he asked Martha to stay at the house with her, but Martha would be tired from her day in Tyler and he didn't want to ask her to come unless he had to. Anyway, Janey would be happier at Beth's house if it could be arranged.

There was no answer to his call, however, and Jeff frowned as the ringing continued. Now where could they be? Had she and Beth gone off with some other kids in a car or were they merely outside somewhere?

It was probably the latter, he assured himself. Sometimes the girls enjoyed sunbathing in the backyard. Or perhaps they had taken Toby and one of the other horses to go riding. Janey was a big girl, and he would not, he sternly ordered himself, panic and rush home to check. She would only be more furious with him if he did.

Still, he continued to call home intermittently throughout the afternoon and the phone went unanswered. In spite of himself, Jeff was growing increasingly concerned and promptly at five o'clock, he left the office and drove straight home.

The house was silent as he entered. "Janey?" he shouted. "Janey, where are you?"

No one responded and Jeff sensed by the quiet that pervaded the house that he was alone. Even so, he ran up the stairs at a lope to check Janey's bedroom. He paused briefly to knock and then opened the door. Janey wasn't there, so he wasted no time going inside. He turned and ran downstairs again and through the back of the house out to the lawn. He saw no one there either, so he headed toward the corral to check whether the horses were there.

They were. Toby neighed at him and came toward the fence, hoping for a sugar cube.

"Sorry, fellow, not this time."

With a growing sense of urgency, Jeff ran back to the house. His heart thudded and he couldn't seem to breathe. He was truly alarmed now. The nightmare he'd experienced when Janey had been kidnapped was beginning all over again.

Yet surely it couldn't happen again! "Calm down," he told himself as he reentered the house. "Stay calm. There has to be a simple explanation."

That's when it occurred to him to telephone Beth's house. Perhaps her mother had come and taken both girls there. Janey probably hadn't expected him home this early and intended to call and let him know her change of plans.

Jeff went into his study and hurriedly looked up Beth's number. Then he punched the numbers with an unsteady hand.

Mrs. Winston answered and Jeff felt a measure of relief just to hear her calm, sane voice. He identified himself, then asked, "Did Janey go home with Beth?"

"Go home with her?" Mrs. Winston echoed, sounding baffled. "She hasn't been with Janey at all today."

Jeff was stunned. "Did...didn't Beth come over this morning and spend the day with Janey?"

"Why, no. She's been home with me all day. We've been repainting her bedroom."

A chill shivered down his spine. "I . . . see. Do you happen to know whether Janey called Beth today?"

"No, she didn't. As I said, we've been really busy and Beth hasn't talked on the phone at all."

"I see," Jeff said slowly. "If you hear from Janey, would you ask her to call home, please?"

"Certainly."

When he hung up the phone, he was rigid from the shocking blow he'd just received. Janey hadn't planned to have Beth visit her today at all! She had deliberately lied to him, something he'd never known her to do before. Now he didn't know what to do next or where to turn. This was all so unlike her.

Why? Why?

No answer came to him. For some time Jeff simply stood immobile as he tried to think where his sister might have gone, tried to figure out why she had deceived him.

After a while, with leaden feet and heart, he went upstairs to her room once more. He couldn't have explained why he went there. It was merely that something pulled him toward her room, a need to be among her belongings in order to feel close to her. It had happened to him before, while she'd been missing after the kidnapping.

He went into the room and stood gazing around at the familiar things, as his heart filled with an aching poignancy. Then, heavily, he sank down to sit at the foot of the bed and buried his face in his hands.

After a moment, he rubbed his face and raised his head, staring blankly at the mirror above the dresser. But gradually his gaze lowered and that's when he saw the pink envelope propped up in front of the row of perfume bottles. His name was scrawled across the front.

Lila was mildly annoyed when the telephone rang. She had just added the vegetables to the roast and gravy and replaced the pan in the oven and was about to take her bath. She hoped it wasn't Amy Mathis calling and wanting to carry on a long conversation.

"Hello?"

"Jeff here."

Warmth flooded through her and Lila smiled to herself. "Hi," she said. "I was just thinking about you...about tonight. I—"

Jeff cut in on her words and his voice was hard as rock. "I'm at home," he said succinctly. "I want you to come here right now."

Sudden alarm hammered through Lila's veins. "What's the matter?" she questioned urgently.

"Just come."

He hung up without another word. Lila was so surprised she ceased breathing for the space of a couple of heartbeats. Something had radically changed Jeff since she'd seen him at noon. Something was terribly, terribly wrong.

A shiver of apprehension raced through her.

Lila paused only long enough to switch off the oven and then she grabbed her purse and went out to the car.

Within ten minutes she was ringing Jeff's doorbell and when he opened the massive front door and she saw his black expression, her heart sank. Here was no eager lover; here was a man with loathing in his eyes.

"Come in." The words were a command rather than an invitation. Completely at sea over the change in him, Lila followed on shaky legs as he led her into his study. There he waved a hand toward a chair, indicating she should sit. Then he walked over to his desk, picked up a pink slip of paper and tossed it without ceremony into her lap.

"Read it," he said flatly. He leaned against the edge of the desk and crossed his arms.

For a second, Lila looked at him uncertainly, trying to read his face, but except for the overt hostility she saw there, it told her nothing.

Then she looked at the paper in her hand. After a moment, she sat up straight, every nerve in her body tense, while alarm poured through her veins like hot lead.

It was a note to Jeff from Janey. There was a lot in it about how she loved him, but couldn't bear his strict, over-protective ways anymore and how she wanted to be free to get on with her life. The last paragraph applied most to Lila. Janey wrote that she intended to make her own way, to begin her career, as Lila had done. Jeff was not to worry; she had money she'd been saving up for years and was sure it would tide her over until she found a job to support herself while she pursued her career. A friend with a car had picked her up today and driven her someplace where Jeff couldn't find her. She was sorry she'd had to deceive him, but it had been the only possible way. The missive ended with Love and XXXXX's and a postscript: *Maybe someday when I'm a success, you'll finally realize that I'm all grown-up and not just your baby sister.*

The paper flitted out of Lila's hand as numbness overtook her. For a long time there was utter silence in the room. She searched for words to comfort Jeff, but there were none.

Finally she looked up. Jeff's dark eyes seemed to sear her very soul. "Well?" he asked harshly. "What do you have to say to that?"

Lila spread her hands. "What can I say, except that I'm terribly sorry? Have you called the police?"

"Oh, yes, I've already put the word out, but the law really isn't all that interested in runaways, it seems. They have so many of them."

"I wish she'd come to me," Lila murmured. "Confided in me. Maybe I could have talked her—"

"You've done quite enough talking to my sister already," Jeff snapped, interrupting her. "That's precisely why this has happened!"

Lila got to her feet. "What are you saying? You can't possibly blame *me* for this!"

"Oh, but I do!" Jeff's voice was seething as he uncrossed his arms and took a menacing step toward her. "None of this would've happened if you hadn't filled her head full of fantasies and daydreams about a modeling career!"

"I did nothing of the sort!" Lila protested vigorously.

"Don't give me that! You fed her a steady diet of nonsense about what a grand, glamorous life it is, so that all she could think about was being beautiful and famous and successful like you! Now this is what it's come to," he said, pointing a finger directly in her face.

Lila was trembling, now as angry as he. She slapped his hand away from her face. "Stop trying to place *your* blame on *my* shoulders!" she said hotly. "I refuse to accept it! You drove her to this extreme, not me!"

"You're crazy! I'm her brother and I love her. I'd never do anything to hurt her."

"You already did! The poor kid felt as though she was living in a fancy prison!" Wildly, Lila flung her arms out, indicating the house itself. "She told me how you refused to let her do anything she asked! I know you were trying to protect her and keep her safe, Jeff, but you went overboard!"

"I thought you agreed with me. You even backed me up!"

"Sure, about something clearly out of the question like that trip to Houston, I did, but not about everything! She's almost sixteen years old, for heaven's sake, but you treated her like a five year old. Janey felt smothered; she couldn't breathe. To tell you the truth, I'm not at all surprised she ran away from you!''

Jeff inhaled deeply and shuddered. His brown eyes were black with fury. "Get out," he said in a low, controlled voice. "Get out of my house and out of my life! I thought I loved you, but I was wrong. I never want to see you again after all the trouble you've caused."

"That's fine with me," Lila answered steadily. "I certainly wouldn't want to be married to a man who can't admit his own mistakes!"

Lila raced from the house and out to her car. Her chest was heaving laboriously with churning emotion, her eyes stung, but she drove home with a cold, angry calm.

She smelled the roast that was still in the oven as soon as she entered the house. She no longer had any appetite for it and so she ignored it. In the morning she would throw it out. She couldn't possibly eat the food that had been meant for her engagement dinner.

The night was a long one as Lila paced the floor. She was hurt and angry with Jeff, so much so that it didn't bear thinking about, but at the moment she was more concerned about Janey. No matter who's fault it was, no matter who had influenced her most to run away, it didn't alter the fact that she was a young, inexperienced girl all alone out there somewhere. Dangers lurked everywhere for an attractive girl that age who didn't know how to take care of herself and Lila was terrified for her.

When dawn came, Lila was still up, exhausted but alert and clearheaded. She'd busied herself throughout the long hours rearranging her kitchen cupboards and listening to the radio. Now she made a fresh pot of coffee, then carried a cup with her out to the front porch.

Sometime during the night had come an inner light. She felt certain that she knew where Janey had gone. Or rather, where she would be going. All that remained for Lila to do was make a telephone call and try to wait in patience.

Clotilde Gold had always had a habit of being at her desk by precisely eight o'clock in the morning, so on Friday morning at seven, Texas time, Lila placed her call.

"Lila, darling, how *wonderful* to hear from you! Have you *finally* come to your senses and decided to come back? I *knew* it was only a matter of time before you'd want to brush the hayseed out of your hair and get back to work!"

"Sorry, Clo," Lila replied. "I haven't changed my mind. But I am calling you about something very important and I need your help."

The following Monday Lila got the call she was waiting for. It was Clo and, dispensing with the pleasantries, she got straight to the point. "She just left. We did what you asked and Frances gave her an appointment to come back at ten a.m. Wednesday. Can you make it?"

"Even if I have to sprout wings of my own. Thanks a million, Clo. I owe you. You're a real friend."

"Hmmph. Remember that the next time I have a modeling assignment that would be *perfect* for you. Quite frankly, Lila, my income has dropped *considerably* since you left me."

"I don't believe that for one minute," Lila answered. "There are too many beautiful, young, up-and-coming girls to take my place. Anyway, I've definitely retired. See you day after tomorrow."

The next day Lila drove to Dallas, left her car in the long-term parking lot and boarded a plane for New York. She had tried to call Jeff to let him know she had tentatively located Janey, but she'd been told that he was away. She supposed he was off somewhere searching for Janey himself. She left word with his secretary to tell him that she thought she had located Janey and had gone to find her.

Lila's only hope now was that Janey would keep her appointment. If she didn't ... But she didn't dare think about that. It was impossible to try to locate one lone girl in New York City. It would be like searching for the proverbial needle in a haystack.

She spent the night with another model, Gina, who had been her closest friend when she'd lived in New York, and who also was a client of Clo's. They stayed up late catching up on news, but even with little sleep, Lila had no trouble awakening the next morning. Her nerves were taut as she silently prayed that Janey would show up at the agency for her "interview."

Lila entered the Gold Modeling Agency at eight-thirty and Frances welcomed her warmly before admitting her to Clo's inner office.

Clo was a woman in her late fifties, stylishly attired in a white linen designer suit. Her makeup was flawless on a face that seemed perpetually young. Only her hair was at odds with the rest of her. It was uncompromisingly gray and wispy, always sticking out every which way no matter what Clo or her hairdresser tried to do with it.

They talked over coffee while they awaited zero hour. But by ten of ten, Lila was fidgety, casting frequent glances at her watch.

"She may not come, you know," Clo said. "She may have thought it over and realized it's a trap."

"That occurred to me, too," Lila replied. "Oh, Clo, I couldn't bear it if any harm comes to that girl."

"Who exactly is she?"

Lila was bluntly honest to her old friend. "The sister and ward of the man I was supposed to marry."

Clo's eyebrows quirked. "Supposed to?"

"He blames me for this...he thinks that I influenced her to run away by making modeling sound so glamorous and exciting, but I swear I didn't, Clo! I always told her the un-varnished truth."

"Hmmm. Don't go around doing *that,*" Clo chided. "You'll *ruin* my business." She reached across the desk and patted Lila's hand. "It'll be all right. Even if she doesn't come back here, she'll probably get discouraged soon enough and go home on her own. I—"

A knock sounded on the door and Frances came inside. Lila tensed.

"She's here."

"Thank God!" Lila breathed.

"Show her in at *once,*" Clo ordered. "Don't *let* her get away!"

Frances nodded and went out again. A moment later the door opened once more and Janey entered the room.

She wore a cute little outfit befitting a teenager—blousy white cotton trousers with a white tank top and a large pink overblouse tied at the waist. Her hair hung straight, shiny and well-groomed. Flashy pink earrings dangled next to a face that wore too much makeup.

Except for the excess of makeup, Janey looked pretty and presentable. A nervous smile was plastered on her lips, but it faded the instant she saw Lila. Then her eyes grew large and dark with alarm.

Lila stood up and said pleasantly, "Good morning, Ja-ney."

"What're you doing here?" Janey was too surprised at first to be resentful.

"School begins Monday. I came to take you home."

Now the resentment reared its head. Janey's face took on a definite pout. "I won't go."

"Your brother is worried sick. You ought to be ashamed of yourself for putting him through this."

Janey flushed beneath the makeup and lowered her head. "I didn't want to hurt him, but it's time I made my own decisions."

Clo got up and came around the desk to stand in front of the girl. "It's *easy* to make the wrong decisions. People do it all the time. It's *much* harder to make the right ones, especially if it goes against weak self-indulgence." She stepped closer to Janey and placed her hand beneath the girl's chin, then turned her face to each side as she studied her profile, noting her bone structure and skin with a professional eye. "You have the right basic equipment to become a model, Janey. If you *also* have the self-discipline and determination to match, you just might manage to make it in this business. Someday. But *this* isn't the time. Go back home and finish school."

Janey stepped back from her touch and her eyes flashed. "You just told me I have the right looks to make it. If you don't want to represent me, there are other agencies."

"Wrong." Clo gave her a stern look. "I know *everybody* in this business, and very few agents would be willing to take on a minor without her parents' or guardian's knowledge and consent. I can guarantee you'll never even get past the front desk."

Janey faltered. "That's not fair!"

Clo shrugged. "And *that's* a juvenile statement if I ever heard one. Go home and finish growing up, child. I don't have time to be a *nursemaid* to infants." She smiled then to relieve the harsh words. "Tell you what, though . . . as a favor to Lila, I'll see what I can do for you the day you come back and show me your diploma."

A slow smile came to Janey's lips. "You promise?"

Clo patted her shoulder. "I promise. And let me give you one more small piece of advice. Wash off ninety-nine percent of that makeup. You're *hiding* your best asset of all—the natural beauty and glow of a youthful complexion. It's to *die* for, and if you want to work for me, you won't clog up your pores with all that *gloop.*''

Janey grinned and nodded. "Thanks," she said thickly. "I'll be back in two years."

"It's a date."

Janey faced Lila then and her voice was soft, no longer defiant. "Actually, I've been wanting to go home ever since the second day, but I just didn't have the nerve to call Jeff for the plane fare. Is he very angry with me?"

"I think he's been too busy being scared to death," Lila replied.

"I've been scared, too," Janey admitted. "What I did was pretty stupid."

"Now *that's* what I call a mature remark," Clo said. "I think in a couple more years, you and I will get along just *fine.*"

Lila had booked two seats on a flight to Dallas that departed late that afternoon. At the airport, before boarding, Janey tried to telephone Jeff. Bud told her he was due home in a few hours. He'd been in New York himself a couple of days ago, as well as Dallas, searching for her. Today he was coming in from Los Angeles where he'd also tried to find her.

The news that Jeff had been all over frantically searching for her sobered Janey more than anything else and she suffered heavy guilt as the plane carried them back to Texas. Lila thought it was a good idea to let her stew in her mistake a while, so though she offered a willing ear, she gave no sympathy.

Neither of them had expected it, but Jeff met their plane in Dallas that evening. A tearful, apologetic Janey went straight into his arms.

Lila stood to one side, quietly watching the reunion. Tears choked her throat as she saw Jeff trembling during the embrace.

At last they drew apart and Lila and Jeff faced each other for the first time since that awful afternoon in his study. Lila's heart ceased to beat as they gazed at one another. Would he see now how wrong he'd been, she wondered, or would he still blame her for what had happened? Could the love they'd had for each other be resurrected, or was it really over for good?

She got her answer an instant later. "I must thank you for bringing Janey home," he said at last. The words were polite, civil enough, but there was a chilling coldness behind them. "Naturally," he went on, "I'll reimburse you for your expenses in going to get her."

Lila swallowed hard as sensations of defeat and hopelessness overwhelmed her. She fought back tears and shook her head. "It isn't necessary," she answered, proud of the steadiness in her voice. "I was happy to do it. Now, if you'll both excuse me, I'm going to collect my luggage and my car and head for home."

Chapter Fifteen

Jerri dabbed a white, kidney-shaped spot on the side of the tiny brown rocking horse she was painting. "I wish you'd reconsider, Lila. Rob's friend in Kilgore is not only presentable, but he's also got a terrific sense of humor and he doesn't shovel his food like a backwoods clod. He's even a good dancer."

"In short—every woman's dream, hmm?" Lila applied a small black dot for an eye to her rocking horse, then carefully set it upright in the center of Amy Mathis's newspaper-covered dining room table. "No thanks, Jerri," she answered in response to the renewed offer of a "fix-up" date. "I detest blind dates. I don't intend to stay for the dance, anyway. I'll just go to the banquet, visit with everyone for a couple of hours and then leave."

"But you'll miss the best part of the evening that way!" Jerri protested.

Lila shrugged. "I can live with the disappointment."

Amy returned from the kitchen, carrying cups of hot spiced tea. She set them down and said, "If you won't go with a date, at least stick around for the dance. Maybe Jerri and I'll be generous enough to allow you a couple of dances with our husbands."

Lila grinned. "One each will be sufficient, thank you very much. I'm not about to land myself in hot water with the pair of you over the subject of husbands! I may want to visit this town again someday!"

Amy's expression became glum as she took her chair. "We're sure going to miss you when you leave. I wish you'd change your mind."

"So do I," Jerri echoed. "I've enjoyed working with you on community projects as well as having you for a friend. Are you positive it's what you really want to do? Your art career is blossoming . . . you can't be going back to modeling because you need the money."

Amy sighed. "I guess we can't blame her, really. Cattail's a far cry from the stimulation that New York offers. Except for something like this CBC banquet and dance, there aren't many exciting social events around here."

"Not to mention the scarcity of eligible men," Jerri murmured thoughtfully.

Lila laughed. "Hey, what're you trying to do . . . talk me out of it or encourage me to leave this minute?"

Amy smiled. "I guess it's just that we can see how dull Cattail must be to a single woman . . . especially to one who had led such a glamorous life before. It's a wonder you stayed this long. To be honest, if I were in your shoes, I'd probably do the same thing."

Jerry nodded. "I hate to say it, but so would I. What have you decided to do about your house?"

"It hurts to let go of it, but it's the only sensible thing to do. I'll never live in it again and it's too difficult to see that it's rented and maintained properly from far away. I'm going to put it on the market at the same time that I leave, right after the new year. I didn't want to be bothered showing it to people myself, and anyway, I'm not sure I'd really be able to handle seeing strangers trotting through grandmother's rooms." Lila glanced down at the row of still unpainted ornaments on the table. "We're falling behind, girls," she reminded them as she reached for another rocking horse. "If we don't get a move on, we'll never be finished in time."

It was two weeks before Christmas and they were painting the ornaments, which could be hung on Christmas trees, to be used as table decorations and party favors at the CBC banquet Saturday night.

CBC stood for the Cattail Betterment Club, an umbrella organization from which sprang almost all of the local civic-oriented groups. Once a year it sponsored a banquet and dance at the community center in honor of all volunteer workers. Anyone who had done any sort of civic work—from teenagers involved in paint-and-fix-up-for-the-elderly projects to the Medical Center Support Group, which raised funds for a new ambulance—was recognized and honored at the affair. It was Cattail's grand gala event of the year and practically everyone in town over the age of thirteen participated.

Lila had considered not attending for the simple reason that Jeff was bound to be there as well. But since she had headed the ticket sales for the event, the proceeds of which would go toward a local family who had recently lost their home and possessions in a fire, she was expected to make a short report during the dinner. She had finally decided to bite the bullet and attend. After all, she had as much right to be there as Jeff did.

During the past three and a half months, her life had entered a different dimension. In many respects it had become easier, smoother, fuller. In other ways, it had been far more difficult.

Since the night Jeff had met their plane in Dallas, Lila had had no communication with either Jeff or Janey. She knew that Janey had settled into school life again because she'd seen her prancing around doing her cheerleader routines before the stands at a couple of high school football games she'd attended with Amy and Dave. Since the girl had neither called nor visited her, she concluded that Jeff had forbidden it, which meant only one thing...that he still blamed her for Janey's running away.

At the same time, during the past few months Lila's painting ability had deepened, expressing beauty, grace and meaning. Even she could see the startling change, not to mention the ever-increasing number of sales that told its own story. She was actually a bit in awe of her developing skill, and when she pondered the reason for such a dramatic improvement, she finally came to the conclusion that being introspective and unhappy, having experienced an extremely painful loss, must somehow have plumbed her artistic soul.

In spite of the utter and final ending of her relationship with Jeff, her recent life hadn't been bad, all things considered. Besides the fact that her work in the studio had been going unbelievably well, she had alleviated much of her loneliness by getting involved in community activities. In the process she'd discovered that there were far more things that needed doing than there were people with enough time, energy or resources to do them. She found that she was both needed and warmly accepted by the town's citizens and she had also learned, to her surprise, just how much she actually enjoyed being involved. In New York, there had never seemed to be enough free time for such things. Or perhaps it had been that she'd just been too wrapped up in herself.

An unexpected bonus that she'd found was that by getting involved, staying busy, she'd discovered an antidote to heartache. She was drawn out of herself, mentally and physically stretched, forced to give, and it left little time to wallow in self-pity.

But there were times when the pain came anyway, a lashing storm battering her emotions, such as the day she'd been walking down Main Street and had unexpectedly seen Jeff. Then her heart had lodged in her throat, salty tears had pricked her eyes and she had hurried inside the drugstore to avoid meeting him. Sometimes the emotional assault came late at night, at the end of a long day when she'd pushed thoughts of him aside, only to see them resurface with forceful determination when she tried to fall asleep.

Lila had also lost a considerable amount of weight, enough so that she'd become alarmed and had consulted a doctor in Tyler. His conclusion had been that while there was nothing physically wrong with her, she must be under a lot of stress. "Get rid of whatever is upsetting you in your life," he'd said. The trouble was, Lila didn't know how to perform that magical feat. If she could ever get over loving Jeff, she knew she'd be cured. But how?

After much thought and soul-searching, she had finally come to the conclusion that her personal life was likely to remain a sterile void as long as she stayed in Cattail. Between the two of them, Amy and Jerri had introduced her to just about every available man of their acquaintance, but Lila wasn't interested. That's why she'd known it was a waste of time for Jerri to fix her up for the dance with one of Rob's friends. In every man's face she searched for Jeff's teasing dark eyes and never found them; she looked for a tall, gentle giant and saw only ordinary men; she listened for a deep, yet tender voice and heard merely a functional male voice.

So…the time had come to leave, to cut her losses and get on with her life as best she could. Once she was back in New York where she could meet other men and hopefully resist comparing them to Jeff, maybe she would finally heal.

She had to try.

Jeff knotted his tie and eyed his reflection in the mirror without enthusiasm. Then he slid into his suit jacket. He was ready—like it or not.

This year he could whip up no pleasure at the prospect of attending the CBC banquet and dance. He should have arranged to take a date, he mused, but he hadn't felt like it because there'd been no one he wanted to invite. Since Janey had chosen to accompany him tonight, though, it was just as well. True, once the dancing began she'd be deserting him, but that was okay, too. That would leave him free to slip out at the first opportunity and avoid duty-dances with half the middle-aged matrons in town.

Life with Janey these past few months had taken a turn for the better. Her running away had shaken them both enough to bring about compromise and reasonable effort on both their parts. He'd eased up on his rigid, overprotective ways and had begun to allow her more freedom. She, in turn, had proved that she could be trusted, and not once had she abused her new-found privileges. The day she'd turned sixteen, she had also taken her driver's license test and passed. Jeff threw her a big surprise birthday party and presented her with a small car. She'd also begun dating now and then, but it had turned out to be no big deal. Most of the time she preferred the company of groups rather than that of just one boy.

Tonight, however, was special. Ron, the boy she liked most, was also attending the banquet with his parents. He had asked her to be his partner at the dance afterward and he had offered to drive her home later. Jeff had given his permission since Ron seemed like a responsible boy. Besides, what beautiful sixteen-year-old girl, dressed up in a formal and attending a dance wanted to end the evening by driving home with her brother? Jeff grinned wryly at his face reflected in the mirror. The last few months he had come a long way in understanding teenage girls!

He'd had a bit of help in that department from Beth Winston's mother. He had been so appalled over the idea that his inflexible attitude might cause Janey to run away a second time that he'd gone to the woman, who seemed eminently sensible to him, and confessed his inadequacy as a guardian. First, she had assured him that while there was no rule book to guide one when raising teenagers, he could manage as well as any two-parented families as long as he remembered and abided by one all-important principle. He had to open the lines of communication and keep them open. She had assured him, too, that erring on the side of too much leniency would be worse than too much discipline. So, with a bit of advice and a lot of encouragement from that kind lady, he'd relaxed his vigilance somewhat. On the other hand, when he did forbid something, he sat down and explained his reasons or his concerns and it had benefitted both Janey and himself. They still had moments when they didn't see eye to eye, but at least now they talked things out.

Jeff had come to accept his full measure of the blame for causing Janey to go to the extremes she had, but he had never been able to shake the conviction that Lila had also been at fault. Janey had told him that it wasn't Lila's influence that had caused her to go to New York, but he couldn't buy that. Hadn't she gone straight to the modeling agency Lila had been affiliated with? That was no coincidence. That was premeditated and there could be no other explanation for it than that Lila had encouraged Janey to do it in the first place. And if she hadn't influenced her to approach that particular agency, then how had Lila known exactly where to find her? No, Lila had had plenty to do with what happened, and Jeff would neither forget it nor forgive it. He still went cold whenever he thought of all the things that could have happened to Janey all alone on the streets of New York City. Associating with Lila any further had been the one thing he had since been inflexible about with Janey. He had expressly forbidden it, and had flatly refused to listen to either her pleas or her defense of Lila.

Not liking the direction of his thoughts, Jeff left his bedroom and went downstairs. Janey was waiting for him in the living room and Jeff drew up short at the sight of her. She wore a cranberry-red party dress with huge bows at the shoulders above her bare arms. Another bow was centered at the waist, below which flared a full skirt. Her long dark hair shimmered with golden highlights and her creamy face was flushed with youthful beauty and excitement.

His throat tightened as he went toward her and clasped her hands. A proprietary pride gleamed in his eyes as he smiled at her. "You've turned into a great beauty, honey," he said in a choked voice. "I only wish Mom and Dad could see you now."

Janey returned the smile and stood on tiptoes to kiss his cheek. "Thanks, Jeff. You look awfully handsome tonight yourself, big brother."

Jeff chuckled and tucked her hand in the crook of his arm. "Well, are the Chappels ready to dazzle the town with their incredible good looks?"

Janey giggled and nodded.

The community hall was already crowded by the time they arrived. The huge room was a yuletide wonderland with pine boughs and red velvet bows festooning the walls. Still more decorations graced the centers of the white-clothed tables interspersed by flickering candles. An enormous spruce tree with twinkling lights, colorful ornaments and icicles dominated the front of the room. The star on top of the tree touched the high ceiling.

Jeff and Janey made their way toward the Christmas tree so that they could deposit their wrapped gifts beneath its branches. Tomorrow afternoon Jeff, dressed in a Santa Claus suit, would distribute the donated toys at a party for the children of the neediest families in the area. He'd been doing it for the past three seasons.

George Duncan and his wife Esther were there also placing their packages beneath the tree. When he saw them, George beamed at Janey. "Hey, now, aren't you the beauty tonight? What did you do, grow up overnight when nobody was looking?"

Janey grinned. "Thanks, Pokey."

"Nice collection of gifts this year, isn't it?" Jeff commented to Esther. "Are you going to be one of the hostesses tomorrow like last year?"

She nodded. "Wouldn't miss it. They tell me you're going to play Santa again."

"You better believe it," Jeff answered. "They'll have to fight me to ever take that job away from me. It's the most fun I get to have all year long."

"Ron and his parents just came in," Janey said in Jeff's ear. "I'm going over to say 'hello.' I'll be back in a few minutes."

"Okay, honey." Jeff relaxed and spent the next few minutes chatting with the Duncans along with a few others who had joined them.

When it was time to take their places at the tables, Jeff began looking around for Janey. That's when he saw Lila for the first time and the way she looked snatched his breath away.

She was talking to Mr. and Mrs. Amberson, an elderly couple, only a few yards away from him and her face was glowing with animation as she spoke. Her hair was a fiery halo of glory surrounding her face and her dress was a smashing knockout. It was floor length, made of some sort of green shimmery material and it clung to her body with breathtaking snugness. She was unbelievably gorgeous and her appearance tonight left no room for anyone with eyes to doubt why she'd been such a successful model. She seemed to light up the entire room just by being in it. Even so, he couldn't help but see that she was thinner now than he remembered and he frowned slightly, wondering at the reason for her loss of weight.

"She's really something isn't she?" Janey asked.

Jeff hadn't realized his sister had come to his side until she spoke. Even then, he couldn't draw his gaze away from Lila. All the old feelings he'd had for her, that he'd striven so hard to banish these past few months, came surging back over him with the suddenness and intensity of a tornado striking ground. It wasn't just her beauty that riveted him, exquisite as she was. It was also the acknowledgment within the quiet chambers of his heart that he'd not stopped loving her for one single instant.

"She'll be leaving soon."

Janey finally had his attention. Jeff looked down at her and his eyes narrowed. "Who's leaving?"

"Lila. She's going back to New York right after the new year."

"Where'd you hear that?"

"Amy Mathis told me a few minutes ago." Her huge dark eyes were accusing. "I'll bet it's all your fault, too, Jeff."

Jeff stiffened defensively. "What makes you say that?"

Janey shrugged. "Look at how you shoved her out of both our lives after she brought me back from New York. You were hardly even civil to her that night, when you should have been grateful to her for going to the trouble. *I* sure was. If it hadn't been for Lila, I might not be here tonight. What's more," she added with a suddenly trembling lip, "I've missed her a lot, and now she's going away for good!"

Jeff pulled their chairs out and they took their places at their table. Then he leaned toward Janey and spoke softly. "I know you really liked her, honey. So did I," he added in a masterful understatement. "But she just wasn't a good influence on you. If she hadn't filled your head full of all that nonsense about modeling, you would never have gone to New York. You might've been angry with me, but I don't believe you'd have actually run away if you hadn't been convinced you had someplace, something to run to."

"Yes, I would. I was determined, Jeff! It wasn't Lila's doing at all. She was always trying to tell me what a rough life modeling really was...how hard it was to get a break, but I wouldn't listen to that. I didn't want to believe her. But once I got there, I was terrified and I was never so glad to see anyone in my life as I was when I walked into that office and saw her. I didn't even mind too much when she chewed me out for hurting you so badly. I knew I had it coming. And her friend, Clo, the owner of the agency...she told me what a baby I was, how immature I was! But in the end, she was nice to me. She promised that for Lila's sake, if I still wanted to model after graduation, she'd do whatever she could to help me. But neither of them left me under any illusions that I stood a chance if I stayed there on my own then." She paused and tossed him a look of pure defiance. "You may forbid me to visit or call Lila, but you can't stop me from talking to her this evening, and I intend to do just that as soon as dinner is over."

"No," Jeff said with unexpected meekness, "I won't try to stop you."

When the various speakers stood at the podium throughout dinner to congratulate this group or that, or to make brief reports on what their particular groups had accomplished during the year, Jeff tuned them out. He was too busy thinking about Lila...that she was leaving Texas for good, that Janey was right that it was his fault, and that he'd been a first-class fool not to listen to Janey's explanations concerning Lila before. From the sound of it, he'd blamed her unjustly for encouraging Janey about a modeling career when in fact, she'd done everything she could to discourage Janey. Together, Lila and her friend, Clo, had done him, as well as Janey, an enormous service, a favor of incalculable magnitude, and for thanks he had cut Lila out of his life.

When Lila got up to make a brief report over the microphone, Jeff gazed at her with such longing that he felt sure she must feel it, even from across the room. But if she did, she didn't show it. Not once did she so much as glance in his direction. Miserably, he wondered if there was any chance he could ever win her back. In his black mood, he doubted it and he had nothing but contempt for himself for having ruined the finest thing that had ever come into his life. All because he'd been stupidly proud and couldn't see his own faults at the time. He'd had to blame someone, and so he'd dumped the load on Lila's slender shoulders. Well, now he was paying dearly for his mistakes, and likely he'd go on paying for the rest of his life.

The long dinner finally came to an end. While the tables were being cleared, people got up from their seats, mingling sociably before the dancing began. Janey darted from Jeff's side and a minute later he saw her dark head close to Lila's red-gold one. His eyes misted with love for them both.

"I'm so happy things are going well for you now, Janey," Lila said after they'd been chatting for a couple of minutes. "I've wondered many times how you were."

"I would've called or gone to see you, but..." Janey paused and caught her lower lip between her teeth. Then she shrugged helplessly.

"I understand," Lila said softly. "Tell me, how are—"

She broke off when two things happened simultaneously. The band struck up the music, a slow, romantic tune, and a deep masculine voice spoke beside her. "Good evening."

Lila looked up into Jeff's dark eyes and what she saw in them made her feel light-headed and breathless. "Good evening," she managed to reply with just the right inflection to her voice ... cordial but reserved.

Jeff turned his gaze on his sister then and smiling, utterly shocked Lily by saying, "Will you please get lost while I tell this lady how much I love her?"

Janey giggled, clearly delighted. "Consider me lost," she replied. And good as her word, she melted away into the crowd.

Despite the throng of people surrounding them, Lila felt as though she had suddenly been washed upon a small, private island for two. She saw no one else, heard no one else. There was only Jeff, smiling at her with heartbreaking tenderness, and the soft strains of the music.

She wasn't aware of exactly how it happened, but all at once she was floating, drifting around the dance floor, her feet light as wings. A hazy warmth enveloped her, the warmth of Jeff's possessive embrace. For the time being she allowed herself the luxury of it—surrendering to the dizzying sensations that held her in their grip—the wonderful pressure of his hand at her waist, the fingers of his other hand curled tightly around hers, his soft breath fanning her cheek, the irresistible scent of his after-shave lotion. Her entire body softened, melted, melding into his as though she'd been turned into fluid.

"I meant it, you know," Jeff whispered into her ear. "I love you, Lila."

Reality, which she'd kept at bay, now came crashing over Lila like the swell of tides tumbling toward shore. She put space between their bodies, at once missing the intimate heat of his, but knowing she couldn't indulge in fantasy any longer.

She shook her head and swallowed. "Don't say things like that. It's over."

"No," he protested harshly. "It doesn't have to be."

Lila nodded sadly. "I think it does. I didn't trust you for a long time and then you didn't trust me. There's nothing to build on there...no security or permanence or commitment."

"I want to *marry* you!" Jeff exclaimed.

Her eyes were sorrowful. "So you told me once before. I don't believe it anymore, Jeff. And I can't—" For the first time her composure broke. "I just can't bear being hurt anymore. Not ever."

With lightning suddenness Jeff released her hand, but his other arm remained firmly around her waist as he led her away from the dance floor. "Where's your purse and wrap?" he demanded.

"Over there." Vaguely she waved her hand in the direction of the table where she'd been sitting. "But I'm not going anywhere with you."

"That, my dear, is where you're very much mistaken."

They arrived at Lila's table and without ceremony, Jeff picked up her dainty gold evening purse and her velvet cape and thrust them into Lila's hands. With his hand now gripping her arm, he all but pulled her across the room to the door.

Once they were outside, Jeff continued to pull her across the parking lot until they reached his car. "I can't go with you," Lila protested once more. "My car is here."

"Leave it. I'll send Bud and Lionel for it in the morning."

Lila balked beside the car and glared at him. "You haven't been listening to me. I don't *want* to go anywhere with you."

"Who asked you what you wanted?" Jeff opened the passenger door and said in a voice of steel, "Get in by yourself or I'll put you there myself."

Lila sighed. She supposed they would have to have it out before the final curtain could ring down. She got inside the car, and while Jeff went around the car and slid beneath the wheel, she wrapped her cape around her shoulders for warmth. Moments later, they were off.

They drove in silence through a slumbering countryside. It was a cold, wintry night and the only sound inside the car was the whine of the heater. Since Jeff seemed in no rush to speak, Lila didn't bother to do so either. She felt too tired to argue, now or later, yet she knew the words would come. Her mind was made up, no matter what he said.

Instead of taking her home, Jeff took her to his house. Lila was somewhat surprised, but again, she didn't argue about it. What did it matter where they said their final words to each other? Goodbye was goodbye.

Jeff flipped on lights as they went through the dark, silent house. When they arrived at the study, they appeared to have reached their destination.

"Have a seat," Jeff said. He indicated she should sit in the same chair she had taken that last day when he had told her he no longer wanted to marry her. Lila did, then looked up at him warily.

Surprisingly, he turned his back to her then. Bracing one arm on a bookshelf, he lowered his head as though studying his shoes. "I'm told you're planning to go back to New York soon."

"That's right."

"Back to modeling?"

"Yes."

Jeff turned then and his eyes were dark and glittering as he looked at her. "Why?"

"Why?" Lila shook her head. "Because it's what I do."

"What about your painting?"

"I'll keep up with that, too."

"Don't you think you're being a bit selfish, returning to modeling?"

Lila's eyes widened. "Selfish? How?"

Jeff grinned. "Well, if you go back, you'll be taking assignments that might otherwise be offered to a newcomer...say, like Janey in another year or so. I call that pretty selfish. There's no way those young girls can compete with you."

Lila's lips twitched in spite of herself. "You know," she said slowly, "I never thought about it like that."

"Well, you should," Jeff said briskly. "And another thing..."

"Yes?"

Jeff crossed to her swiftly and knelt on one knee. He took both her hands in his and said simply, "If you leave me, there won't be any purpose to the rest of my life."

Lila's eyes squeezed shut. "Ah, don't, Jeff. Please, don't."

His hands tightened over hers. "Don't shut me out, Lila, please. I was so wrong about everything—blaming you because Janey ran away. I was afraid and angry that day. I wouldn't listen to you or later, to her, but tonight she made me see the truth, that you had been doing everything you could to discourage her all along. I can't blame you if you hate me now, if you carry out your plan to go away and never see me again. But I want you to know that you can't go away without carrying my love with you. These past few months of being without you have been sheer hell. Even though I rationalized that you were wrong for me, I kept on wanting you. If you'll reconsider...if you can find it in your heart to forgive me enough to marry me, I swear you'll never regret it. I'll be yours through all eternity. I...I don't know what else I can offer you."

Lila's eyes were moist, her voice husky. "That...that's the longest speech I ever heard you make."

He smiled wistfully. "I think it's the longest one I ever did make. Did it do me any good?"

Lila laughed softly. "You said you didn't know what else to offer me—"

"Yes? Anything!" he promised recklessly.

Her eyes began to twinkle through the tears that had turned them into glazed emeralds.

"How about something to eat while we make our wedding plans?"

A vast relief rolled over Jeff. She was his, after all! He relaxed and found a renewed sense of humor. "Food again? We just came from a banquet! And anyway," he added, frowning as he allowed his gaze to drift over her body, "it looks to me like you've been on a strict diet or something."

"Food just...just didn't taste as good once you weren't around to tease me about it anymore. And tonight, when I saw you there, I couldn't eat because I kept looking at you all through dinner and wishing..."

"Yes?" he prompted.

Lila entwined her arms around his neck and leaned forward until her lips were almost touching his. "I kept wishing that somehow a Christmas miracle would happen—that you'd stop me from going back to New York by convincing me you really wanted me to stay."

"Has the miracle happened, then? Have I finally convinced you?"

She nodded. "I love you, too, Jeff. I never stopped, and I know I never will."

His arms slid around her waist. "That's all I need to hear," he whispered huskily. "As to the wedding plans... how about simple and quick? We'll get the license first thing Monday, visit the judge and make you mine forever.''

"That's fine, Jeff," Lila said dreamily. "Whatever you say. But meantime..."

"Meantime?"

"I'm still hungry!"

Jeff made a sound that was a cross between a growl of exasperation and a chuckle of amusement. "I absolutely insist upon a kiss first," he said, "to seal the bargain. Then we'll see what we can do about you and your appetite!"

His lips moved against hers, warm and sweet, with the taste of forever on them. Lila forgot all about her hunger for food as she quickly developed an entirely different appetite... one that would only grow stronger and more intense as time went on.

* * * * *

The passionate saga that brought you SARAH and
ELIZABETH continues in the compelling,
unforgettable story of

Catherine

MAURA SEGER

An independent and ambitious woman earns the disap-
proval of Boston society when she discovers passion and
love with Irishman Evan O'Connel.

Silhouette Romance™
Legendary Lovers Trilogy

BY DEBBIE MACOMBER....

ONCE UPON A TIME, in a land not so far away, there lived a girl, Debbie Macomber, who grew up dreaming of castles, white knights and princes on fiery steeds. Her family was an ordinary one with a mother and father and one wicked brother, who sold copies of her diary to all the boys in her junior high class.

One day, when Debbie was only nineteen, a handsome electrician drove by in a shiny black convertible. Now Debbie knew a prince when she saw one, and before long they lived in a two-bedroom cottage surrounded by a white picket fence.

As often happens when a damsel fair meets her prince charming, children followed, and soon the two-bedroom cottage became a four-bedroom castle. The kingdom flourished and prospered, and between soccer games and car pools, ballet classes and clarinet lessons, Debbie thought about love and enchantment and the magic of romance.

One day Debbie said, "What this country needs is a good fairy tale." She remembered how well her diary had sold and she dreamed again of castles, white knights and princes on fiery steeds. And so the stories of Cinderella, Beauty and the Beast, and Snow White were reborn....

Look for Debbie Macomber's *Legendary Lovers* trilogy from Silhouette Romance: *Cindy and the Prince* (January, 1988); *Some Kind of Wonderful* (March, 1988); *Almost Paradise* (May, 1988). Don't miss them!

SRT-1

 *Silhouette Intimate Moments*

Rx: One Dose of

DODD MEMORIAL HOSPITAL

In sickness and in health the employees of Dodd Memorial Hospital stick together, sharing triumphs and defeats, and sometimes their hearts as well. Revisit these special people next month in the newest book in Lucy Hamilton's Dodd Memorial Hospital Trilogy, *After Midnight*—IM #237, the time when romance begins.

Thea Stevens knew there was no room for a man in her life—she had a young daughter to care for and a demanding new job as the hospital's media coordinator. But then Luke Adams walked through the door, and everything changed. She had never met a man like him before—handsome enough to be the movie star he was, yet thoughtful, considerate and absolutely determined to get the one thing he wanted—Thea.

Finish the trilogy in July with *Heartbeats*—IM #245.